The Hidden **Game**

By Richard Donald Groves

Published by

köehlerbooks™

3705 Shore Drive
Virginia Beach, VA 23455
800–435–4811
www.koehlerbooks.com

THE
HIDDEN GAME

RICHARD DONALD GROVES

VIRGINIA BEACH
CAPE CHARLES

Dedication

To Ferol and Sally for their never-ending love and support,
from the present back to the very beginning of this great journey.

To my mother, who fostered in me a love of reading
and the magic of the printed word.

Finally, to Lily, my constant four-legged companion,
always praising and never a critic.

CHAPTER ONE

Tony Stravnicki's world began to unravel when he realized he had seen too much to merely be coincidence. Coincidence, he believed, is random, and today was anything but random. As the defensive backs coach for the Columbus Colonels of the National American Football League, he saw the yellow flag near his player for the fourth time today and slammed his clipboard—a special gift from his players—to the ground. He could live with random, but not with this fear that he was being played. If this was done on purpose, it meant his passion, his life's work, all he had ever done, was rigged.

His gum chewing accelerated to such a frenetic pace he could barely get words out.

"C'mon, ref, no foul there. They were both going for the ball!" His booming New York accent cut through the sideline noise like a frustrated parent at a ten-year old's soccer game.

"Shit, that one's gonna hurt us. I can't believe this," he complained for all to hear, green eyes blazing. His signature backward baseball cap, topped by a headset, hid his flattop brown hair. His powerful build and frenzied pacing, evoking a caged tiger, were hard to ignore and created his own personal no-fly zone. He strode the sideline, oblivious to the controlled chaos swirling around him, his mind trying desperately to make sense of what was happening. He swallowed hard to push down the fear and forced himself to refocus on the game, ignoring the roar of screaming fans, loud music, and buxom, provocatively clad cheerleaders. "Stay sharp, Strav, stay sharp," he whispered.

—————

As side judge Frank Ohlendorf walked over to the meeting of the other officials, a deep, gnawing pain gripped his stomach and an icy shudder ran down his body. *I must maintain control. I didn't think I would feel this way.*

As an NAFL official with thirteen years experience, he had received many accolades for his cool decisions in pressure situations when much was at stake. His mind had tried to tell him that today would be no different, that his calls would be just like all the other ones he had ever made and would not cause suspicion. How wrong he had been in thinking it wouldn't bother him to compromise his integrity this way.

I'm in control. This is just another game. No different.

The officials were waiting for him, impassive looks but questioning eyes.

"Number thirty-two, pass interference. No question about it."

As he had done two other times today, he stated this decisively and looked into the eyes of each official after he said it, daring them to challenge him. None did. The head official simply said, "Okay, Frank. You were the only one in position to see it."

Frank jogged back to where the flag lay, its yellow cloth in vivid contrast to the dark-green turf. He ignored the hostile, glaring looks from the defensive team.

His heart rate slowed as the wave of emotion passed. Focused again, he allowed himself a slight sigh of relief. *I got away with it again.* He picked up the flag as the referee keyed his mike and said authoritatively, "Pass interference, number thirty-two, defense. The ball will be placed at the spot of the foul. First down."

The disapproval of the home crowd was instantaneous, and the crescendo of the noise reached an almost unbearable level. Houston scored on the next play, taking the lead.

———————

The home crowd's frustration slowly became evident as their cheers decreased in volume. Their beloved Colonels had been favored to win this division rivalry game and, most importantly, advance in the standings, qualifying for a playoff spot. But as the weather changed from blue sky and sunshine to gray and blustery by the fourth quarter, so too had their hopes faded.

Tony glanced back to the stands where he knew his family was sitting and locked eyes with his wife of fourteen years, Maggie. She smiled, held her hands out, and slowly pushed down, signaling him to relax. He returned a weak smile and held his hands up in frustration. He nodded, took a deep breath and turned back to the field, watching as the officials met.

Shit, we're gonna lose this one! What the hell is going on?

Curtis Bond, the cornerback who had drawn the alleged foul, came directly to Tony with his helmet in hand, eyes bulging, along with the veins on his neck.

Bond spit on the ground. "Coach Rocky yanked me! That wasn't my fault, Coach T! That's bullshit man! Wasn't nothin' there!"

"I know, Curtis, I know . . . "

"Second on me, fourth on us. What's going on, Coach? They targeting me? How do I play against that, huh?" A desperate, pleading look filled his eyes.

Grabbing Curtis's shoulder pads and looking reassuringly in his eyes, Tony lowered his voice.

"I don't know what's going on, but it's not us—and not you—man. Let it go. Remember your fundamentals. Keep giving it your very best and rise above it. You can elevate your game, Curtis. I know it and you do too. It's not over yet." This last statement was for the player's benefit. Tony now had no faith it was really true.

Curtis nodded, gave Tony a fist bump, mumbled, "Okay Coach. Thanks," and walked away muttering. A couple of nearby players watching the interaction came up to Curtis, and one said, "Chill, bro. Coach T got yo' back."

With hands on his hips and head cocked to one side, head coach Rocky Jones gave Tony a withering look.

"What crap, Rocky! These calls aren't on us! They're bogus! Those zebras are taking this friggin' game right away and giving it to Houston." His voice rose in intensity, words rapid-fire, hands waving in frustration. Tony jammed his third stick of gum into his mouth, his face crimson with rage. "Something crazy is going on out there, Rocky. We're being played!"

"We'll talk later, Tony. I don't have time for this now. Gather your players and settle them down."

"My comms keep cutting out too! What's up with that?"

"Just do your job, Coach!" Rocky yelled, pointing a finger at him, then turning away, too frustrated to argue, having comms issues of his own.

Great! Rocky's blaming me! I sure don't need that.

Having played ten pro seasons as a defensive back, Tony had learned a thing or two about fouls, their increasing complexity and subjectivity. *With all the camera angles, slow-motion replays, and live feeds to the league officiating office at NAFL headquarters, why do they screw up so much? How are they getting away with it? They're changing outcomes and standings. Something I can't control is hurting the sport and really screwing me, once again! Will it cost me my job?* He buried these thoughts for now, but just barely, concentrating on getting through the game.

───────────

Up in a lavish skybox, two powerful men toasted each other over a successful day. One man, casually dressed, took a sip of expensive white wine, winked at his much younger wife, and said, "What a game. Boy, are things working out!"

"Yes, honey, it's a great game. I'm glad you're pleased," she agreed, as always, with her perfect smile, looking every bit the former Playmate model, a stunning green dress revealing her ample cleavage.

"Working out, indeed," the other man said, pride resounding in his commanding voice. A former player, his white shirt and red power tie, framed by a custom-tailored navy-blue suit, emphasized his powerful build and projected the exact image he craved.

"Well done, sir. Kudos to your visionary plan," said the casually dressed man, raising his glass in salute.

His colleague began to reply when he was interrupted by an assistant who handed him a note. Scanning it, he turned to his associate and spoke in a hushed voice that only they could hear and then departed, leaving the man to entertain his bored wife. The game ended a few minutes later, and the wife joined others at the bar while he ambled over to the large window overlooking the field, now empty except for stadium personnel. A smirk on his face, he mused about the deceit that had occurred today, known only to a select group. *We, the very select few*, his mind boasted as he recalled a special meeting over a year ago. Jolted from the memory by his wife, he took her arm, planting a kiss on her cheek, and they headed off to dinner.

CHAPTER TWO

Afterthe game, Frank quickly left the field, down the narrow but brightly lit corridor lined with impassive security guards toward the referee's locker room. He exchanged nods with one he recognized. *Thank God for NAFL security so I don't have to worry about problems from teams, aggressive media, or upset fans.* He changed, not bothering to shower and avoiding contact with other referees. He took the exit used exclusively by VIPs, this one guarded by police, where his limo with tinted glass waited to take him to the airport. As a senior official, he was awarded this highly prized perk and it was very useful today.

His head was spinning as the driver pulled away from the stadium. The first thing he tried to do was to pour himself a stiff Johnny Walker Black from the well-stocked bar. This was no easy task, as his shaking hands were almost uncontrollable. He pounded down the first one, not bothering with ice, wincing at the burn in his throat but grateful for the anticipated effect.

The second one, over rocks, he savored more leisurely. The thirty-five-minute ride to the airport could not go by fast enough, but he slowly began to relax with relief that his covert job for today was done. There would be other such jobs; he would be contacted soon enough.

Four minutes later his burner phone rang. *That was fast.* Ignoring it was not an option.

A raspy smoker's voice with a thick Russian accent said, "Good job, Mr. O. You no fuck up. Da. See you Thursday at diner. Same time."

Before he could respond, the phone went silent.

Frank crunched down on the ice so hard he was afraid he would break a molar. He closed his eyes, a dark cloud enveloping him, negating the scotch, returning him to the series of events that had cornered him into this horrible position.

CHAPTER THREE

Tony had spoken to each of his players after the game and tried to defuse their anger over the manner of their loss and bolster their spirits, having mixed results. As he was finishing, he ran into the defensive coordinator, Hank Naples—his direct boss.

"Rocky wants to speak with you for a moment, Tony." Naples followed him into the head coach's office, closing the door behind them.

Coach Jones looked up from his desk, eyes dark and a scowl on his face. "That was a subpar performance by your group today, Tony. Your D backs have to be better."

Tony stared in disbelief, slack jawed by the timing and abrupt tone of Jones's words. Finger-pointing was always reserved for Monday, following review of game film. He swallowed hard before replying and wished he hadn't just spit out his gum.

"You're not telling me you think those calls on my guys were all justified, are you? You haven't even reviewed film." He looked over at Naples, arms folded, silent, making no effort to speak.

"Those fouls cost us the game and our standing. You realize that, Tony?"

"Of course I know that, Rocky. But you've got to admit those four calls on my guys were suspect at best. Right? The one on Bond was totally bogus. We saw this last year too. Remember the Richmond game?" Rocky remained steely eyed. "Today was the worst. I tell you, somethin's going on. I saw O'Brien here with you and Mr. Cane. What did ya say to him about the calls and our comms issues?"

"I expressed our concerns, and he said he would review the game and get back to me. As team owner, Mr. Cane's conversation with the commissioner was private," Rocky replied, evading the question. "There's not much else I could say."

He looked first at Tony and then at Hank. "I don't want to see this again. You guys have to get a handle on this!" Hank stared at Tony and opened the door, signaling an end to the meeting. Tony walked out, a grim expression on his face.

———————

He retreated to the privacy of his small office, slamming his clipboard on the desk and sulking into his chair, furious at Rocky. And Hank hadn't even tried to help—not a word! What was up with that? Opening his desk drawer, he pulled out his favorite after-game medication. He savored every bite of the full-size Milky Way, marveling at how something as basic as chocolate could have such a calming effect. As his blood pressure slowly returned to normal, he replayed in his mind the critical points in the game where things went so wrong.

The black cloud continued until Dennis Jalmond, his assistant, knocked on his door. Five foot six, with a slim build and outsized glasses accentuating his expressive eyes, the young man was well thought of around the team and had a reputation as being something of a whiz kid with technology.

"Hey, Coach, some game," he said, eyebrows raised, more of a question than a statement.

"Yah, Dennis, it was," Tony answered sharply, only briefly glancing at him.

Dennis took a quick step back toward the door. "I'll leave you alone, Coach T. Don't mean to bother you."

"Dennis, my door is always open for you." He sighed. "Just trying to relax."

"Milky Way time, huh?"

"Yep. Want one? I've got more," he said, now focused on him.

"Nah. But thanks, Coach. Just wanted to see how you doin'. You were a mite upset today." His voice was low, matching his diminutive stature, a slow drawl his trademark.

Tony shook his head. "Something happened out there today that doesn't feel right, Denny. We all work our butts off and then we have something like today. The head coach and owner complained to the commissioner, but nothing will change, like we don't matter. I get chewed out before they even reviewed the game. CYA time and I'm the scapegoat. Just an expendable pawn in somebody's chess game and it stinks," he said, his tone rising.

He took a long pause as he took a bite of the Milky Way, a fan in the stuffy office the only sound. "The implications got to me today. Not that I can do anything about it." He stared with a distant look at a picture from his playing days. "I don't like how or where the game is going. It all seems so phony to me at times."

He looked up, noticing the concern on Dennis' face. "I'm just rambling, Dennis. Wah, wah, wah. Poor me." He laughed. "I'll be fine tomorrow. Thanks for stopping by."

"Sure thing, Coach. See you tomorrow."

Tony let out a long sigh, puffing out his lips. *What if I am a pawn? What if there is a wizard behind a screen, pulling levers, controlling everything? How do you prove that? How do you fight that?* He again reached into his drawer. It was a rare two Milky Way day.

CHAPTER FOUR

Two hours later, Tony drove into his quiet cul-de-sac and pulled into the long driveway of his brown Colonial. He always looked forward to coming home after a game, even more so after a tough loss like today's. It provided a sanctuary of calm from the frequent turbulent storms of his profession.

He parked the Volvo wagon and noticed the kids had put their bicycles off to the side, not dumping them smack in the middle of the garage—a pleasant surprise. Tony entered the kitchen to a mouthwatering aroma and was soon greeted by his tribe; nine-year-old Hope led the way, followed by Zach, age twelve. Maggie was right behind.

"Daddy, Daddy!" Hope yelled, ending her run to him with a leap into his arms.

"Hello, Peanut," he replied, enveloping her in a soft bear hug.

"Sorry about the tough loss, Pop. You got screwed," offered Zach, a talented Pop Warner player.

"Zachary Taylor Stravnicki, you will not use that kind of language in this house," Margaret Flaherty Stravnicki warned in her no-nonsense nurse's tone.

"Even if it might be true," she whispered in Tony's ear, planting a kiss on his cheek.

Putting Hope down, he wrapped his buxom, athletic mate in a warm embrace, inhaling the fragrance of her long red hair. "Might? No might about it, Mags." Separating from each other, he turned to Zach while Maggie set the table for their dinner. "Yeah, it was tough, Zach. We'll just have to play smarter and try harder, that's all. The refs have a tough job, too."

Zach looked up at him with bursting pride. "You'll get 'em next time, Dad."

"Okay, kids, you've got five minutes until dinner. Get your clothes and bags ready for school, and we'll check homework after supper," said Maggie.

They ran off as Tony grabbed a beer from the fridge and sat down, exhaling loudly.

Maggie pulled the roast from the oven, shut it off, and turned toward Tony, a concerned look on her face. "So, how you doing, Tony? Rough day at the office."

"Thanks for the 'calm down' signal today. You know, I *was* gettin' cranked up. Four crappy calls—all at critical times. A loss that shouldn't have happened. Rocky called me on the carpet about it. Hank just stood there, not saying a word. And the worst part was I didn't have any gum. You woulda been proud of me, Mags. No gum and I still maintained control and challenged him."

Maggie looked over her glasses, frowning. "What did you say?"

"I told him that it wasn't the players' or my fault, and I pointed out that he hadn't seen the film yet."

"And his response?"

"Pass-the-buck time. Said Hank and I need to get a handle on it."

"Wow. Sounds like a threat."

"Nah, just frustration. Maybe I was just the low man to take it out on today. I'm not worried."

"Don't be naive, Tony! It's not good that Hank didn't say anything supportive. They know your history in Phoenix. That you were on shaky ground even before the new owner let everyone go. Don't give them any ammunition against you. We need this job. Take the threat seriously!" Her Irish temper began to simmer, honey-brown eyes wide with concern.

The comments stung. He lowered his eyes but avoided a direct response. Now was not the time to rehash the past. "I'll review the film so I can be ready for the game critique. See how he handles it then. I'll defend my guys if it's warranted, outline drills for practice to try to prevent a recurrence. I can only take it so far without support from Hank."

"Tony, you're a player's coach, but you know that doesn't always sit well with management. I get nervous when I hear things like today. You've got to play by their rules."

He took a sip from his beer, then banged the can on the table, scowling as he looked at Maggie.

"Thanks for the lecture, Mags," he said, his voice rising. "I hate their rules and how the league is changin'. You know, so big business now. So *Hollywood*. But that shouldn't affect the sport itself. That's gotta stay the same, right?"

"I don't know; everything is so complex now. Nothing's simple anymore. Life isn't black and white even if you think it should be."

"Yep, gray *is* hard for me. But I gotta believe the essence of the game is still there. That hard work, discipline, and commitment matter, and are still what it's really all about."

He drained the beer and threw it in the trash. "Maybe Rocky's right. I'll work on doing better," he said in a whisper.

The kids burst in just as Maggie was about to respond. Mealtime as a family was special for them, as Tony was gone so frequently during the season. Banter about school, homework, friends, and activities filled the time and redirected Tony's thoughts. But that ended during dessert when Zach startled Tony. "So, Pop, what's gonna happen about those calls today?"

Tony looked closely at his son. "It's my responsibility, Zach, working with the players and other coaches to figure out what we're doin' wrong. You know, we all have responsibilities in life. Your Mom has incredible responsibilities as a nurse helping people, and you and Hope have responsibilities to try your best and do well in school."

"Yes, sir."

"I always try my best, Daddy," said Hope, with an ear-to-ear smile.

"We know you both do, Peanut," added Maggie. "You guys may be excused. We'll be up in a few minutes to check homework, then read and get you into bed.

"Dad can read to us in *my* room tonight, Hope," Zach could be heard saying as they scampered upstairs.

"It's been a long day, Tony."

"It sure has," he replied as he helped Maggie clean up. "I'm just going to give them a quick kiss goodnight. You can read to them. I'm too tired and have too much on my mind." He was distracted enough that he missed this ongoing flash point, one of several in their marriage.

"No, Tony. You *will* read to them tonight. Didn't you hear how excited Zach was? I'm tired too, and you haven't been around much. They miss you. How do you think they'll feel if you don't? Put your family first for a change!" She threw the dish towel down on the counter and stormed upstairs.

Another zinger! *I don't need this!* He stood at the sink, staring out the window, needing a minute alone to process her comments and the day. He feared that the present might lead to a repeat of the past in more than one way: a lost job, a failed marriage. That a single bad decision could affect the family, like the one his father had made so many years ago.

CHAPTER FIVE

Frank's commute home from the airport that night was uneventful, and he lost himself in a talk radio show. Entering his kitchen, he was greeted by his wife's warm smile.

Nancy took one look at his haggard expression and gave him a hug.

"You look beat," she said.

"That bad, huh?"

"Yes. Dinner is in about ten minutes. Why don't you grab a beer and relax for a few? You deserve it. I'm all set here."

"Good idea. I'm gonna do just that." He plopped into his recliner in the family room, taking long pulls from the beer as he reviewed the Saturday mail. The monthly invoice from One Step Forward Treatment Center stood out from the pile, and he quickly tore it open. *Damn!! Another increase. They're already ridiculous. How high can they go? How long will this last?* He took another swig of the beer, took the bills to his office, and threw out the junk mail. He returned to the kitchen a few minutes later.

"Perfect timing, hon. You take a look at the mail?"

"Yep, I did. Another increase from One Step Forward, I'm afraid," he said in a low voice.

Nancy frowned, a concerned look accentuating the lines of her face.

"Is it a problem, Frank? Can we do it? This one seems to be working."

Frank paused, upset he had allowed his frustration to show, bothering his easily worried wife. "No problem at all, Nancy. We're fine. Yes, it does seem to be helping Paul," he said with a smile and an upbeat tone. "Sometimes I think I should go into recovery services. They seem to be able to print money." He laughed.

Her smile returned. "You're my hero, Frank. You know how grateful I am for your patience and understanding with Paul. We certainly couldn't manage it without you. How you're doing it is a mystery, but it's wonderful."

"Things are finally coming together for me, and the bonus should be pretty big in a few more weeks," he lied.

Frank took care of all the family finances, so he was able to keep Nancy in the dark about the true state of their money problems. His tales of stock market successes and company bonuses had kept her from asking too many questions. Up until three months ago, his financial plate-spinning and juggling act had worked well, but with their home equity line of credit and ability to take loans against his retirement account at their maximums, Frank was against the wall. And then the solution appeared.

All he had to do was sell his soul.

Nancy grasped his hand, caressing it. "You work *so* hard for us, Frank. The pressure must be enormous," she whispered, almost in tears.

He squeezed her hand back with a well-practiced, staged smile. "Anything for you, hon."

If only she knew what that really meant. He turned his head away, taking a minute to hide his shame.

CHAPTER SIX

Tony arrived at the team facility at seven thirty Monday morning a troubled man. He decided to take a circuitous route to his office, and he paused for a few moments in the empty locker room. Walking around, he took in all the sights and smells that were so familiar to him. Although the room was cleaned and sanitized each evening and was outfitted with the most advanced HVAC air filtration system, it still retained unique scents common to most sports locker rooms.

Tony inhaled deeply, energized by the primal mixture of sweat-soaked uniforms and body odor only slightly masked by the clean smell of camphor and menthol in various topical pain relievers. To most people the aroma might be offensive or repugnant, but to him it was just the opposite. Here was his soul, infused with comfortable, ordinary, and reassuring smells that had been a part of his life for over twenty years.

He savored the quiet, knowing that soon the room would be bustling with activity and filled with boisterous voices. He smiled at the memories of wisecracks, tongue-in-cheek insults, and off-color jokes with some serious conversations here and there. Tony was grateful that this team had a few key experienced leaders who set the tone not just for the room but for the team itself, fostering the right amount of seriousness and levity, contributing to a cohesive camaraderie. Many teams lacked this intangible advantage.

The dynamics of such a testosterone-rich environment were complex. Not every personality meshed, but they usually put aside personal differences for the common good of the team. Tony took great pride in mentoring players to help accomplish this.

He knew well this emotional place of highs and lows, vividly remembering ecstatic euphoria following an important win and the bitter pain after a loss. Tony replayed personal achievements and tragedies, honors received, and goals not met. He had witnessed memorable media interviews with players holding court, and the dreaded appearance of "the Turk," a lowly team assistant coming to take your playbook on orders from the head coach because you were being cut or traded. *Never for me, thank God.*

A virtual highlight film from his playing days spun through Tony's head as he roamed the locker room. Here he was grounded and at peace.

Tony made his way to his office. Not having the aura of hallowed ground that the locker room possessed, the space nonetheless still held its own vibe of Tony's football life. He completed his film review of yesterday's debacle, replaying the penalty segments multiple times, taking copious notes for the coach's review that afternoon.

Immersed in the organized chaos of his desk, Tony failed to see Dennis standing in the partially open door, observing his boss. Dominated by a large monitor for watching game film, the desk's periphery was covered with stacks of paperwork, a white erasable clipboard and whistle, and the team playbook. One corner was reserved for Tony's favorite family photos, which he updated regularly.

"Mornin', Coach. How you doin' today?" Dennis asked after a few moments, depositing a backpack on his own neat and orderly desk. "Looks like you've been at it for a while."

"Feeling pretty frustrated right now, Denny," Tony replied, his jaws already hard at work with gum. "Just reviewed the game. Those penalties. Curiously, the camera angles were not great for three of them. So, they were totally judgment calls by the side judge."

"That's convenient."

"Convenient for sure. Our guys had a hard time maintaining confidence after the last one. Completely changed the tone of the game."

"For what it's worth, Coach, I've noticed other strange calls too, going back to last year. I wasn't sure, so I didn't say anything. I've been keeping some statistics on 'em, among other things. I think I'll just take a closer look, on my own time of course."

Tony cast Dennis a bewildered look. "Well, statistics might be interesting, but I don't know what good it'll do." He paused, shuffling some papers. "Hey, it's too much for me to think about now. I've got to get ready for the meeting. See what Coach Rocky says now that he's seen the film."

"I should have the reports for you within the hour." It was his job to compile a set of specific statistics developed by Tony and distribute them to the head coach and defensive coordinator.

He turned to go but then stopped and wheeled around. "Can I ask you somethin', Coach?"

"Sure. What's on your mind?"

"Yesterday, you said somethin' about 'a pawn in somebody's chess game.' What did you mean?" He looked intently at his boss, awaiting his answer.

Tony thought for a moment before replying. "Denny, somethin's happening to the sport. It's all about ratings and TV revenue now. The league will do anything to impress fans, the media, and to generate ratings and market share." He paused, his gum chewing the only sound. "The game seems more show than sport, all that stuff, but they don't care about the integrity of the game, or the players or coaches. I feel powerless when this crap happens, just like a pawn, to be used up for the king." He toyed with a paper clip and gave his prized bobblehead—a football player wearing number twenty-three, Tony's playing number since high school—a whack. Given to him years ago by Maggie, it was a constant reminder of his foundation.

"You know, Denny, Commissioner O'Brien rarely uses the word *football* anymore. He keeps referring to it as 'the product.' At times I think the NAFL is simply another Fortune 500 company, with similar marketing and manipulations of their audience."

His volume rose, gum chewing accelerating, and he pounded the desk with his fist.

"Are they making us just another phony reality show?" Tony stared at the still moving bobblehead. "That's not the game I've known—or want to know."

"I hear you, Coach. But I *sure* do love the game, despite how it's changin'. See you tomorrow," he said with a huge smile as he closed the door behind him.

Tony appreciated Dennis's upbeat attitude. He was a great kid and had been a lucky find. Behind Dennis's slow, heavy drawl was a keen intellect with an encyclopedic knowledge about football statistics. He had been invaluable to Tony since he hired him two years ago.

After Dennis left, Tony stared at his computer screen while tapping his pencil furiously on the desk, disgusted at the possibility that somebody was playing him and his players. He snapped the pencil in half, flinging the pieces into the wastebasket, and returned to his film review. *At least* this *I can control.*

The mood in a Monday game-review session was always tense after a loss and particularly so after this one. Tony came prepared, already pounding two sticks of gum with a new pack in his pocket. Coach Jones's criticism of the plays involving Tony's defensive backs was pointed yet less scathing than he had expected, and the head coach's summation to the assembled team hadn't mentioned Tony.

"I don't really know about those calls yesterday," said Coach Jones. "I do know we need to improve how we handle those situations, how we respond to them. We can't get down, can't ease up. That's on us."

That was his *official* response to the team and later to the media. When the players had all left and it was just the coaches, a different message was delivered. Jones wasted no time in venting his frustrations on Tony.

"Just so you know, I spared you in front of the team and media, Tony, but I place this loss squarely on you and your players."

"Did we watch the same film, Rocky?" asked Tony, voice rising. "You didn't see anything wrong with those calls? It was all on my guys?"

"Like I told you yesterday, their performance was subpar and must be improved." He said this in a monotone, avoiding the question and not making direct eye contact with Tony.

Tony chewed vigorously for a few seconds and looked over to Coach Naples, who remained impassive. "My guys played well, Rocky. I reviewed those calls and only found one that possibly could be considered their fault."

Head coaches do not like to be challenged by assistant coaches, and Jones was no different. "Don't blame the officials for your deficiencies and those of your players. Coach 'em up, Tony!" he shot back with a finality signaling the end to the topic.

Tony fumed in silence for the remainder of the meeting and then headed to his office.

———

He worked hard to put the rebuke behind him, immersing himself in preparing for tomorrow's practice. He planned to review the pass interference rules with the players and run a series of drills to try to avoid these penalties. A glimmer of self-doubt crept into his mind. *Was that game my fault, bad luck, or something else?*

The thought was just beginning to depress Tony when Dennis walked in, upbeat as usual. "Well, that didn't go so poorly, did it, Coach T?"

Tony looked up at him with a sour expression. "Oh, it went *great*, Denny. You weren't in the coaches' meeting. Different story there. Jones said he 'spared me in front of the team.' Refused any comment on the calls other than to blame my guys." Tony paused, staring at his bobblehead. "I dunno, maybe it *is* me."

Dennis walked over to Tony's desk, placed his palms flat, and leaned in. "Now don't go beating yourself up, Coach. We *know* what we saw. Coach Rocky is talking two different stories. I have a buddy who saw Mr. Cane and Coach Rocky give the commish an earful yesterday. The commissioner was not happy with their tone and let them know it. Warned them that further complaining could lead to *consequences*. Put 'em right down," he said, eyes wide with a knowing smirk.

Tony thought about that for a few seconds. There was a system of back-channel gossip involving the lower-level team assistants that was well known. Dennis's info had always proven reliable. Tony's gray mood brightened slightly. "That's very interesting, Dennis, and I appreciate you telling me that, but the buck still stops with me."

Dennis straightened up. "I realize that, Coach. Just wanted *you* to know the real scoop. If you don't need me for anything, I'll go pull some film and take a closer look at other games this season."

"I got nothin' else for you today, Dennis. See you tomorrow. And thanks for the info."

Dennis's face lit up. He simply nodded and said, "No problem, Coach. My pleasure."

Tony returned to his work with a wry smile on his face. *Jones just couldn't deal with me straight, had to shift the blame to someone. He also doesn't approve of my rapport with players or going to bat for them over injuries.* Tony's smile faded. *Naple's not backing me was a bad sign. Could they be looking for an excuse to get rid of me?* The thought raised the hair on Tony's neck, turning his mood dark again.

———

Dennis left Tony's office and headed for the film room, anxious to go home and begin his review. He made his request to the team employee, waited, and when the man returned, he signed for the films. The man raised an eyebrow but said nothing when Dennis said he would need the films for several days, an unusual request for a low-level employee. The film guy was aware of Dennis's position in the organization and didn't know more about him than that, but his request was suspicious. He put a *Back in 10 Minutes* sign on the door of the film vault and went to a secluded area behind the building where he could have a cigarette and make a phone call. It might not be important information, but in his unofficial job he was paid to report anything suspicious—and not to someone on the team.

CHAPTER SEVEN

His Monday morning had been routine, even boring. As an accountant with a major firm, Frank Ohlendorf was grateful for that. Yesterday's emotions were fresh and raw, and the diversion of work was welcome, but short lived.

As a cost-saving measure and because his wife Nancy made such a great lunch, he almost always brown-bagged it, eating at his desk while continuing to work. Today he had decided to leave the office, thinking that the crisp, early autumn weather in the nearby park would help to soothe his troubled soul.

It almost did.

Frank was doing great until a guy sat next to him with a cheesesteak sub. The aroma assaulted him and brought Frank back to exactly a week ago . . .

========

It was eight o'clock in a poorly lit diner with cracked, peeling, off-yellow walls and a dirty linoleum floor. Frank sat at a table scarred by many years of use, staring out the window, his half-eaten cheesesteak sub not yet cleared away. The glass hadn't seen Windex since the place opened a decade ago, and Frank was sure that was the reason his reflection looked like hell.

Yeah, right.

He went to the men's room, splashed cold water on his face, combed his salt-and-pepper hair, and took another look, shaken at what he saw. "Shit, I've got to pull myself together," he mumbled to himself.

He returned to the booth, due to meet someone named Steve any minute. He slowly sipped the tepid coffee, oblivious to its temperature, and thought about last week, and the meeting which had led to today. He kept wondering how they knew about Paul, his addiction, and the financial hole Frank was in. *Does it really matter? I'm out of options.*

Steve entered the diner three minutes later, slowly scanned the few patrons there, and located Frank in the last booth in a far corner. He walked confidently up, towered over him, and asked in a low, gruff, heavily accented voice, "You Mr. O?" He knew the answer but wanted to see Frank's reaction.

Frank began to rise as he answered but was quickly cut off with a sharp "Sit down!" and a downward gesture from the man's massive left hand. Tall and built like a linebacker, Steve eased into the booth, unbuttoned the top two buttons of his expensive leather coat, and pulled out a thick envelope, placing it on the table between them.

As a referee, Frank was used to being around large men, but he found Steve's size and demeanor menacing. A prominent, jagged scar ran down the side of his face, adding to the thug's sinister look.

Steve leaned forward and barely whispered, "This all you need. Read, then burn. Leave no trace. Do your part, everything cool. Da?" He paused, eyes dark, deep emotionless pools boring into Frank like a laser. "I know your house, your wife, your kid. Don't fuck up," he sneered before Frank could say anything, and then quickly began to leave.

Frank started to speak. "I—"

Steve spun around, glowered at him, took two steps, and leaned over until he was so close Frank was almost overcome by his fetid cigarette breath.

"Don't fuck up, Mr. O," he said again through clenched teeth and disappeared into the night.

Sweat poured down Frank's brow. His mouth felt like cotton and his lips stuck together. His hands trembled as he scooped up the envelope, wishing this were a bar rather than a diner. *What the hell did I expect?* He paid the bill, thoughtlessly leaving way too much tip, and hurried to his car. Part of him couldn't wait to open the envelope while another part wanted to throw it away. But ten grand was a lot to toss away, and if all went well, it was just the beginning . . .

———————————

". . . it cost how much? Ten grand? That's exorbitant," Mister Cheesesteak Sub bellowed into his cell phone, jolting Frank back. *So much for the relaxing lunch. At least accounting ledgers shouldn't have any triggers.* Frank returned to his office, burying himself in work. Anything to be at peace for just a little while.

CHAPTER EIGHT

James O'Brien toiled in his opulent office, poring over financial and media reports. His day had begun this Tuesday morning at five thirty with a full hour of weight training and cardio, and now at three he was not yet slowing down, having only taken a short midmorning break. This relentless work ethic had served him well over the course of his fifteen-year career, culminating in his being elected to his top position five years ago.

O'Brien's concentration was broken by a series of sharp knocks on the door. Since his assistant was on an errand, the visitor was unannounced. O'Brien said, "Come on in."

Phil Townsend, senior VP of corporate communications and internal security, marched in, consistent with his former military background. He had a wrestler's muscular build with a square jaw and piercing blue eyes, projecting a confident, no-nonsense attitude.

"Hey, Phil, what's up?" O'Brien asked of his most important employee.

"Just wanted to touch base on a couple things, Jimmy. Macafee told me you were pleased with Sunday's outcome."

"Yes, a perfect example of what we're trying to accomplish on several levels. Any problems you're aware of that I don't know?"

"No problems, just things to keep my eyes on. Yesterday afternoon, one of my sources on the Columbus team reported that a low-level assistant checked out extensive game film from this year, far more than is usual."

"Who does this assistant work for, Phil?"

"The defensive backs coach, a guy by the name of Tony Stravnicki. Former player, well thought of by players and most coaches. Some think he sides with the players too often. He got let go when the Phoenix Rattlers' owner cleaned house a few years back. I don't have anything more on him. My source did say he heard Stravnicki and Jones got into it a bit after the game."

O'Brien thought for a moment, tapping a pencil on his desk. Typical Townsend briefing: a lot of information quickly. "Probably nothing. Stravnicki *would* be the one in the crosshairs after Sunday. I'm guessing he's just going to review a lot of film to see what he can do about it. Get off the hot seat."

"Yeah, that's logical. He's on my radar now, nonetheless. We can't be too careful."

"That's for sure. Phil, keep me informed. See you tomorrow." O'Brien returned to his computer as Townsend replied, "Roger that," and departed.

O'Brien decided it was a good time for a break, calling down to the dining room for a lunch delivery. He walked over to the credenza bar and poured himself a short scotch. Returning to his desk, he propped his feet up and enjoyed the spectacular view. On top of his world, *his* empire—literally and figuratively—he thoroughly enjoyed this perk of his success, part of his grand quest. He was smart enough to know he needed men like Townsend to fulfill that vision. Men who were willing to bend the rules, live on the edge, and do whatever was needed.

O'Brien sipped the scotch. He didn't know this Stravnicki, but he knew Townsend. People were justifiably afraid of him. The man was ruthless and paranoid: a bad combination unless you were chief of security. Never a good thing to be on *his* radar. That coach better not make any waves.

CHAPTER NINE

Returning to the team facility early Tuesday, Tony was determined to get past the rebuke from Rocky and put on a strong showing at the afternoon practice. He had put together a series of drills for his players that would emphasize minimizing pass interference penalties, and he was anxious to put these to use. When he entered his office, he was surprised to see Dennis hard at work. Two computer screens were open, and multiple piles of paper were arranged on his desk.

"Well, this is unusual. What's going on, Dennis?"

"I've finished my little side project. Found some interesting stuff you might wanna know about," he said, eyes wide and sparkling.

"Really? You've got me curious, Denny, but I've got a full schedule until just before noon, so we'll meet here and work through lunch."

Dennis nodded and closed his computers. "Sure thing. See you then, Coach."

Tony went back to his preparation, skeptical about what his assistant could have found.

Today's meetings were routine, with none of the rancor with Jones from the previous day. Complaints were made about erratic communications problems during the game, and some players and coaches were critiqued, but nothing further was said directly to him. He picked up some sandwiches for himself and Denny and headed back to his office, locking the door behind him. Dennis had the laptops ready to go.

"Okay, Dennis, what have you found?" asked Tony.

His assistant cleared his throat, and a poised, confident look came over him. "Coach, I've reviewed every game in the league this season and made a spreadsheet of all penalties. I gave each data point a numerical value from one to five and correlated these with what effects these penalties had on the outcomes of the games versus the pregame projections and then correlated these with the media numbers from all networks and sports radio and television talk shows in their individual markets." He looked over at his boss, who was wide eyed, fully focused.

Dennis continued, explaining his statistical software programs in detail until Tony's eyes glazed over. He spoke in a matter-of-fact tone just above a whisper so that their conversation could not be heard outside the office. "Any questions so far, Coach?" asked Dennis.

"I won't pretend to understand the technical aspects of this, Dennis, but I guess I understand what you're trying to do. Continue, I'll hang in there."

"Great, Coach. Not too much more." He said this like a professor encouraging an overwhelmed student. He continued for a short time before summarizing his findings. "These programs and data points strongly suggest these events are linked. The question is, what do we do next?"

"How reliable's this stuff, Dennis?"

"Very, but it's a limited sample size. Coach, I look at this as telling us we are not imagining things or victims of our own biases." Maintaining eye contact with Tony he said, "I really believe in what I've found."

Tony had never seen Dennis so passionate about something, so he took his time to respond, choosing his words carefully. He let out a long sigh. "I really don't want to believe this, Denny. I was hoping that you wouldn't find anything. *You* need to look further and get more data, and *I* need to come to terms with this. Really think it out. It's normal now for teams to be looking at tons of data, so I don't think you'll draw much attention if you're careful, which I know you will be."

"Not a problem, Coach. All my computers have multiple levels of security, and I'm not using team equipment." He gathered his laptops and notebooks, put them in his backpack, and simply said, "See you at practice."

After he had gone, Tony spit his gum out and reached into a lower drawer of his desk. His supply was getting low, but so far it was only a one Milky Way day. He reviewed his conversation with Dennis. *That was an impressive presentation, but the kid looked worried when he left; not scared exactly, but like he knew enough to be concerned. All that statistical stuff? Does it really mean anything?* Tony trusted Dennis but decided to do a little research himself with human connections—not some computer.

Tony got up and locked his door. Using his old-fashioned Rolodex, he looked up three numbers and began making the calls.

———

Once again, Dennis went to the film room and placed his request, this time for significantly more film than yesterday. The same employee waited on him, saying nothing, but was alarmed by the amount of material. He filled the order and decided it was an important time for another cigarette break. He puffed nervously, waiting for the call to be answered, not daring to leave a message, and was just about to hang up when the gruff voice answered.

"Yes. What is it?"

"Sir, Johnny in Columbus. Just had the same individual as yesterday but requesting far more film this time, going back to last year."

His contact was silent for only a few seconds before replying: "Johnny, do you remember what I gave you and trained you to do?"

"Yes, sir. I've got it handy, and I know how to use it."

"Good. You need to get it into that coach's office. Stravnicki is his name. Remember there are two parts for his office, and the retransmitter in your film room."

"Yes, sir. Coach Stravnicki. I've got the master key you gave me. I'll get in there tonight. You can count on me."

"I'm sure I can. I also need you to text me the home address of that coach as soon as you can."

"Yes, sir. I can get that for you by the end of the day."

"Good. There'll be a bonus for you. Keep me informed." He hung up.

Johnny the film guy went back into his office and retrieved the equipment, carefully checking the devices in a secluded corner of the film vault, looking forward to his bonus.

———————

The afternoon practice went well, and Coach Jones approved the drills Tony had put together, pleasing Tony. However, the three phone calls he had made earlier in the day weighed on him. He arrived home consumed with his meeting with Dennis and the calls. When he walked through the door Maggie greeted him as usual.

"Hey, Tony, you're home earlier than I expected. That's a nice change," she said with their customary hug and kiss. Tony went through the mail, saying nothing. He normally was pretty good at leaving the team and coaching stuff behind unless something really big was bothering him, but tonight he was off.

Dinner with Zach and Hope was animated as always, and Tony interacted normally, but he only ate some of his favorite meal, chicken marsala, which just never happened. He and Maggie completed their usual kitchen cleanup and kids' pre-bed routine. It was her turn to read to them, and when Maggie came downstairs, she found him staring blankly at an inane game show he hated. She picked up the remote, shutting off the TV while looking at Tony.

"What's going on, Coach? My marsala didn't seem to have its normal effect on you. Too many mushrooms or too little wine?" she joked, sitting down in a wing chair.

Tony's laugh rang hollow, devoid of joy. "Sorry, Mags. Great dinner as always." He picked up a throw pillow and tossed it on the sofa with a sigh. "I'm having a hard time wrappin' my head around somethin'and I have no clue how to handle it," he said, his voice barely audible. "I'm not even sure I believe there is a problem, but if there is and I screw up how I handle it, I could get hurt. *We* could get hurt."

Maggie jerked up. "You need to talk to me about this, Tony. Let me help. Whatever it is, I can tell that this is not a problem you've faced before."

"No, it sure isn't," he replied. "This is going to take a while, so let's get some tea for you and decaf coffee for me."

A few minutes later they were settled back on the sofa and Tony began a detailed review, starting with the last game and continuing with his meeting with Dennis today. Maggie took it all in, asking a question here or there but letting Tony talk.

When he finished, she shook her head, saying, "What does Dennis know about statistics, Tony? I wouldn't put too much faith in that."

"Well, he did get a minor in informatics at Georgia Tech, along with his sports management degree, so he sure knows more than me. But there's more, Mags. I've been in contact with three other assistant coaches as quietly and low-key as I could. These were guys I played with, thought I knew well and had a good rapport with, and a couple at one time I considered friends. I asked only general questions about officials' calls, not naming specific names or games, just asking if they saw any patterns or irregularities that bothered them. Well, Maggie, I got three totally different responses. The first guy, normally someone who would talk your ear off, got really quiet, told me that he had, in fact, been bothered by some things he had been seeing and had his suspicions. He then abruptly said he had to run and hung up on me." Tony took a sip of coffee, seeing a puzzled look on Maggie.

"The second guy totally refused to talk about anything to do with the officials, even in general terms, and he told me not to make any waves about this. This from a guy who always had an opinion about everything and would tell you it. He was one of the most fearless guys I ever played with, but I tell you, Maggie, there was unmistakable fear in his voice. I touched a nerve, and he didn't like it.

"The last guy was the most talkative, probably because we played together longer and had a tighter relationship than I had with the other two. He admitted certain calls and their timing seemed strange, but he had been so busy with coaching and family issues he hadn't had time to really think about it. He said he would contact me if he saw or found anything suspicious. We'll see if he does."

Tony stared up at the ceiling for a few seconds before looking back at Maggie, a somber look on his face. "What do you think, Maggie?"

"Really, Tony? Did you think these guys would risk getting in trouble over you because you *think* something funny is going on? You know how competitive the league is. Why do their actions surprise you?"

Tony face was blank. "I just thought I might find something out. I didn't really know. Where do I go from here?"

"Is there a *here*, Tony? Some statistics from a kid and random short phone calls? The league plays rough; do I have to remind you? You can't risk your career and damage to the family over something that *might* be going on. You certainly need a lot more than this."

"Then what do I do? Pursue it or just let it go?"

"You and I both know that you are not the type of man who can let this go, presuming there is something to it. You can't just drop it. To do that would eat at you constantly."

She tapped her foot on the floor, her nervous tic, and let out a sigh. "But I'm really concerned about all of us getting hurt over something out of your control. We've been down that road, and it wasn't good."

"I know, Mags, I know. I'm concerned too." After an uneasy silence, Tony said, "My mind has been running wild with thoughts of who could be screwing with the game. Organized crime from inside or outside the country? We hear talk of the Russian mob trying to get more of a slice of sports betting. But they're not the only bad guys around now." He paused. "I know I'm rambling, Maggie. Thinking up all sorts of whacked-out stuff."

"It might not be whacked out, Tony. We don't know yet. Only time will tell if something is really there. I'm not telling you to forget about it, but you and Dennis must keep a low profile as you pursue this. Be careful Tony—for all of us."

"We will. We won't attract attention," he assured her.

But that ship had already sailed.

CHAPTER TEN

B ill Macafee shifted in his seat for the fifth time. His boss, James O'Brien, had been on the phone for more than ten minutes with no end in sight. Macafee studied the many pictures of O'Brien with famous dignitaries, but his focus was drawn to the most prominently displayed photo, one of O'Brien from his Notre Dame playing days, inscribed *Big Jimmy #75*.

O'Brien put down the phone, rubbing his hands together, a broad smile lighting up his face. "That's what we've been waiting for, Bill. TNI is in!" he said, referring to Television Networks International, an up-and-coming network anxious to challenge the monopoly the major networks had on sports.

"That's great, Jim. It's a thrill to have a network court *us* for a change."

"Damn right! Their style of production is exactly what we need to catapult the league to the country's leading entertainment product. We're gonna ride them all the way to the bank."

"*If* we handle them properly. You know I'm not in favor of pushing the contracts to the max. This is their first rodeo. Can't come on too strong—"

"Too hell with that, Bill," O'Brien cut him off. "They're anxious to get their foot in the door. Now is exactly the time to go big, when they're hungry. It's a huge opportunity to grow our brand and revenue and to *control* how we do it." His eyes sparkled, wide with enthusiasm, his voice rising. He had become a master at projecting his power and getting his way. Few could really challenge him, and Macafee was not one of them, as his strength was finance and taxes, not politics and power plays. "Bill, I want all the projections we've discussed complete for tomorrow's meeting."

"No problem, I—" He was interrupted by the buzzing of O'Brien's intercom.

"Yes, what is it?" O'Brien answered sharply.

"Mr. Townsend to see you, sir," his assistant, Kate Forsythe, replied.

"Just finishing something. Send him right in . . . and coffee and a snack too."

Macafee gathered his notes. "I'll call you," he said, and simply nodded to Townsend as the two passed.

Townsend did not sit and waited for the door to close. "Just a quick follow-up on that coach, Stravnicki. His assistant pulled even more film yesterday, way out of the ordinary."

O'Brien huffed. "Do we really have to worry about some insignificant defensive backs coach and his assistant?"

"This is twice in two days. It's still most likely nothing, but you don't pay me to wait for a problem to happen," he shot back. "I'm looking into this assistant and ramping up oversight on Stravnicki, just to be sure. Simply wanted to give you a heads-up before the meeting," he said, heading for the door.

"Okay, Phil. See you there."

Three minutes later, Kate rapped twice on the door and entered with a tray of coffee and pastries. He barely acknowledged her, saying nothing, merely pointing to his desk. She poured a cup for him and then immediately left.

Grabbing a bear claw, O'Brien sipped his coffee and reflected on why he had been short with his security chief. After all, the man had an impressive resume: Naval Academy graduate, Marine Corps special ops, National Security Agency. O'Brien had hired him to improve security in the league, on several levels, which he had done in ways approaching fanaticism, so today wasn't unusual. *I've got to trust him and let him do his job.* Still, O'Brien had a fleeting sense of concern about the assistant coach. *Probably nothing,* he chided himself.

CHAPTER ELEVEN

The four handpicked men rode the private elevator in silence from the lobby of the commissioner's suite to a corridor deep in the basement of league headquarters. From there, it was only a few steps to a small, seemingly insignificant room. Access to the elevator, corridor, and room was controlled by keypad codes known only to the commissioner, his trusted assistant, and these four men.

The room was spartan in appearance: only a rectangular wooden table and five chairs, with none of the high-tech computer and audiovisual capabilities which were widespread throughout the league offices. The room was an electronic dead zone. No signals could penetrate its special walls, ensuring complete privacy, so no cell phones were permitted. No written records were kept. The room was meant solely for use by five men whose existence as a group was unknown within the league, except to the assistant. She had been told it was a select team whose function was to brainstorm the future of the business.

That was only a fraction of the truth.

Small talk ensued among the CFO and three high-ranking VPs, until their boss marched in, acknowledging them with a sweep of his hand and saying, "You are part of the greatest opportunity in your lives . . . to transform a sport from merely a game into the premier entertainment product in America. In effect, you will be creating a reality show the magnitude of which has never been seen. You have been carefully selected by me, and we share a common vision. Our initial meetings have created the framework for our goals, and you have each contributed with your specific areas of expertise. Secrecy is absolute. There is no turning back," he said, looking hard at each man.

He paused for a few seconds to emphasize the point. "Phil Townsend will brief us on recent accomplishments."

"Thank you, Commissioner," Phil responded. His blue eyes, as cold as a mountain lake, with their laser-quality ability to pierce right into a person's psyche, scanned each member.

"Prior to the formation of this group, last season the commissioner and I created test cases for our project. Using a very small number of officials and players, we experienced good success in our attempts to influence game outcomes and standings. We expanded that to eight people in total, and that number may increase."

"How is that number broken down, and how secure is your control of these people?" challenged a member.

Staring him down with a withering look, Townsend answered, "The number is comprised of two officials, four players, and two game-day frequency coordinators. Control is not a factor because of how carefully they were chosen and because the alternatives to not cooperating would be very unpleasant." The chilling tone of his voice projected an unsettling finality.

"In performing covert background checks on select players, officiating personnel, and game-day communications technicians, I was able to discover individuals in all three categories whose life situations left them vulnerable to influence. They are involved in situations in games where their performance can, under the right circumstances, alter the outcome. We help solve the problems in their lives, and they in turn do what we tell them to do. My operatives have extensive experience in this sort of thing and are very good at what they do. They make it very difficult to decline their offers."

"What's the possibility any of these individuals could stop doing what you've told them to do or even refuse in the first place?" asked another. "They are, after all, supposed to report contacts such as this to their coach. What safeguards do you have in place so that none of this can be traced back to us?"

"Very good question," replied Townsend. "As part of league internal security regulations, if an individual were to report such contacts to their coaches or directly to the league, my contacts would know about it. I want to emphasize that the way my associates approach these people strongly warns them of the consequences of not doing what we tell them to do or going to the authorities. The situations in these individuals' lives are such that they are desperate to find a solution and they are deemed *highly* unlikely to refuse." There was a finality in his tone that was not lost on the audience. The man who had asked the question shifted nervously in his seat.

"We've had several meetings about this program, and I can assure you that he has set up a system with extraordinary safeguards and redundancies to prevent anyone from knowing the true source of the influencing party," stated the commissioner.

Townsend continued. "A part of the program is to plant a series of false impressions with these individuals so that they are led to believe that the people who are contacting them represent Russian or Eastern European mob activity. By knowing game schedules and standings, team rosters, game-day personnel assignments, and officiating crew assignments, we are able to target which games we want to influence." He folded his arms across his chest and asked, "Any questions or comments?" There were none.

"Thank you for that brief report. That is the overview; there are many aspects to our plan that will be reviewed in the future. You will be contacted about the next meeting."

The commissioner stood and headed to the elevator. It was established policy that the others would wait five minutes before taking the elevator as a group to the top floor, so that the commissioner could get back to his office and it would appear that they had been in a regular meeting. The commissioner's assistant nodded to her boss as he breezed past her without comment. Six minutes later the private elevator opened, and they scattered to their individual offices. She shook her head and once again contemplated why such secrecy was necessary for just another of the countless meetings held every week.

CHAPTER TWELVE

Vincent Taranto settled into his seat in the Top of the Town, waiting for his mark to arrive. He had carefully reviewed the extensive file his boss had provided on the subject player and would be able to instantly recognize him. Taranto, who would be introduced as Mr. Thomas, had rehearsed his role and was already supremely confident in the outcome, having much experience in this sort of thing. For security, he was wearing an electronic device that could detect any type of recording instrument within fifteen feet.

Twenty minutes later Travis Dustin arrived and settled into his usual corner table. The Top was his favorite place in the city. The young celebrity enjoyed its fine food, quiet environment, and the fact that he usually wasn't bothered by fans while he was there. In the two years he had been in New York, he had found the place to be a relaxing getaway from the pressures he encountered while playing cornerback for the New York Pride.

He was surprised and annoyed when a waitress handed him a note and said it was from a gentleman over at the corner table. He opened the note and was astonished at its message: "Mr. Dustin, if I could have a brief moment of your time, I think you would find it most beneficial to your future." It was signed by a *Mr. Thomas*. He instantly became angry that someone would dare to disturb his privacy with what was probably a frivolous business pitch, attempting to make a buck from his name and status. But the night was young, and his friends had not yet arrived, so he figured he'd go give this guy a piece of his mind and maybe even have him thrown out.

He quickly finished his drink, motioned to the waitress to bring another, and said he'd be right back. He rose to his six-foot-three height and, projecting his best image of toughness, marched confidently over to the table where Mr. Thomas sat. When he approached the table, an impeccably dressed man started to rise, extending his hand, but Travis instantly cut him off.

"I don't know what bullshit plan you think you can pitch me, but I don't appreciate my privacy being disturbed here. I don't know how you got in, but I'm probably gonna have your ass tossed outta here."

Mr. Thomas continued extending his hand, which Travis ignored. His engaging smile with perfect, brilliant white teeth set against his tanned face contrasted with a chillingly serious voice.

"Oh, I'm pretty well known here, and I assure you this won't be a waste of your time." He withdrew his hand. "We need to discuss your college academic record and how that could become a serious issue to your future professional football career and endorsements. We can also talk about your Vegas troubles. You're in pretty deep."

Travis was momentarily stunned but then recovered. "I have no idea what you're talking about. This meeting is over. Who do you think you are, trying to shake me down?" He started to walk away,

"Does the name Tina Bishop ring a bell with you, Mr. Dustin? We know all about her. You wouldn't be here without her help, and your career won't last long without ours." His tone was confident, direct, and soft spoken, but his eyes were frigid pools.

Stopping in his stride, Travis blinked rapidly and tried to swallow the lump in his throat. Looking around quickly to make sure no one was noticing, he turned back and slowly settled into a seat opposite Mr. Thomas. Leaning forward, he said in a very low voice, "That's history and can't hurt me now. And my Vegas issues are under control."

"Joey out there says otherwise," Thomas countered. "And the college issue can definitely hurt you if we *want* it to. Your past isn't as buried as you think. Here's my card. When you've thought it over carefully, call me and we can discuss how we can help." Mr. Thomas got up, put his hand on Travis's shoulder, and said, "I'll be looking forward to your call real soon. Enjoy your evening."

A few seconds later a numb Travis slowly walked back to his table. *Shit! They know about Joey in Vegas and Tina in college. How?* Fortunately, his companions had still not yet arrived. His drink was ready, and taking a big belt, he let his mind drift back to a few years before.

A poor student in high school, only his rampant cheating allowed him to get marginal grades so that colleges could pretend to be interested in his academics. He had many colleges to choose from, and he ultimately chose a major conference school.

He enrolled as a sports business major because he had been advised this would be the easiest for star athletes. But even in those courses he struggled, despite the best efforts of special tutors used for the football team. He was heading for academic ineligibility when salvation arrived in the form of Tina Bishop, a classmate. A very smart, personable young lady, she mentioned one day that she had noticed he was having difficulty in class and offered to help him. In return, she asked him to get game tickets and access to the social circle of his football teammates.

Travis struggled with the idea of being beholden to anyone, but his desperation overcame his pride, and he agreed. The university had very lax academic oversight when it came to athletes, and in her part-time work-study job in the school IT department, she had access to the main school computer. She soon figured out how to change grades, all without arousing suspicion, as she was considered above reproach by her boss. She did many of Travis's assignments, changed a few grades, and with minimal effort on his part, he was able to maintain eligibility. With the help of key alumni supporters, who provided him and other players with cash payments, he was also able to pay her something for her efforts. He accepted this situation as just another compromise in life and buried the thought of any consequences.

They maintained this arrangement for almost three years, without a hint of trouble or suspicion. He didn't obtain his degree but became a top NAFL prospect, ultimately being picked up in the second round of the draft by the Pride. He became a starter for the Pride midway through his first season and gained accolades for his rookie performance.

Unfortunately, like many NAFL players in general and rookies in particular, his newfound wealth went to his head. Vegas became his second home; gambling, strippers, and partying now dominated his life outside football. It didn't take long for the gambling to get addictive, and Vegas was eager to oblige. Because it didn't interfere with his playing, he wasn't too concerned. He felt on top of the world.

Until tonight.

Though he was never one to be intimidated or scared easily, Mr. Thomas's ominous tone got his attention. It had been a very long time since Dustin had this hollow, queasy feeling. He hadn't felt this emotion since he was a boy.

Raw fear.

He was instantly embarrassed by this forgotten sensation. For most of his life he was the one who had cowed others through his physical presence and aggressive posturing. He had been in control of his life since he was twelve, and that control was now gone. Pacing back and forth later in his condo, his mind ran wild. He was alarmed at what they knew about his academic problems in college and high school, and he couldn't think about how they could help him.

Travis went to his well-stocked bar and poured three fingers of Glenlivet. He normally did not drink during the week while in football season, but he desperately needed to regain some control of his emotions and to think this whole mess out clearly. He considered how he should approach the next meeting but soon realized it was not his to control. This thought made him even more anxious, and he needed a distraction. His current companion would be more than up to the task.

He quickly dialed her number, and she was thrilled at the

opportunity. However, she was not one he could confide in. He had no one he could talk to about these issues, but she would certainly know how to keep him happy for the evening.

That would have to be enough for tonight.

CHAPTER THIRTEEN

The electric company truck pulled into the driveway of Tony Stravnicki's house at ten thirty in the morning, and a man dressed as a utility employee went to the meter with his toolbox. After seeming to examine it, he proceeded to the secluded back door of the house and picked the simple lock. Once inside, his real work began. With practiced ease he connected a recording device to the telephone wiring in the basement and hid separate units in the kitchen and living room. His boss had felt this combination would be sufficient, and he *never* challenged his boss.

Exiting as he had entered, he was certain he had left no trace of his visit. He then went to a far corner of the yard, and in a location hidden by dense landscaping he placed the sophisticated retransmitter. Returning to the electric meter, he once again made a show of checking it before departing in the vehicle. To any nosy neighbor it had the appearance of a routine service call.

———————

Tony was reviewing Tuesday's practice film when Dennis entered after a knock, an excited look on his face.

"Hey, good morning, Coach. I've got some news for you. Found more interesting stuff."

"That's great, Dennis, but I'm slammed right now. I really want to hear what you've discovered, but it'll have to wait. How about dinner at my house tonight at seven?"

"I understand, Coach. No problem. It can wait until tonight. Looking forward to cooking that's not mine! See you at practice."

Tony was concerned he was on thin ice with Rocky and didn't want to take a chance that anything Dennis found could be overheard and used against him, so that morning Tony had spoken to Maggie about Dennis coming for dinner and she agreed, being fond of him and grateful for how helpful he was to Tony.

Dinner was low-key, and Tony and Maggie enjoyed Dennis's interaction with their children. After dessert she said, "Tony, I'll take care of the kids while you and Dennis relax in the family room. I'll join you later. I want to hear what Dennis has to say."

"Of course, Mags. I want to hear what you think of all of this."

While Dennis set up and they waited for Maggie, Tony reviewed the three conversations with the other assistant coaches and Dennis listened without comment. When Maggie came down, Dennis explained to her the concepts of the statistical analysis process and what he had discovered. He outlined how he had expanded the project to the end of last season, including the playoffs.

"I'm afraid to tell you, Coach T, that it's more of the same correlations. Nothing to discredit what I've found before."

"Well, there's another thing which I haven't told you both yet," said Tony. "You know we've been having some problems with our comms during games: poor audio, weird interference, or simply not working. I thought they were just random tech glitches. But in the third quarter of the last game when it happened again, I was near the league comms equipment box. Just at its worst, something caught my attention, and out of the corner of my eye I see some guy who

I've never seen before, no official jacket, just a sideline badge. He's standing in front of the comms box with his back to the field and his hands in his pockets, and he starts to walk slowly around the area. I've never seen anyone do this before, and as I started to walk toward him, someone called me from the sideline, and I turned around for about a minute. When I turned back to look for him, he was at the far end of our sideline near the exit, and the comms were back to normal. How about that?"

"The guy walked around the box but didn't actually touch it?" asked Maggie.

"Yeah. The regular uniformed comms guy was busy and didn't seem to notice."

The silence hung heavy, each person processing these new bits of information, not understanding their significance.

"Very sketchy, Coach. I think that's another avenue for me to check. Comms issues and their effects."

"Dennis, I know this is a lot to ask, but I want you to review the entire last season, looking at every game, every possibility you can think of. How did the standings change throughout the season— any correlations with injuries? Anything odd with the most popular teams that have the most popular players, the superstars who get the most media coverage? Look at penalties per player and the outcome of those penalties on the game. Look at all the officials and the effect of their calls. Any technical problems with comms or computer systems? Once you've gathered all this data, Dennis, run it through your programs twice. I want this to be the most comprehensive analysis you're capable of, and I wouldn't ask if I didn't know you're up to the task. And you've got to do all this while maintaining your regular duties and, of course, without anybody knowing anything about this."

Tony looked at Maggie. "Do you think this is a good idea, hon?"

"It sounds harmless, so sure."

They both turned and were startled by what they saw: Dennis had a huge grin on his face, like he had just won the lottery rather than being given an incredibly time-consuming, Herculean task of unknown significance.

"Coach T, I'm grateful and humbled at your trust in me," he said as he packed up his gear. "We do think alike, because I've already started doing this very same thing. I knew I needed a lot more data points. Don't worry about my normal duties sliding. I can handle it. This is exciting stuff to me." He paused as he reached the door. "I really don't have a life outside the team anyways," he said with a frown.

Maggie remained in the family room when Tony saw Dennis out. He returned carrying two glasses of wine, and she accepted hers with a frown highlighting her serious look.

They touched glasses, and Maggie asked, "What's your next step Tony? Just see what Dennis finds?"

"No. I'm going to touch base with Freddie Wilmington. Denny is his nephew, and I'll also contact Brad Vanderbilt from college. Do you remember them?"

"Just the names. I can't picture their faces."

"Brad was a solid player in college, who knew his limitations and realized he would never make it in the bigs. Smart guy. Lives in Columbus. Got his degree in criminal justice, was in the Army in special ops. I understand he has his own company doing private eye and surveillance work now. We had a great relationship in college, and he was always considered someone you could count on. I'll call him, sound him out, but not tell him everything. See if he's interested in doing some on-field surveillance work and observation during games. I'm sure I can get a field pass for him for a few games. My only concern is what he might charge. What do you think?"

"Great idea to get outside help you trust. To help you keep a low profile. How does Freddie fit into the picture?"

"He's another really stand-up guy. I hear he has connections in the league and has a good reputation. At the very least, he can be a potential source of information. I'm not thrilled about using outside people, Maggie, but I need other opinions. If Brad decides to work with me, I bet he's got knowledge of electronic surveillance, and one of the first things I'll have him do is sweep the house to make sure we're clean here and to advise us on how to maintain security."

Maggie's head shot up, her eyes wide. "Sweep the house? Maintain security? Tony, what are you saying? This is serious talk!"

"It could be, Mags. I just don't know. That's why I'm trying to get help I can trust."

"I agree, Tony but we need advice from a *professional* who can help sort out whether there's something to this or not."

Tony looked quizzically at Maggie. "Who are you thinking about, Mags? I can't just go to the police or Coach Jones with this."

"I know that, Tony, but what about Nick? Remember, he's an FBI agent? I know we haven't seen him in a while, but you were always his favorite uncle. You gave him a lot of advice then, and now he can return the favor."

"I never thought about Nick. That's a great idea. Got his number?"

Searching her cell phone, she said, "Here it is," and wrote it on a slip of paper, handing it to Tony. "If there is something to this, Nick will know what to do and how to keep us all safe."

"Thanks, Mags, for hearing me out. For coming up with a great option. I'll call him the very first thing tomorrow."

"Tony, how about getting a special cell phone for all calls about this stuff? Keep it separate from work and personal."

Her tone was not lost on Tony, but he laughed, thinking she was overreacting. "Really? Isn't that a little James Bondish, Mags?"

He had touched the third rail again.

"Yes, it is, Tony. I've told you my concerns about protecting the family. Respect them. If you're going to do this, be smart about it! Don't treat it lightly!" She grabbed the wineglasses, stomping out to the kitchen and then upstairs.

Tony was wounded by her biting comment. He had Dennis come here specifically because he *was* concerned about security. *She didn't give me credit for that.* He shut the light off and sat in the dark for a few minutes, deep in thought, before heading to bed. Fortunately, Maggie was already asleep.

CHAPTER FOURTEEN

Travis's companion did indeed take his mind off Mr. Thomas for the night, and by the time he was back in his condo the next morning, he felt better and was planning on ignoring the meeting. Then his cell dinged with a text.

He casually glanced at it until his eyes locked on the sender. Sweat formed on his forehead and his mouth became a desert as the adrenaline rush skyrocketed his heart rate, and he dropped the phone. His hands trembled as he picked it up.

The caller ID glared at him. *Joey$$$.*

You overdue, bro. Don't make me get ugly.

He called Mr. Thomas just before nine.

Fortunately, Travis's schedule demanded his attention, and he performed so well during practice that he had his swagger back when he left the team facility at five. As he made the drive home to his condo, his thoughts about the meeting were very different than those he'd had that morning. He actually believed that no matter what was asked of him, he could deal with it. He had handled countless other roadblocks, adversities, and holes he had dug himself into during his life. This would be just another.

He had not wanted to be early and appear too eager, but he wore his best suit and projected his most confident image. He kept telling himself, *I've got this.*

Mr. Thomas greeted him with a handshake, saying, "I've taken the liberty to order us some drinks. I believe Glenlivet is your preference."

They raised glasses as Mr. Thomas toasted, "To a successful business venture for us both." Travis merely nodded.

While the room was private, Mr. Thomas was again wearing his electronic device. His boss didn't think Travis would be bright enough to attempt to record their meeting, and Taranto was pleased when the device did not indicate any threat.

"Mr. Dustin, as I indicated at our first meeting, the people I work for are aware of your past. It is very unlikely you would ever have been eligible for the NAFL because you probably would have become academically ineligible to play by midway in your sophomore year without the help you received. You essentially defrauded the university by the illegal manipulation of your grades with the help of Ms. Bishop," he said, sipping his drink.

"Your gambling losses in Vegas are very serious. We know who you owe, and they don't tolerate that sort of thing. They will get their money or their pound of flesh." Mr. Thomas maintained steady eye contact with Travis, using a matter-of-fact tone of voice. Travis blinked quickly but remained silent.

"Mr. Dustin, my employers are in a position to help you with these issues, and as with any business dealing, we expect you to help us in return. We can eliminate your Vegas obligations and potential threats to your safety, and we can make sure that the academic issues never surface. On the other hand, if you decide against doing business with us, you will be completely on your own. Good luck with Vegas, and we will make certain that your academic past becomes a major issue for you. You can say goodbye to your football career, endorsements, and your lifestyle."

He took a long sip from his drink, motioned to the waiter by holding up two fingers, and returned his steady gaze to Travis, who had remained silent. Mr. Thomas's delivery had been simultaneously sinister and professional in a way that Travis had never experienced before, and the effect was profound. He had the instant startling realization that he was in deep trouble. Whoever this man worked for held all the cards, and he had no ability to bluff his way into a negotiation or compromise; he could only hope to salvage his career by doing what they wanted. Time to find out what that was.

"Mr. Thomas, what is it that you want me to do?" Travis asked in a low voice.

"Mr. Dustin, my employers need you to affect the outcome of certain games your team will be playing this season."

"What? You want me to throw games?" He kept his voice low but looked around nervously.

"You are in a unique position where you can subtly influence how you play in favor of your opponent. Done carefully, no one will notice."

"Like hell they won't! I've got a good rep, you know!"

"We do know that. The subjectivity of calls allows skilled players like you to get penalties that won't seem unusual. We won't have you do so much as to bring too much attention to yourself. Your ego may get a little bruised, but you will still make enough legitimate plays to be valuable to your team."

"You're asking a lot for someone who hasn't shown me any proof," he said, jutting his chin defiantly.

Mr. Thomas glared back, eyes boring into Travis. "Heard from Joey recently? Wouldn't want to see Tina hurt, would you?"

That had the desired effect, deflating Travis.

"How do I know that I can trust you, that you will do as you say?" mumbled Travis, eyes lowered.

"That is a valid concern, Mr. Dustin. Ten percent of your debt will be paid before the first game, and we will take care of half of it after the first three games. The balance will be gone by the end of two seasons, and they will leave you alone, provided you are not foolish enough to repeat your mistake.

"With all business relationships, there is some measure of trust necessary, isn't there?" he stated. "The truth is you really don't have much choice in this, but you need to realize my employers prize their assets. You have the potential to be a very valuable one, an asset that they will protect to ensure their success. Does this make sense to you?"

"Yes, I see that it does." After a short pause Travis continued. "How does this actually happen? What is the next step?"

"I will continue to be your contact. We will meet here with more detailed instructions as the season progresses."

With that, Mr. Thomas extended his hand. Travis accepted it as Mr. Thomas stated, "To a mutually successful season." He reached into his pocket, extracting a cell phone, which he placed in front of Travis. "This is only to be used for our contacts, nothing else. I will contact you within the week. Please stay and enjoy your dinner." With that, he grabbed his coat and left.

A waiter came over with a menu, and Travis ordered his favorite steak. While his head was spinning, he still had his appetite. His ego told him that he could work with these guys, and that a bad call here or there would not really hurt his reputation. His arrogance told him they needed him too much for anything bad to happen. Street smarts convinced his rational side to devise a plan should that not be true. As he finished his meal, he outlined that plan. *They think they hold all the cards, and they sure have most. But I've got a couple of my own. Just hope they're never needed.*

CHAPTER FIFTEEN

Phil Townsend arrived in his office the next day and accessed an encrypted program on his computer. The program's function was to collect and transcribe voice recordings forwarded from wireless devices he had in place as part of his surveillance of several individuals. The program could recognize key phrases and tonal inflections of individual voices, which were used to quickly screen recordings.

This morning he had a particular person of interest, Tony Stravnicki. This would be the first time Townsend had reviewed recordings of the man, as the devices had just been placed in response to suspicious behavior by one of Stravnicki's assistants.

Townsend listened first to the device from the coach's office and quickly zeroed in on a meeting yesterday between the coach and assistant. The assistant had come into Stravnicki's office proclaiming that he had "found more interesting stuff." Townsend had high hopes that this would lead to something, but unfortunately that was the end of it, with the coach referencing a meeting that night at the coach's house. It was unlikely Stravnicki knew his office was bugged, but the abrupt change in direction of the conversation was puzzling.

Townsend next accessed the recordings from the coach's house last evening. He distinctly heard the wife say, "You and Dennis relax in the family room," followed by "I want to hear what Dennis has to say," and then nothing of value after that.

Townsend realized he had committed a tactical error. He had failed to have his associate check out the entire house, telling him that devices in the kitchen and living room would be sufficient. It was apparent that the family room was in the basement. It would be easy to rectify the mistake, but Townsend decided that what little he had heard from the office and the home was enough to warrant some type of action. Stravnicki and his assistant were up to something, and Townsend didn't like it. He had a gut feeling about this and had acted in the past on even less information. A not-so-subtle warning to the coach would be arranged today.

———————

Nick St. Angelo had arrived at work with the FBI by seven fifteen, long before his required eight o'clock start time, but by nine he was nowhere near as caught up as he had hoped to be. He was annoyed when his phone rang at five past nine. When he picked it up, his mood changed. The familiar voice of his favorite uncle, Tony, was on the other end.

"Hello, Nick. It's Tony. Sorry to bother you so early. How ya doing?"

Nick detected an edge in Tony's voice. This was not a social call.

"I'm doing well, Uncle Tony. Is everything all right with the family? I don't think you've ever called me at work before."

"No problems with the family, Nick. Didn't mean to alarm you. I'm calling because I need your advice on something, and Maggie thought you might be able to help."

Nick sighed with relief as he wondered how he could be of help to his uncle. In his eight-year career with the bureau, he had shared few details of his job with anyone, and this was the first time a family member had ever called him at work.

"What's going on, Tony? How can I be of help?"

"Nick, I need to speak with you in person. I have too much to tell you over the phone. Can I come into your office? I can get an early flight to New York tomorrow if you have any time available. Is that possible?" Tony asked, each sentence clipped and running together.

Nick was alarmed at the stress and unusually subdued tone in Tony's voice, neither of which was normal. The fact that he was going to jump right on a plane amplified his concern. This request was a complete reversal of roles for Nick and his uncle. Nick had often sought out Tony's advice in the past, and Tony had been a major influence in his high school and college football career.

"Sure, Tony, I've got time tomorrow, late morning. How about eleven?" he said, glancing at his schedule. He then gave Tony directions to his office.

"That's great, Nick. I'll see you then. Thanks for getting me in on such short notice."

"No problem, Tony. I just hope I can be of help. You've got me very curious. Have a safe trip."

"I think it's something, Nick, but I'll let you be the judge of that. Till tomorrow."

Nick replaced the handset as his mind raced through possible scenarios. Something had gotten to Tony. The fact that he had talked it over with Aunt Maggie and she had recommended Tony contact him gave the issue a level of legitimacy Nick couldn't ignore. His thoughts about his aunt and uncle continued until his phone rang, bringing him back to reality.

"Good morning, Nick. It's Scott. How are you this morning?" said Nick's boss, Scott Thompson. Before waiting for an answer, Scott continued, "How are you coming along with the Cayman file? Any progress since last week?"

This was typical behavior for Thompson. He was a hard-charging, very experienced and highly regarded special agent in the FBI Criminal Investigations branch. Tall and fit, he still favored the high-and-tight hairstyle from his Marine Corps days. He was a great mentor, and Nick thanked his stars that Thompson was his boss. As such, he was not offended by his abrupt shift from pleasantry to inquiry.

"I'm doing great, boss, and I've had a productive week on the

Cayman file. Something is clearly going on down there, and our contact has been very helpful so far. I haven't been able to work backward from the Cayman accounts yet, but I have been able to confirm a lot of suspicious activity, with simultaneous payments to five unusual accounts on a recurring basis over the last year, and the amounts deposited have been increasing."

"At least that's something. Other aspects of this investigation are going nowhere. I want to review what you have tomorrow. Let's meet after lunch, say one, in my office."

"Yes, sir. I'll bring all that I have."

"Okay, Nick," his boss said with his typical to-the-point manner.

The timing of tomorrow's meeting was perfect, right after his meeting with Tony. If anything was going on with his uncle, Nick could ask for his superior's advice. While he hoped his uncle was not in trouble, Nick was gratified by the possible opportunity of being able to help Tony out.

———

Tony had used a burner phone to call Nick, one of several he had picked up after his meeting with Dennis and his talk with Maggie. He felt a little foolish about all of this, acting like he was a fledgling spy in some novel, using burner cell phones and calling his nephew at the FBI. Maggie was the next call. "Hey, Mags. I just got off the phone with Nick, and he can get me in tomorrow morning."

"That's great, Tony. How did Nick sound? Did he seem surprised?"

"Yeah, he did, thinking at first that there was a family emergency. He was pleasant and his usual self while I'm sure I sounded crazy, acting so mysteriously. I tried to act normal, but I don't think it fooled him. We didn't talk any specifics, and he didn't press me for details."

"When can he see you?" she asked.

"I've got a flight out at six tomorrow morning, and Nick will see me at eleven. Lucky it's a bye week, so no practice. I'll put a little extra time in today, so I should be home by seven thirty."

"Okay, Tony. I'll feed the kids something early and have dinner ready for us by eight. See you then."

"Great, Mags. Thanks for holding dinner. See you then."

As Tony reviewed it all like a movie on a continuous loop, he hoped Nick could offer some logical explanation for his observations. The irony of the reversal of roles with Nick was not lost on Tony and only unsettled him more, another something to rock his world.

―――――――

It had been a busy day for Tony, and he was glad for the bye week. Lost in the music of his favorite station, he barely noticed the dented, late-model sedan pull up next to him. Before he could react, the car swerved toward him, sideswiping his car. Tony reacted quickly, maintaining control and coming to a stop on the shoulder. Breathing hard, he shook his head and was grateful he was uninjured. When the driver of the car that hit him backed up parallel to Tony, he expected the driver to apologize. The man, wearing sunglasses and a cap pulled low on his brow, looked at Tony through the lowered passenger-side window, pointed a finger at him, and yelled, "You better be more aware of what you're doing in life, bud, and the consequences. You could get badly hurt, you know!" The perpetrator laughed and sped off, burning rubber and leaving a cloud of dust in his wake.

A stunned Tony yelled, "What the fuck?" as his heart rate skyrocketed. He jumped out to examine the car, finding the damage to be more cosmetic than functional. Shock gave way to questions. *"Be more aware of what you're doing in life . . . " What the hell was that about? I certainly wasn't at fault!*

He reported it to the police, but he didn't have much hope they could do anything. They saw it as a random event and, with no injuries involved, probably wouldn't give it much more than a cursory investigation. He would describe it to Maggie as a simple hit-and-run. *Was that really all there was to it?* He sharply inhaled, and a shiver ran through him when the real possibility dawned on him.

Tony showed Maggie the damage as soon as he arrived home, trying to pass it off as just a simple accident, but she pressed for details.

"Tony, thank God you weren't injured. You say he came out of nowhere? Did the guy seem drunk or high? What did he say when you passed papers?"

"Nothing really, Mags. We didn't pass papers; he just made some random comment and sped off laughing. I couldn't tell anything about him, everything happened so fast." *Please let this go. I don't want to play twenty questions.*

"Sped off laughing? That's some crazy type of accident."

"The police thought it was nothing much, I'm afraid. I'll deal with the insurance company tomorrow after Nick," he said, staring blankly at her, hoping to end the inquisition.

She stared right back, tilting her head slightly. "Some random comment, huh?"

Tony withered under her glare. "He might have said something about 'being more aware in life.'"

"You weren't going to tell me that? What does that even mean? Were you driving distracted?" she demanded, the words staccato, her tone accusatory.

"I don't know what he meant, and I didn't tell you 'cause I didn't want to upset you. Maybe I wasn't driving as focused as I should have been," he offered.

Her lips curled into a frown, and her eyes softened. "I'm sorry I barked, Tony. I admit all this talk lately has got me a bit on edge."

"That's understandable, Mags. Don't give it another thought." *Although I certainly will.*

Maggie headed into the kitchen just as the kids came downstairs, their happy, cheerful banter in sharp contrast to Tony's turbulent thoughts.

CHAPTER SIXTEEN

Tony's trip was uneventful, and he made it to Nick's office twenty minutes ahead of schedule. When Nick appeared, they shook hands warmly, but seated in Nick's office, an awkward silence ensued. Tony looked down at his hands, unsure how to begin.

Nick leaned forward in his chair. "Tony, tell me what's going on. I'll help you whatever way I can." He noticed Tony's jaws were going into overdrive with gum chewing.

"Starting at the end of last season, in the regular season before the playoffs began, I noticed that there were controversial calls from the officials, not just against my team, but against others too, that often altered the outcome of the games. Now, controversial calls by officials have always been a part of the game, especially as the complexity of the game has increased, but it seems that more and more of these calls are not justified. The result can change the standings, and therefore the playoff picture. As a coach, it's very frustrating for me to see players work so hard and be penalized for things that are not their fault. You know that I always preached hard work, discipline, and desire as keys to succeeding in football, but too often it seems like that doesn't matter anymore." He paused, looked out the window and back to Nick.

"I know this sounds paranoid, but as I continued to observe things, I mentioned it to my assistant, Dennis Jalmond, a really bright young guy whose background is in sports analytics and statistics. He had noticed similar irregularities but really didn't think much of it until I brought it up. We both agreed to quietly look into this further."

Tony continued with a detailed review of his conversations with the three assistant coaches and Dennis's in-depth use of the software. He mentioned the accident, omitting most details. He ended by reviewing his talk with Maggie, and her idea to contact him.

Nick said nothing during Tony's long discourse, listening and paying close attention to his uncle's tone and body language. His uncle appeared somewhat embarrassed. As the details from Tony's conversation emerged, Nick remained expressionless but was astounded by what his uncle was telling him. Tony had never been an alarmist or a conspiracy theory nut, but Nick understood that as a play-by-the-rules guy, Tony could become upset if he thought his beloved game of football was somehow being compromised. Nick's mind churned with the possibility that his uncle might be right. He needed to be cool and objective about this and not say much.

There was an uncomfortable pause for several seconds until Nick replied, "Tony, as you have described it, and as your assistant Dennis has indicated, these are only a few events. When you think of all the calls the officials make during a season, surely some will be seen as questionable by someone. We both agree that the game of football is changing and evolving, not necessarily in ways that either one of us likes. These events are most likely random and not indicative of anything else. The timing of the accident is curious, but you're sure you've been careful? Nobody in the organization knows what Dennis is doing?"

"We've been very careful. I haven't told anyone but Maggie about it."

Nick nodded. "Okay, I'll put out some feelers to agents involved in anti-gambling and anti-organized crime to see if there's any noise about anything being linked to the NAFL."

"That would be great, Nick."

"In the meantime, continue being aware, but be very careful in how you and your assistant do this. If you stumble upon anything really startling, call me, and if I hear of anything out of the ordinary, I'll contact you."

"Well, thanks, Nick, for hearing me out. Maggie will be grateful and relieved that you gave us your input. I've got her pretty cranked up."

"No problem, Tony. I'm glad you contacted me, and I'm happy to try to help you after all the advice you've given me over the years. We'll stay in touch." They shook hands, and Nick walked Tony to the door.

The meeting with Nick's boss began promptly at one, and Nick reviewed in detail his efforts with the Cayman file. The bureau had a presence there primarily for drug money investigations, and based upon several tips from a confidential informant working in the banking system, they were looking at wire transfer records involving large amounts of cash to a select group of accounts. It was a very complicated business that included looking at tax shelters and limited partnerships, establishing links, and following trails, all requiring intensive effort.

The informant had overheard conversations suggesting that revenue associated with these transfers originated in the States and involved a pro sport in some way but did not know any more than that. The informant had access to important documents, and had provided the bureau with an enormous amount of paperwork. A team had been assembled to try and sort this out but made very little progress until Nick got involved.

He brought his laptop to his boss's office and in fifteen minutes had Special Agent Thompson fully briefed on the progress that he had made.

"So, Nick, where do you think this is heading? It's clear something is going on, but what is the source? We've got to find where it originates. This is all just academic without knowing that."

"Yes, sir, I agree, but we're not there yet. Have you heard anything from OC that could be associated with this?"

"No, nothing. We know the Russian and Eastern European syndicates would like to make it into the big leagues in sports, but so far they're small players with big ambitions."

For a moment Nick thought to tell his boss about the visit with his uncle, but he caught himself and remained silent. The moment was not lost on Thompson, however.

"Something you were going to add, Nick? Anything else on your mind?"

Nick recovered and replied, "No, boss, just thinking of the multiple possibilities we may be dealing with here. But I'm confident we'll unravel this and find out what's up. As long as our source is good, we have an advantage. I just hope she continues to be careful. We really need her."

"We do have a second asset in place in George Town whose job is to protect her. No backup coverage is ever foolproof, but it's better than nothing. That's all I'll say about it now. Okay, Nick, let me know if you find anything big, and if I don't hear from you, we'll meet here next week, same time." He nodded as a sign of dismissal, and Nick headed back to his office.

He grabbed a coffee on the way, amazed that his boss had told him about the protection. he took it as a show of confidence in his efforts. He was glad he had not said anything about Tony and decided that he would not involve Thompson without something more concrete about Tony's concerns. He would spend tomorrow morning contacting other junior agents about anything that would support Tony's observations. He wanted to believe his uncle but not look like a fool in the process.

———————

Tony returned to the team facility later that day. He had decided not to tell Dennis about the accident or his meeting with Nick yet, wanting to review the meeting with Maggie and think things over about how to proceed.

After dinner he sat gazing into his wine, until Maggie exclaimed, "Tony, I thought you'd be anxious to tell me about your visit with Nick. How did it go? What did he say? How did he react?"

Tony took a sip, leaned back in his chair, and exhaled forcefully.

"Uh, good, I guess. He listened to everything I told him, didn't interrupt me, and didn't act like I was crazy. But by the end of the meeting, he seemed distant and reserved."

"Well, Tony, he probably didn't know what to make of it. Any comment on the accident? Did he say anything helpful or give any indication that the FBI was aware of something going on?"

Tony twirled the wine in his glass. "Nah, nothin' like that. In fact, he did make the point that perhaps what I've been seeing is just part of the game evolving, and not out of the ordinary. He didn't comment on the accident. He did say that he would check to see if there was any information on organized crime activity, perhaps from outside of the country, involved with the league. It seemed like it was more of a statement just to placate me, really."

"Well, come on, we didn't expect him to have a definite answer. The important point is that you contacted him. He knows and trusts you, and I'm sure he realizes you wouldn't have contacted him on a whim. He's now aware of your concerns and will look into it, make a few phone calls. That's all I was really hoping for. The question is, what were *you* expecting?"

"Shit, I really don't know what I was expecting," he answered, shrugging. "The problem is that I don't know what I don't know about this whole thing. The big thing to me, Mags, is something *just doesn't feel right*. My gut feeling, my intuition, screams at me that somethin' is going on. It's rare that I feel this strongly about anything, just based on some sort of sixth sense. I can't ignore what I'm feeling," he said with emphasis.

"Nor should you, honey. Give it a few more weeks and see where it goes. But again, I say, be careful. Hearing 'organized crime' bothers me."

"I know, Maggie, me too." Thirty seconds passed with no words, each deep in thought. Tony broke the silence. "One day at a time, Mags. One day at a time." *Whenever I've ignored my gut feelings in the past, bad things have happened. No matter what anyone says, I won't let that happen again.*

CHAPTER SEVENTEEN

The following Monday morning, in the team parking lot before work, Tony dialed Brad Vanderbilt's business phone number, using a burner cell phone. He identified himself, stated that the call was not expected, and waited an agonizing thirty seconds, self-doubt surging through him like an electric shock. He was reviewing what he would say when the silence on the line mercifully ended.

"Tony Stravnicki, great to hear from you! Are you calling to recruit me?" Brad asked, his Midwestern accent with a touch of Southern drawl a pleasant combination. "How've you been, and is this personal or business?"

"Brad, I've been good, and it may be both. I hope you might be able to help me. It's been a long time since we last connected, and if I heard right, after college you were in the Army for a while, Special Forces."

"Yeah, I had some adventures for a few years before I got hurt and was given a medical discharge. Then I opened my PI business here in Columbus, and it's gone really well. What's up, Tony?" His voice was confident, professional, and frank.

"I have a very sensitive issue I'm dealing with now that requires the utmost caution. I think it best if we meet in person."

"Tony, this sounds serious. Are you open for lunch today at half past twelve?"

"Yes. That's great. How about Panera on South?"

"Okay, see you there. You've got me intrigued." The line went dead.

Three hours later, Tony arrived at Panera early enough to grab a secluded table in the corner. Brad arrived exactly at twelve thirty, quickly scanned the restaurant with practiced eyes, and found Tony. They embraced with a handshake and man-hug with back slaps, both exhibiting wide smiles and sparkling eyes. No observer could tell that they hadn't seen each other in over fifteen years, their chemistry displaying a bond of fondness and respect forged years ago but still as palpable today. As they placed their order and waited at the pickup counter, each man sized up the other. Their conversation over lunch was a quick review of their family situations, with the two men avoiding any specific talk about this meeting until they finished eating and got second cups of coffee. Brad was the first to speak.

"Tony, my company is just me and an office assistant who you spoke with on the phone. I also have trusted men I use as needed. I'm sure you remember that my degree was in criminal justice, and I've got a wide range of experience, both civilian and military. Information gathering, surveillance, and counter-surveillance are my bread and butter. I've worked in corporate espionage, and I have extensive training in electronics and communications, far more in-depth than most civilian PIs. I'm quite confident in my skills and experience. So, tell me in depth how this can possibly relate to you."

Tony spent the next fifteen minutes reviewing his concerns and observations, everything that had happened the past few weeks. "Brad, I need another set of eyes and ears on the field during games. Specifically, I want you to go undercover on the field as my former college teammate who's getting background for a novel. But what I really want you to be watching out for are any irregularities in the master communications area."

Brad paused before replying. "Tony, I've never known you to jump into anything without thinking it through. Maybe there is nothing to this and I'll find squat. But if you're right, some people aren't going to like this, and you and your family could be at risk. I can evaluate your home security and upgrade as needed. I'm more than happy to help. Being on the field during a game is a plus," he added with a grin.

"I'm sure I'll have no problem with that. I'll get working on that today. How soon can you evaluate my house, and what are your rates?"

"Tony, I'm honored with your trust about such a sensitive issue. I'm not going to charge until I evaluate things both on the field and at your house, and then I can give a teammate discount. I'll begin with your house tomorrow. If you're right, I want to bring the bad guys down, too. Football was a big part of making me who I am, and I don't like to think somebody's screwing with it."

Tony gave Brad a house key and burner cell phone number, walking out of Panera with a smile on his face.

Brad watched Tony leave Panera but stayed to finish his coffee. He replayed the conversation and thought about the Tony he'd known years ago, and the one he had met again today. Brad knew Tony never would've contacted him professionally without serious concerns. He and Tony had fought many battles together on the football field once upon a time, and Tony's integrity and heart were legendary. *This is crazy, but I feel the same initial tinge of excitement I used to feel when we were first briefed before a game. Are Tony and I going into battle again, but with higher stakes than a number on a scoreboard? Has he stumbled on some serious shit?* Brad also walked out of Panera with a smile on his face and a spring in his step. He had a mission to prepare for.

Tony obtained Brad's credentials in the morning, with the afternoon spent in an intense practice for their upcoming opponent, the New York Pride. It promised to be a tough game with New York the favorite to win.

Tony was eager to call Freddie Wilmington, and he placed the call from his car. Freddy was a busy guy, so Tony was surprised when his former teammate answered on the second ring.

"Tony, how you doing? I've been thinking about you, wondering how my nephew was working out."

"Freddie, that's one of the reasons I'm calling. I'm embarrassed that I haven't called you sooner. Dennis has been a godsend. I'm a better coach because of him. Can't thank you enough for that referral."

"That's fantastic! I thought he might be a good fit. Tony, you said he's one of the reasons you called. What else is going on?"

"Freddie, how much contact do you currently maintain with the league? With players or coaches? Do you go to many games?"

"Actually, quite a bit of contact, Tony. A lot of the current players come to my dealerships. I don't have much contact with the coaches, and my schedule is so busy I don't get to go to as many games as I would like, probably a half dozen a year. Why do you ask?"

"Freddie, what do you think about the game now compared to when we played?"

"It's so commercialized now, Tony. The money they throw at players is incredible and that can lead to all sorts of problems if they're not careful. The sport itself is changing, and the environment it's played in is also. Tony, I feel there's a bigger question here someplace you want to ask me. No offense, but you were never known as a philosopher," he laughed.

"You always cut to the chase, Freddie. I need your help to be another set of eyes and ears for me." Tony spent several minutes reviewing his observations and Denny's analysis, clearly stating that he just might be imagining things.

Freddy took it all in without saying a word.

"Tony, I'm so busy I really don't give it a second thought, but if I did, I could see where there have been some unusual events during games. I'll tell you, the fact that Denny believes some of these events aren't random holds a lot of weight with me. So, sure, I'll see if I hear anything. But let's say you're right, and I do find something; what happens then? Where would you go with this?"

"I haven't gotten that far, Freddie. I just need someone I can trust to tell me if they notice things too. That's as far in the future as I can see right now."

"Okay, Tony. Let's give it a couple of weeks. Contact you then."

After the call ended, Freddie grabbed a power drink from his office cooler and thought about the conversation. He hoped his friend was wrong but wouldn't be surprised if he had stumbled upon something. Money, status, and power had become such a big part of the game, and he saw the negative effects of this as he interacted with the younger players. Freddie had never backed away from anything, but the thought of something like this was unsettling. He wondered what the endgame would be, if they did find something, realizing they could be up against powerful people who would go to great lengths to protect themselves.

———————————

A week of demanding practices preceded the game on Sunday. Brad's presence at the game gave Tony peace of mind and allowed him to concentrate on his duties as a coach. Although the Pride were the favored team, Tony's Columbus Colonels played well and were only down ten points going into the half. They scored a field goal on their first possession and held New York on downs, forcing them to punt. Columbus got to just past midfield, their drive seeming to stall, when New York cornerback Travis Dustin appeared confused on a passing play and let his man get by him.

He caught up to the receiver and could have made a clean play for the ball. Instead, he clearly pulled the receiver's shirt and was called for pass interference, which gave Columbus the ball on the seventeen-yard line. Simultaneously with this, the New York defensive coaches informed the officials that they were having problems communicating with their defense. Columbus was not having any problems with theirs, and then New York's comms came back as if nothing had happened. Dennis Jalmond was close by Tony when the penalty was called, and Tony turned toward him, saying, "That was a real lucky break for us, but I'm shocked that Dustin did that."

The penalty caused the Metropolitans to come unglued, and Columbus scored on the next play. They tried for two points and were stopped, giving New York a one-point lead going into the fourth quarter. Neither side was able to do much, and with less than four minutes left in the game, Columbus barely made two first downs, and still had over fifty yards to go. In desperation, they tried a long pass to their best receiver, who was covered by both Travis Dustin and the free safety. All three players converged simultaneously, the ball moving between them and falling to the turf. Two officials immediately threw flags, and they had a conference before announcing the call. It was another pass interference call on Travis, and he hung his head, shaking it in disgust. The slow-motion review from one angle, projected on the large-screen stadium TVs, seemed to show that Travis had momentarily grabbed the receiver's face mask. The ball was placed at the nineteen-yard line, Columbus easily kicked a field goal, giving them a two-point lead, and they played great defense for the final three minutes, sealing the win.

In the locker room after the game, the Columbus players and coaches were elated. Tony enthusiastically participated in the celebration, but he was bothered by how they had won. The two penalties had been game changers. Was it luck or something else?

———

Deep in the bowels of the stadium, Phil Townsend met in the security office with two members of the league's internal security staff. These were not members of the stadium's own security, who had finished their post-game briefing and left, but separate security personnel directly under Townsend 's personal control.

"What do you have to report, Mike?" Townsend asked of the more senior member.

"Everything was routine, boss, nothing out of the ordinary, except for a brief issue with New York's comms in the second half. We spoke with the frequency coordinator, and he didn't have an explanation. It was very brief and resolved itself. This isn't the first time this has happened this season. We did notice two people on the Columbus sideline who we could not account for at game time. Here are their pictures."

Mike showed the cell phone images to his boss, who nodded and said, "The first guy is one of mine on a special project. I didn't tell you guys about him, as he's part of my quality control," Townsend said, looking authoritatively at Mike.

"Understood, boss. But how about the second guy? He is not in our database."

"I don't know him. Check with Columbus security; he may have been a late entry they didn't tell you about. Let me know as soon as you find out tomorrow. Was his behavior suspicious in any way?

"No. He took a lot of notes on a clipboard and used his cell phone a fair amount. We'll also check with the frequency coordinator to make sure he registered that."

"Okay. Good job today, guys. Critical that you stay on your toes. I appreciate your efforts."

"Thanks, boss. I'll call you tomorrow."

Townsend stomped away, not hiding his annoyance. He was not happy about this unknown person near his "special project" guy but would wait until tomorrow before getting too excited. He believed in the tightest security and control possible, and a degree of paranoia was closely associated with that.

CHAPTER EIGHTEEN

After completing his postgame duties, Tony headed to his car and dialed Brad, who picked up on the first ring. "Well, Brad, that was an interesting outcome. Anything jump out at you for your first game?" Tony kept his voice in a monotone, trying to sound tired, when he was really trying not to sound too anxious.

"Being my first game, Tony, I didn't know what to expect. There's so much activity on the sidelines with so many people. I kept it low-key, pretending to focus on the game and taking notes as if I was actually following the game. I know your team won, but that's all I can tell you. I did locate the official league game-day frequency coordinator, who was identified by his jacket. He stayed close to his communications console throughout the game. But at one point in the second half, he seemed momentarily disturbed by something that happened.

"Coincidentally, I noticed a guy who did have an official-looking badge but whose jacket was unmarked standing just a few feet away. I got a picture of him, which I'll send you. He only stayed there for maybe fifteen seconds and then walked away, and I lost him when I looked toward the field after the crowd roared. What was interesting, Tony, is at the same time the official league guy was upset, my combination field strength meter and frequency analyzer recorded a very brief anomaly. I had been monitoring it the entire game, and it was normal up to that point and was normal again after that. It is disguised to look exactly like my real cell phone, which I had to registered with the officials pregame, so it shouldn't have caused any suspicion. I don't know the significance of that anomaly."

"Brad, that's important, because the 'anomaly,' as you call it, was probably exactly when New York complained that their comms with their defense went down. At the same time, their cornerback made a bad play, and I heard he blamed it on the comms confusing their coverage. The net result of that call was that we scored, and the momentum of the game clearly changed."

"I didn't know that, Tony. That's really suspicious. Another thing I observed is that it appeared that at least two other guys on the sideline were there to observe everybody else. We call it overwatch surveillance, and it may be normal procedure during these games. Tony, I would recommend that you get my credentials expanded so that I can go to games in the league other than just yours. The more I observe, the more I'll know what's normal."

"That's a great idea, but I'll have to go to the league itself for that. It shouldn't be a problem. Send me that picture, and I'll call you back tomorrow with more information. Thanks, Brad," Tony said.

"Glad to help out, Tony, and it was a great experience. Hear from you tomorrow."

What a great start, thought Tony. Two minutes later he was not surprised to see that the picture Brad sent him was the same suspicious guy Tony himself had noticed in a previous game.

———

Maggie met Tony at the door, beaming. "Great win, Tony. And I know you guys weren't favored. It must feel good!"

Tony embraced his wife, caressing her long red hair. "Thanks,

Mags. Yeah, I'm happy, but I've got a nagging little voice in the back of my head telling me we were given one. Did you see those two plays by their cornerback in the second half? They changed the whole momentum of the game."

"Tony, don't look a gift horse in the mouth," Maggie said with a laugh.

"Yeah, I know, hon. But I know Travis Dustin's style of play. I scouted him when he was a senior in college, and I recommended to Rocky that he considered drafting him, but New York got him first. Both plays were really unusual for him. On the first one, the defensive coordinator was screaming that their comms went down, and Travis blamed it on that. And his second foul seemed flagrant on replay. He'd been having a great game until that second half. Very strange."

The telephone rang and Maggie answered it. She looked at Tony quizzically and said, "It's Freddie Wilmington. Says it's important, and he'll call you on your cell in a couple of minutes."

Tony almost jumped out of his chair and motioned to Maggie that he would take the call outside. He took a couple of deep breaths to slow his heart rate after the adrenaline kick.

He picked up the cell just as it rang, and before he could even say hello, Freddie started, "I apologize for interrupting your supper after a long day, Tony, but I wonder what you thought of your win today? Great play, good luck, or something else?"

Tony paused before he replied. "Honestly, Freddie, I'm not sure. Everything changed on those two calls on Dustin. They were highly unusual to say the least."

"Tony, I told you I mentored a lot of young athletes, and Travis was one of them. I've known him since his sophomore year of college, he just doesn't do what he did today. I'm very surprised."

"I agree, Freddie. He's developed such a good reputation. Everybody can have a bad day. That's what I want to believe."

"Me too, Tony, me too. Here you and I talk about weird stuff just this week, and I'm a little skeptical, and then I see this. It's got my attention now, I'll tell you."

"This is what I mean, Freddie. Denny is going to do a complete review of Travis since he entered the league and see if anything else pops up. We'll just keep looking, paying attention."

"As will I, Tony. Just wanted to get back to you right away with my thoughts. I'll stay in touch."

"Thanks, Freddie" was all Tony could say.

━━━━━━━

Tony was reserved during dinner, talking with Maggie and the kids quietly. The night after a win, Tony was often boisterously happy, and the kids noticed the difference.

"You okay, Pop? You don't seem so happy, considering you guys won," said his son.

"I'm really happy, Zach, just tired. Thanks for thinking about your old man."

Maggie gave Tony a pass tonight and got the kids in bed. She came down to the living room where Tony had tossed the paper, barely opened, on the ottoman. "Penny for your thoughts."

"Another issue. People who I trust now seeing things, too. I really hoped I was wrong about all of this, Maggie, maybe just having a midlife crisis." He then turned and looked at her, frowning. "This could get intense. I've been asking myself just how far I'd take this, what am I willing to risk. And for what. But I haven't come up with the answers yet."

Maggie sat next to Tony. "I can't answer that for you. What is more important, Tony? Football or us?"

"The family, of course, Maggie. But you basically said I couldn't handle it if I just ignored it, and you're right. Outside of the family, football is my *life*. It's all I've ever done or wanted to do. I'm good at it, and I think I make a difference. What would the kids think if it came out I'm right and I did nothing? That I was afraid? Is that the man you want their father to be?"

His words rang true, and her words reflected the same truth. "No, Tony, it isn't." She stood and turned to Tony. "It's hard for me when I think my family could be at risk. A mother's instinct is to protect her children."

"I'm doing my best," he answered, as Maggie headed upstairs without replying.

━━━━━━━

At twelve fifteen the next day, Tony had just reached his car on the way to get lunch when his burner phone rang. It was Brad Vanderbilt.

"Hi, Brad. Didn't expect to hear from you until tonight. What's up?"

"Hey, Tony, I wanted to contact you right away. I swept your house this morning and you *are* bugged," he stated. "I found devices on your phone lines and in the kitchen and living room. Curiously, none were in the basement family room or anywhere else. I removed these devices and placed two other units: one will let me know if other devices are ever placed again, and the other will totally jam these devices until I can find them. I plan on checking weekly, but as an additional measure, I left another unit in the family room that you will turn on when you use that as your meeting room. This will create an electronic wall that will guarantee nothing can leave that room. Just another layer of security."

"Damn! Someone was in our house!" Tony said in a low voice.

"Yeah, Tony. You're certainly in somebody's shit who doesn't like it."

"Great. You can't trace these devices to anybody, can you?"

"No, that's not possible. They won't hear anything from your house, and I'll recommend a good security system, along with upgrading all the locks. There's no such thing as one hundred percent anything, but I'll get you damn close."

Tony sighed. "Thanks so much, Brad. I know you'll do all you can. I'm working on expanded credentials for you but don't have them yet. I'll call you when I do."

"Okay, Tony."

Tony sat in disbelief, having lost his appetite, wondering how he would tell Maggie.

CHAPTER NINETEEN

The meeting was due to begin at one o'clock in the afternoon. At two minutes to one, Commissioner James O'Brien strode into their special meeting room and greeted the other members: the CFO, Bill Macafee; the VP of Media and Properties, Paul Johnstone; and the VP of Contracts and Negotiations, Thomas St. George. He took his seat with a nod to his security chief, Phil Townsend, who simply nodded back.

The commissioner began. "Today, we will review the progress we have made in enhancing our product as indicated by revenue and ratings numbers. We will also outline our goals in this regard for the rest of the season." He took a sip of water, cleared his throat, and continued.

"Our first objective was to improve revenue and ratings numbers.

These are trending upward due in large part to the increased competition we have been able to develop. We constantly review the schedule to determine which games have the potential to produce the biggest impact and study our ability to affect the outcomes. Several of the games have resulted in controversies of one type or another, again generating buzz.

"A second primary objective was to dramatically improve the entertainment value of the games themselves, separate from the actual football being played. Things are moving forward in this area, and the best is yet to come. The games are more fun to watch now and appeal to a broader range of viewers. Similarly, we have increased halftime activities, which run the gamut from entertainers to recognition of our military, to encouraging youth football participation with contests that generate prizes and scholarships. Bill, will you review the ratings and revenue numbers for us please."

"Thank you, Commissioner. These are indeed exciting times. Compared to this time last year, our ratings for games televised by TNI in time slots identical to last season are up a significant twenty percent and pull larger ratings points and market share," said Macafee. "The demographic analysis clearly shows that we are gaining in our target audiences, and TNI tells us that their secondary markets have improved also. All of this has resulted in significant revenue increases in advertising for the network, thrilling TNI.

"Our contracts stipulate we get fifty percent of all advertising revenue above a baseline. As the commissioner has indicated, our efforts to improve the entertainment value of the games continues, and we have recently hired the Austin Agency to improve our presentations. These efforts have been extremely lucrative for us, as virtually all of this is provided by our preferred vendors and subcontractors, which are linked to our shell companies. Tom will review that aspect for us now."

Thomas St. George rose. "The system we have set up using preferred vendors and subcontractors is actually fairly complex and the shell companies to which they are linked are even more so. Working with Bill, we have made these virtually impossible to track back to us. There are six main preferred vendors. All bill out as actual costs plus a fifteen percent fee directly to us. There has been some grumbling about the use of our preferred vendors from some team owners and the production companies of some entertainers, but these have been easy to handle, as everyone is pleased with the result."

"Our only real complaints have come from team owners, coaches, and players about the communications issues they've been having," commented Macafee.

"That's the perfect introduction to Phil's report," said Commissioner O'Brien.

"As the commissioner stated, there have been some complaints about comms. These problems are being well covered by the media and are generating a lot of talk. The fans have hatched all sorts of conspiracy theories over this, which has been fun to watch," he said with a smirk.

"Of course, we're behind this and the results have been very gratifying, contributing to our goals. We use sophisticated equipment based on military electronic countermeasures, virtually undetectable except with specialized hardware, and we control when and how it's used, so the random nature of the events is very frustrating for the teams and the operations personnel. It's impossible for anyone to trace this back to us," he said with an arrogant confidence. "I again emphasize that I have set up a system with multiple safeguards for our protection, all with the approval of the commissioner. Our official media response is that all equipment checks out from our personnel, thereby shifting the blame to individual teams," said Townsend.

O'Brien nodded at Townsend and looked around the table. "Gentlemen, Phil and I have worked closely together on this program, and I have complete confidence in him and his systems. Let me remind you that we are all in this together. Mutual trust is critical to our success. Meeting adjourned."

———————

When the commissioner returned to his office, Kate Forsythe handed him two messages from his wife, Justine, the second one requesting that he call her right away. He read these in front of Kate, looked at her, and grimaced.

"It's probably about the damned house again," he grumbled as he walked to his office and closed the door. At his desk he slumped into his chair, opened his "special" drawer and removed a tumbler and a small flask. Pouring himself two fingers, he took a sip, let out a deep sigh, and thought about how he would handle his wife's latest demand. His rise to prominence as commissioner of the NAFL was paralleled by Justine's rise in social circles and an insatiable appetite for the trappings that accompanied that lifestyle. Her current focus was a quest to redecorate their Fifth Avenue penthouse while also badgering him to consider a bigger house in the Hamptons. He understood her need for social equivalency to his position, but her near-constant push for more and more material things was wearing on him. He took a deep breath and dialed her number.

"Hi, hon, how's your day going? Sorry I couldn't respond sooner, but I was stuck in an important meeting," he said, hoping to soften what was sure to be a whiny complaint.

"Jimmy dear, I know you're so busy and I hate to bother you, really I do, but I've got to have your answer on the redecorating options we talked about over the weekend. If we don't commit soon, it's going to take forever to get done. What have you decided? And did you check your schedule to see if we can meet with our realtor in the Hamptons this weekend?"

"Justine, I have complete faith in your choices, and as I said, I was happy with all the options you presented. Let's just not break the bank," he said. "Yes, we can meet with Frances this weekend and look around a little to see what might be available."

"That's wonderful, Jimbo. Frances has already done a lot of legwork for us, so hopefully we can find something soon. I'd like to be in for Christmas. Thank you for trusting my selections on the penthouse," she purred.

"You are great at decorating, Justine. I just don't know if it's feasible if we can get into a new place by then. That's pushing it."

"Well, if we went all cash, Jimbo, that might do it."

"Whoa, Justine. We'll have to think more about that. That's a chunk of change. Might not be the best option. Let's see what we find this weekend, and I'll have our CPA firm run some numbers."

"Oh, Jimmy, I really want this to happen. And did you follow through with the invite to Fergie for the twenty-fifth?"

He rolled his eyes, annoyed that this was one thing he had forgotten.

"Yes, hon. We just haven't heard back from her people yet," he lied, deciding to push Paul Johnstone hard to make that happen. "Justine, I've got to run, but we'll talk more about this tonight."

"Okay. I'll get going with our decorator. Thanks! See you tonight," she said, no longer purring, having gotten what she wanted.

"Yes, hon, I should be home at a reasonable time. Enjoy your decorating." Finishing his drink, he thought about pouring another one before his resolve took hold. *I won't let that woman get under my skin!*

He put away the flask and thought about his increasing annoyance at Justine's constant requests. This was cut short when Kate Forsythe's voice came over the intercom, announcing Phil Townsend wanted a quick meeting with him. Townsend strode in, and O'Brien motioned to a chair.

Townsend got right to the point. "Jim, I'm not happy with the attitude Johnstone showed today. I think he's becoming a liability."

"I knew you were annoyed, Phil, but I don't think your concerns are warranted at this time. Your methods are foreign to most people, and Paul will become more comfortable with them as we continue to get results. We'll watch him closely, of course, and it's a wise idea to not go into details about your work unless pushed. Quite honestly, I don't expect him to push on this. I thought I made a strong point about our group at the end."

"Yes, I think you did. Good idea to remind them from time to time that there's no turning back. I'll keep close tabs on him, and I'm looking into that coach's assistant also. Find out what, if anything, he's up to." He rose. "I've got to run to a meeting with two of my key people. I'll keep you informed."

O'Brien just nodded, not wanting to know anything about Townsend's people. He turned his thoughts back to Justine as he dialed Paul Johnstone's direct number, thinking not only of his Fergie problem but fervently hoping Paul behaved himself; the ultimate consequences would be in the hands of Phil Townsend if he didn't.

———————

Two men were already seated in an isolated corner of the exclusive restaurant, awaiting the third. One was a large man, well over six feet tall, with a square, rugged, weathered face marked by a distinctive jagged scar on the left side. His jet-black hair was combed back haphazardly, and he was dressed in an expensive leather coat.

The other man was shorter, perhaps five foot ten, with a stocky build but a polished image projected by a handsome face with perfect white teeth that were a focal point the few times he smiled.

The first man's thick Russian accent was in sharp contrast to the second man's refined, educated East Coast tone. Their physical dissimilarities notwithstanding, the men had certain skills not considered mainstream, and they had been employed by the same man, performing unconventional jobs, for some time. They waited for their employer in silence, one sipping a fine red wine while the other enjoyed his preferred brand of vodka.

When their employer arrived promptly at his designated time, he proceeded to their table and ordered coffee from the already present waitress, who left menus. They exchanged brief greetings, ordered dinner, and got right down to business.

"Pavel, please report on your trip to the Caymans," stated their boss, Phil Townsend.

In his thick accent and barely above a whisper, Pavel Lyubov replied, "I contact the woman our people were worried about. Warn her to mind own business. Stop asking questions or she might have accident. She acted like she know nothing about it and I was mistaken, but our people report she stopped being nosy, so it looks like she get my message."

"Very good, Pavel, and of course you will continue to follow up on it?"

The thug grunted, "Da."

Townsend continued, "Any issues I need to know about with your league contacts? Any pushback?"

"No. Our meetings quick. I do all talking. I presume you getting results from them you want?"

"Yes. We are very pleased with the results, so your methods are working." Turning his attention to the other man, Vincent Taranto, Townsend asked, "Any problems with your contacts, Vincent?"

Taranto was all business, not smiling now. "I'm not having problems with anyone, but Travis Dustin is obviously uncomfortable with our meetings. He doesn't say anything, but his body language tells me he's under a great deal of stress. He seems to be doing what we want."

"Yes, his situation is more challenging, and he has to be very careful how he goes about doing what we want. So, I can see how it would be stressful for him. Keep close tabs on him, Vincent. Anything else?"

"The two refs and the defensive tackle are cooperating without incident or complaint," said Taranto. "However, our jamming guy has mentioned twice that he thinks he has been noticed and has aborted his mission because of it. He believes he's being ultracautious, but he is concerned. I've reassured him about the quality of the equipment he's using and the safeguards you've put in place. Have you heard anything about him?"

"Yes, I have, and I'm gonna nip this in the bud. You can tell him he has no concerns. Also, I have another subject, a coach's assistant, I want you to contact. As usual, your specific mission assignments will be sent via secure text link to your encrypted phones. Keep close contact with your subjects."

Townsend finished his coffee, threw two C-notes on the table, and departed, leaving them to finish their drinks.

CHAPTER TWENTY

Phil Townsend had just completed his review of the past weekend's security reports when his secretary buzzed him on the intercom and informed him that he had an urgent call. He picked up with a curt "Yes, what is it?"

"Mr. Townsend, it's Mike Stevens here, sir. As you ordered, I'm getting right back to you. I've identified the unknown individual we observed at the game. His name is Brad Vanderbilt, and he runs a security company called Nevis Security Services. He is a former college football player, decent but not professional caliber. After college he joined the Army and served in Special Forces before being hurt and receiving a medical discharge. He was given on-field credentials by the Columbus Colonels, specifically at the request of one of their assistant coaches, defensive backs coach Tony Stravnicki. The reason given was that Vanderbilt and Stravnicki were close friends as college teammates and that he requested access to the field on game days as research for a book he is supposedly writing."

"Okay, that's interesting. What else do you know about him?"

"I wasn't able to find anything negative about his business, and I was unable to determine anything about their relationship as friends. During the game he did a lot of writing on a clipboard, so it's possible he was getting ideas for a book. My men did verify his credentials and he did show them a notebook which contained notes consistent with researching for a book."

"Hmm, not much to go on, but I don't like it. I want to know whenever he's on the field, and he is to be closely watched. Anything questionable, and we pull his badge. There's not enough to justify that yet. Keep me informed of everything. Is that understood, Mike? Good work, by the way."

"Thank you, sir. Everything is understood."

As he slowly put back the telephone, Townsend remembered something else about Stravnicki had crossed his desk recently. It had been an email about three weeks ago from another assistant coach, someone who Townsend had done a favor for, and the guy was now as loyal as a hunting dog. Townsend used him occasionally as a discreet source of information on the man's team and had found him reliable.

Townsend quickly located the email, and as he read it, alarm bells went off. The email mentioned a phone call the assistant coach had received in which Stravnicki asked this assistant coach multiple questions about what he thought of the officiating so far this year. The assistant coach stated he was uncomfortable with this line of questioning and was curt with Stravnicki, refusing to say that he noticed any problems. The email from the assistant coach was brief, and Townsend wanted to make sure nothing had been left out, so he called him on the secure line, catching him in his office.

"Coach Henderson, this is Phil Townsend from league headquarters. I wanted to talk with you about the email you sent me three weeks ago. Sorry it's taken so long to get back in touch with you. Your email was very brief, and I wanted to make sure I understood the phone call you had with Tony Stravnicki. Can you give me any more details?"

"No problem on the delay, Mr. Townsend. I'm sure you're very busy, and I wasn't even sure this was important. The conversation did not last long, but I felt uncomfortable with what Tony was asking. While I know him from our years in the league together, we are not close, and I felt his line of questioning was very direct, like he was fishing for something. It was just shy of being aggressive. He wanted to know if I thought anything unusual was happening with officiating this year. I told him I hadn't noticed anything, and I felt that this was not an appropriate phone call. He attempted to continue, but I told him I had to run and hung up on him. I have not heard from him again. While I didn't want to get him in trouble, I felt you should be notified of this conversation."

"Well, Coach Henderson, you did the right thing by notifying me of this. Thank you and don't worry. Tony won't get into any trouble. This is just normal coach venting. This is all I needed to know, and thanks for your time."

"No problem, Mr. Townsend."

Phil Townsend let out a long exhale as he stared at the email still on his computer screen. *Stravnicki again! His assistant pulling an unusual amount of film and two unusual events connected with his former teammate, who owns a security company! And the bugs stopped working from his house. Coincidences? I don't believe in coincidences. Got to find out why the assistant pulled film. Stravnicki can't possibly have found out anything; my security is too good! I'm going to put some serious pressure on the owner and head coach of the Colonels about Tony Stravnicki's job.*

He found the number for John Cane, team owner, and was pleased when he was immediately connected to him. "Mr. Cane, this is Phil Townsend, vice president of Internal Security for the league."

"Yes, Mr. Townsend, what's going on?"

"Mr. Cane, I must inform you that I have received a serious complaint from an assistant coach of another team about one of your assistant coaches, Tony Stravnicki. Apparently, he called this coach asking questions about league officiating and trying to draw him into making derogatory comments. The coach would have none of this and refused to continue the conversation, but he was alarmed and offended by the nature of the call."

"I know nothing about this, Mr. Townsend, but I'm wondering why I'm hearing from Internal Security rather than Operations, under whose purview officiating lies," Cane said.

"That the source chose to report this to my department rather than Operations speaks to the concern that this individual had about the potential seriousness of the call. I'm giving you the courtesy of keeping this within your house rather than having it escalate into a larger league matter," he said. "I shouldn't have to remind you that your head coach, Rocky Jones, has quite a poor reputation concerning excessive complaints about officiating. Perhaps this even started with him. In any case, I strongly recommend that you let your coaching staff know that this will not be tolerated, and if it continues, serious disciplinary action could follow."

A very alarmed John Cane replied, "I'll have a very serious talk with both coaches today. Thank you for reporting this to me." Cane simply hung up, without waiting for a response.

Townsend was not offended that the call was terminated so abruptly. In fact, he was very pleased with the tone he had used to deliver the warning. John Cane had sounded quite upset, although he had tried to hide it, and with the history of Coach Jones, Townsend felt a strong warning would be delivered.

———————

A furious John Cane called Coach Jones as soon as he disconnected with Townsend. Jones picked up on the first ring, but before he could speak, Cane barked at him, "Rocky, I just had a very unpleasant phone call from Phil Townsend, VP of league Internal Security. Is Tony Stravnicki in the building now?"

"Yes, but what's this all about John?" a mystified Rocky asked. He had rarely heard Cane this angry.

"Get him and both of you report to my office this instant!"

"Will do" was all Jones could manage. He raced out of his office and burst into Tony's office. Without preamble he blared, "I don't know what's going on, Tony, but a very pissed John Cane wants you and me in his office right now. He wouldn't tell me anything about it. Want to clue me in before we get there?"

Tony cocked his head to one side and squinted his eyes into slits. "Huh? Beats me, Rocky."

Sensing this was really serious, Tony popped a new piece of gum into his mouth on the way out. They reached the owner's suite of offices, were shown into Cane's office, and their boss simply pointed at two chairs as he stared at them, arms folded. In the three minutes since he had contacted Rocky, he had pulled himself back from the precipice of destructive anger and was back in control. He settled down into his custom made, black leather, high-backed executive chair, put his elbows on his desk with his fingertips together, and began in a calm yet forceful tone.

"I've been the owner of this team for fifteen years, and I have never received a call from the league like the one I just received from Phil Townsend. I trust that both of you know who he is." Rocky and Tony looked at each other and nodded without reply. Cane continued. "Tony, Townsend informed me that he had received a complaint from an assistant coach of another team, unnamed, that you had contacted him a few weeks ago, asking questions about the quality of officiating in the league, trying to get him to make a negative comment. This guy felt that the tone and nature of the call were serious enough to warrant calling Internal Security rather than Operations, which normally handles officiating. Townsend even insinuated that it was you, Rocky, with your history of officiating complaints, who was working with Tony on this."

Rocky glared at Tony, face red and lips curled in a snarl. "What the hell is this all about, Tony?" he exploded. "I never discussed you talking to other coaches about officiating!"

Listening to John Cane, Tony could not believe what he was hearing, and it took every ounce of his self-control to maintain his composure, chew his gum slowly, and show a neutral facial expression. Tony was not a poker player, but the image he projected would have worked well in Vegas. He answered carefully and slowly, in a matter-of-fact tone. "Yes, I've have made some phone calls this season to a few assistant coaches I've known over the years. The calls were more of a social nature, and depending on the person and the length of the call, we did talk some football in general, which, considering that's our profession and common bond, is only natural. I don't remember any specific talk about officiating."

"That's not what Townsend said, Tony. He views this as just shy of a major league violation and was giving me the opportunity to keep this in-house."

"Mr. Cane, first of all, Rocky had nothing to do with any phone calls I made. You weren't told who made the complaint, but whoever it was clearly misinterpreted and overreacted to our conversation. This is very unfair to not know who my accuser is."

Rocky nodded in agreement and added, "For all we know, it could be someone just trying to mess with us, gain a competitive advantage. Didn't you demand from Townsend to know who made the complaint?" The blank look on Cane's face told the answer. "Great, John, thanks for backing us up!" Rocky said.

That pushed Cane to the edge once again, and he pointed a finger at Rocky, shouting, "Don't give me that attitude, Jones. I've covered your ass with the league several times and you know it. Your whining and complaining has set us up for an incident like this. I'm not going to debate this further. Both of you are on notice: any more complaints from the league will have consequences. That's all. Go back and do your jobs!" He turned slightly in his chair, concentrating on paperwork on his desk to signal that their meeting was over.

Rocky was silent as they walked back to his office. Tony followed, not knowing what to do. When they got to Coach Jones's office, he closed the door and, turning to Tony, snarled, "I don't know what you said or didn't say, but I will *not* be the fall guy for you. You've done well here, Tony, but I know your history. Your ice is pretty thin. You're only an assistant coach and can be easily replaced, and I won't hesitate to do it, even midseason. Is that understood?"

Tony just nodded and walked out without saying a word. Surprisingly, practice went well with no interactions between the two coaches. Tony couldn't wait to leave the facility and get home. Traffic was heavy that evening, giving him plenty of time to think. *I thought I kept those phone calls fairly low-key, but I sure talked to the wrong person someplace. None of the conversations should've caused a response like this. How to tell Maggie?*

CHAPTER TWENTY-ONE

Tony entered his kitchen where Maggie was singing along with the radio. They embraced, and he made a halfhearted attempt to sing along. When the song ended, Maggie remarked, "Well you're certainly in a good mood. I'm guessing you had a great day." Then she looked at his face more closely.

"No, a very bad day actually, Mags. I almost got fired and I might yet." The kids were upstairs doing their homework, so they had a few minutes before dinner to be alone. She got his favorite beer, refreshed her tea, and sat with him at the island.

"What happened? You've rarely been criticized for your coaching, and now you've been threatened with being let go. Tell me what's going on."

Tony took a long swig of beer and recounted in detail the unpleasant interaction with John Cane and Rocky, leaving nothing out.

"I must say, Tony, you seem to be pretty calm about this whole thing considering how serious it is," she said with an edge to her voice.

"Well, I'm not, Maggie. I'm really pretty shaken, but flipping out won't do any good, will it? As I've thought about this over the past few weeks, it occurred to me that I might find out something that could cost my job. But that was just speculating. Now it's real."

"Tony, little by little, things may be adding up. Even I don't believe they're random now."

"It's pretty significant that someone went to Internal Security rather than Operations. I've triggered something that is more than about officiating. I feel like I have a giant target on me now."

"Yes, I'm sure you do. Don't do anything directly anymore; rely on Dennis, Brad, and Freddie. You've got to be a Boy Scout, do the best coaching you can, and maintain as low a profile as you can."

"So, you want me to continue. You're not scared?"

"I'm very concerned, but not scared. Brad has swept our house for bugs, will continue to check it, and has advised us on other security issues, and you've talked to Nick."

"About the bugs, Maggie. Brad told me two days ago that he did find bugs, but he has taken care of them. I've been meaning to tell you. It just slipped my mind."

A wide-eyed Maggie waved a wooden spoon at him. "Slipped your mind? Something that important and it *slipped your mind*? I don't believe you, Tony." She threw the spoon into the sink. "I'm trying to support you in this, but you're not making it easy." She continued making the meal, not saying a word, her body language doing her talking. Tony was smart enough to keep quiet, waiting for the storm to pass.

When she turned around, her anger diminished, a sheepish Tony said, barely audible, "I didn't know how to tell you. I didn't want to alarm you even more." He filled her in on everything Brad had found and done. With his sincere tone and red face, she didn't stay angry.

"As long as there are no more incidents, and you're not perceived as a threat, we should be safe. So, I absolutely want you to continue. We've had this talk, Tony. But I don't want you keeping *anything* from me. Understood?"

Tony nodded. "Absolutely. No more secrets."

"I just hope your team finds something enough to convince Nick to believe you and investigate."

"Let's have Denny over again and see what else he may have come up with, and I'll touch base with Brad and Freddie. I'm sorry, Maggie."

"Well, I signed the contract. We're in this together, but I don't have to like it."

———————

Tony tried to put his best foot forward when he went into work the next day. He couldn't be seen as avoiding Rocky; he had continued to act innocent and be the Boy Scout, like Maggie said. He had just parked his car and was grabbing his briefcase when Brad called. "How's it going, Tony? Anything new on your end?"

"You could say that," Tony replied and reviewed the recent events.

"Gee. That's pretty incredible. You really gotta watch your step, Tony. Somebody's pissed."

"I know, I know. Maggie's not happy—tells me I've got to be the perfect coach, keep my nose to the grindstone, and not draw any more attention."

"She's right, Tony. Let us do the heavy lifting. Hey, I called to tell you about my experience at the Las Vegas–Washington game this weekend. I didn't see our friend, didn't see anything out of the ordinary, but I did have my credentials challenged by two security guys, even though my badge was prominently displayed. It seemed weird and out of the ordinary how it happened. They asked what I was doing there, so I told 'em I was doing research for a book and actually showed 'em my clipboard and notebook, complete with detailed notes. That seemed to satisfy them because they left me alone after that."

"You actually had detailed notes for a book?" Tony asked.

"Absolutely. That's my cover, and it's got to be as realistic as possible. You never know when you'll be challenged like I was. Tony, I think I passed the initial test, but I won't be surprised if I find out that they're keeping an eye on me. I'll just play this out as long as I can."

"That's all I can ask of you, Brad. Be careful. We'll stay in touch." Tony grabbed a new stick of gum but chewed slowly, deep in thought. *I feel like I can lay low, but can the others?*

———————

That night Tony was on his own for dinner while Maggie and the kids went to a birthday party. This gave him the opportunity to get takeout from his favorite Chinese restaurant for himself and Denny, who would arrive soon.

After gorging themselves on their favorite dishes, Dennis set up his latest PowerPoint presentation, a culmination of the intense analytics he had been immersed in for virtually all his time not spent at the team facility.

"Coach, as you'll see over the next few minutes, my research has shown with almost complete certainty that there is some type of *factor*, for lack of a better word, that is influencing the outcomes and standings. Unbiased, completely analytical, statistical modeling confirms correlations across a range of interactions."

"Please, Dennis, the short version only."

"Sure, Coach. No problem. What this boils down to is that these multiple events are not the result of just random acts but are deliberate. I reviewed all of last year's games and all of this season's games to date. Sixty percent of games with communications issues resulted in a non-favored team winning. Twice, a certain defensive player hurt a key player badly enough to have him leave the game, causing that team to lose and alter the standings. This person had the lowest correlation of incidence among everything I studied, but I included it because his events did alter standings. Travis Dustin was the other player, but his correlations were among the highest found, and a profound difference from last year."

Tony had followed closely, nodding in agreement with the summary. "From a layman's point of view, something's up."

"For sure. My work shows it can't be much clearer. What I haven't mentioned yet, Coach, is a secondary correlation that was discovered. There were several games that all had significant entertainment activities pregame or at halftime—more so than other games. There was an extremely high correlation with the presence of these activities and the likelihood that an event would happen that would result in a change of outcome for that game.

"Since these entertainment activities had to be set up in advance of the games, there is a strong probability that the two are related. Someone wants certain games to be wildly popular and will use multiple ways to get this outcome. I correlated changes in standings in all divisions with television market share and ratings. In every case where a team already enjoyed significant ratings and market share, there was a strong probability that there would be some event that would contribute to maintaining or increasing those ratings and market share."

"This is incredible, Dennis. The information on ratings is important news. Great work. I appreciate you simplifying it for me. I presume all of your data is safe?"

"Yes. It all has a very high level of encryption built in. Multiple layers, and I keep a backup copy in a safe-deposit box. What are you going to do with this information, Coach?"

Tony briefly explained his relationship and meeting with Nick. "I'll need to present all your technical data to him. Can you arrange that for me?"

"I'm ahead of you, Coach." He reached into his briefcase and gave Tony a small envelope. "There's two flash drives in there. One is the actual data, the other is the software to run it, with instructions. You'll need a real tech geek to access this, Coach. No offense."

"None taken. You're incredible, Denny. This will go right to my nephew at the bureau."

"Great! They'll know what to do with it. I've got to get going. Thanks for dinner," he said as he packed up.

Dennis never saw the two figures quickly move out of the shadows and approach his car. He had just opened the rear driver-side door to put in his briefcase when he was grabbed from behind and a sweet-smelling cloth was pressed against his mouth and nose.

———————

The next morning, Maggie burst into the bathroom as Tony was shaving. The look on her face startled him. "Mags, what's—"

"Tony, did you see Dennis leave last night?" she asked, breathing heavily.

"Huh? No, he just packed up and left. I didn't walk him to the door. Why?"

"Come with me."

She led him out their front door, and Tony stopped dead in his tracks when he saw Denny's car, the rear door still open.

"I don't know how I missed not seeing the interior light on last night," she said.

Tony ran over to the car, took a quick look, but knew not to touch anything. He ran back into the house, closely followed by Maggie, and dialed Dennis's number. Tony shuddered when it went to voicemail and he heard Denny's upbeat voice. He next called the police, texted Denny, and left three messages while he waited.

The police soon arrived and were questioning Tony when the officer in charge received a radio message that Dennis had been found in a downtown park, beaten up and unconscious. Tony rushed to the hospital and was told only that Denny was unresponsive and in critical condition.

The next day, Dennis Jalmond died, having never regained consciousness. The police speculated that Dennis had resisted a robbery and during the struggle had fallen and hit his head on the pavement. An autopsy would be done. They were unable to determine his assailants or a motive outside of the robbery of his laptop and wallet.

Tony believed in a different theory, which he didn't share with the police.

Despite his own grief, which bordered on depression, Tony tried his best to console the Jalmond family. After the graveside service three days later, Freddie Wilmington pulled Tony aside.

"Robbery? Denny struggling with them? I don't think so," Freddie said, his face a mix of sorrow and anger. "I thought you guys were being careful, Tony!"

"I thought we were, Freddie. Dennis assured me he was taking precautions. He was too smart to slip up." Tony shook his head. "I have no idea how he drew attention. How could anyone have been suspicious of a guy like Dennis?"

"Beats me, Tony, but we've got to find out. Leave this to me. People know I'm his uncle, so it won't seem unusual for me to ask questions. Maybe Brad can help me reconstruct his last couple of weeks, see what we can discover."

"That's smart, Freddie." The uneasy silence was broken when Tony mumbled, "I'm so sorry I caused this."

"You didn't, Tony. Dennis was quiet and reserved, but he was his own man. From what you've told me, he firmly believed in what he was doing, and loved doing it. His work validates your concerns."

Freddie put his hand on his old teammate's shoulder. "We honor him by seeing this through, wherever it takes us," he said and then slowly walked away.

Tony looked at the grave with a heavy heart.

Thanks for all you did for me, Denny. We'll take it from here.

Phil Townsend was seething as he listened to Vincent Taranto's explanation over the secured phone line.

". . . just a couple of jabs, Phil, honest. How did I know the kid was gonna fall backward and hit his head? I didn't even get to question him."

Townsend paused a moment and thought, trying to compose himself before replying. *Taranto is experienced and normally very careful. An operation sometimes goes sideways through no fault. Shit does indeed happen.*

Taranto continued, wanting to change the focus of the conversation. "I got the computer, and the case has a bunch of drives with it."

Townsend sighed. "Well, maybe that's all we need. Meet at the boiler room at six," he said, and then disconnected.

At a brief meeting where little was said, Townsend retrieved Dennis's computer from Taranto and returned to his home office. He had extensive computer security experience from his years at the NSA and specialized equipment, so it didn't take him long to gain access to the files. A quick review revealed nothing suspicious, simply typical football-related software and files.

However, when he ran sophisticated software designed to uncover hidden files, he hit pay dirt. The kid had developed and hidden a subdirectory involving several powerful statistical analysis programs with multiple files linking the programs to games, players, and other league-related events. It was so complex that Townsend realized it would take some time to fully review. *Is this simply the work of a statistics nerd? What was the kid up to?*

CHAPTER TWENTY-TWO

The next few days were a blur for Tony. The practices were sloppy and Tony's coaching erratic. He snapped at his players, threw his clipboard repeatedly, and ran out of gum twice. For now, everyone cut him some slack. Fortunately, the team secured an easy win on Sunday with no controversies.

He returned home that evening out of sorts, and it went downhill from there. When the kids greeted him with their usual excitement, he was cool in his response, instead scolding Zach for leaving his bicycle out and Hope for not putting away her art supplies. Maggie would have none of it, deep in her own funk.

After they slunk out of the room, eyes downcast, she exploded.

"That was uncalled for, Tony. You crushed them. You're not the only one upset about Dennis. Stop thinking only of yourself!"

"I don't need this now, Maggie. Thanks for the support."

"I haven't supported you? Really? Give me a break!"

"I'm under enormous pressure. Don't you see that?"

"Of course I do, but Denny's death got to me too, Tony. You don't think about my emotions at all!" She moved around the kitchen frenetically, Tony silent.

She turned and stared at him, her eyes distant. "I think we need a break from each other. I'll ask my sister if I can use the lake house with the kids for a while."

Tony's jaw dropped, along with his spirit from this emotional jolt. He breathed rapidly, almost hyperventilating, speechless, unable to respond.

———

After eight hours of intense effort on Dennis Jalmond's encrypted files, Phil Townsend loudly exclaimed, "Shit" as he flung his empty beer bottle into the trash can, shattering it. Wildly pacing in his condo, fists balled, he found it hard to believe a couple of pissants like Jalmond and Stravnicki could possibly be figuring things out. He couldn't deny the evidence; they had begun to uncover the very foundation of the Committee's schemes. But it was all speculation on their part, leading nowhere so far.

His rare emotional outburst subsided quickly, Townsend's rational, analytical side taking control.

The misfortune with the assistant was now a blessing, and Townsend decided he would have someone other than Taranto handle Stravnicki. He had other assets capable of quietly eliminating the coach, and they were disposable should something go wrong.

A short call on an encrypted cell set the plan in motion.

———

The week dragged for Tony, somber over his family problems and buried in his own responsibilities and the work that Dennis had done. He sorely missed Denny's upbeat personality and their talks, fueling his depression. Coming home to an empty, silent house only amplified his isolation. He hadn't spoken with Maggie for three days now, and he deeply missed her voice, the embraces when he came home, and the full-of-life antics of Zach and Hope. Cell service at the lake was poor, and he only got Maggie's voicemail when he called that night. He left a simple message: "I'm sorry. I love you all. I miss you all. Please come home." He had no idea if she received it.

He heard Freddie had been at the team facilities but had not run into him. Tony, desperately needing to talk to someone, gave him a call but only got voicemail. Bored and frustrated, he took a walk, and was elated when Freddie called.

"What's up, Freddie? How are you doing, and have you found anything?"

"I'm as good as I can be, Tony. Such a shame, but we must try to move forward. I talked to several people on the team but came up empty. No one really knew him outside of the team, but he sure was highly thought of."

"Yeah, for sure. Quiet guy who made a big impact. I really miss him."

An awkward silence ensued until Freddie said, "Unfortunately, Tony, Brad hasn't turned up anything either. He talked with Dennis's neighbors, but between us we couldn't find any real friends."

"Dennis told me he didn't have a life outside of the team. I guess he was right."

"I did find one thing, probably nothing, maybe you know about it already. The team guy in charge of the film room abruptly quit the day after Dennis died. No one seems to know anything about him. Did you know about that?"

"No. I didn't know him, and Denny never said anything. Interesting timing, though."

"It sure is. I've asked Brad to follow up on him, but I'm not hopeful. The police haven't found anything about Dennis, but the postmortem did confirm posterior head trauma after a blow to the face, so with his other injuries, they're calling it a homicide. I'm hoping they'll find something. That's all I've got, Tony."

The call ended, and Tony resumed his walk, trying to sort out all that had happened in the last few weeks. He tried Maggie again without success and dejectedly headed home to be alone again.

Consumed with his thoughts, Tony failed to notice the two men approaching him from shadows to his right. It was only at the last second that he reacted, and his quick reflexes saved him. One guy swung a bat at Tony's head, but he was able to duck and deflect it, suffering only a glancing blow to his forearm. The other assailant succeeded in delivering a roundhouse punch that caught Tony on his left cheekbone, knocking him backward but causing the man to lose his balance. Tony seized this opportunity to charge the guy, lowering his shoulder and driving him into his accomplice, propelling them both into a parked car. The impact caused the bat to smash the car window, setting off a very loud alarm.

Tony backed up, ready for another assault, when the owner of the car came out with his own bat, yelling, "Get the hell away from my car!"

The two thugs looked at one another, one jerking his head in a *Let's get outta here* signal. They sprinted down the street and took off in a dark-colored vehicle.

Tony was breathing heavily, his arm throbbing, heart rate sky high from the adrenaline rush. The car owner came up to him, asking if he was all right as Tony sat on the curb trying to catch his breath. The police soon arrived, and he and the owner gave their stories, with the police retrieving the bat.

Tony declined medical treatment, and after the police left, he thanked the owner for his quick response. He walked the two blocks back to his house on shaky legs, his head spinning with all that had happened. By the time he returned home, he had the beginnings of a shiner below his left eye and an ugly purple bruise forming on his left forearm.

Jameson for his spirit and ice for his tangible injuries were his preferred medical treatments.

CHAPTER TWENTY-THREE

As the clock ran down to zero and the final whistle blew, Frank Ohlendorf couldn't wait to get off the field. In the fourth quarter he had made a call at a critical moment but had been overruled. Normally he would think nothing of this, but if the penalty had not been overruled, it would have resulted in a game-changing play, which was exactly what he had been instructed to do.

Heart racing and sweating profusely, he wiped his brow with his handkerchief, consumed with worry about the implications of the overruled call. He was almost to the exit leading to the official's locker room when he ran into an assistant coach from the winning team, a man he had known for several years and respected.

The man, just three feet in front of him and looking directly at Frank with searching eyes, simply said, "Frank, what's going on with you? What's with that call you tried to make? And a bunch of others you made this year? What have you become?"

Frank stopped cold, the ambush startling him. He looked away, unable to answer the man, and proceeded rapidly down the exit. He changed clothes and took a cab to the airport, not waiting for the other officials or the NAFL-provided limo. Once there, he was able to make an earlier flight than scheduled and was home by eight, one of the benefits of having the early Sunday game. Entering the kitchen, he was greeted by a surprised and elated Nancy.

"Well, this is a nice surprise. You're much sooner than I expected," she said, smiling. "Great that you were able to get an earlier flight."

"Yeah, I got lucky, and I didn't wait for the limo to the airport," he said as he grabbed a beer from the fridge and picked up the Sunday paper. He sat at the kitchen island but did not engage Nancy in conversation as was his usual custom.

"Everything okay, Frank? You're pretty subdued for after a game. I couldn't watch it today. Did something happen?" Normally an upbeat Frank would review the game with Nancy, who watched Frank's games whenever she could.

"No, everything's fine. I'm just more tired than normal," he said, his voice distant and eyes vacant.

"Frank, I don't believe you. You look troubled. What really happened today to upset you?"

He let out a long sigh, staring at the countertop for a moment before looking up at Nancy.

"Today wasn't my best game. I made a call I was sure of but was overruled," he half lied. "It was pretty embarrassing the way it happened and was portrayed."

"But, hon, you've had calls overruled before. It's rare, and you've disagreed with other guys' calls occasionally. There's got to be more you're not telling me."

He paused before answering. "You know me well, Nancy," he said with a small smile. "As I was leaving the field, I ran into an assistant coach I've known for a long time. I've always had a good relationship with him. He challenged my call today and others I've made this season. But what he ended with really got to me. He asked me, 'What's going on with you?' in a really insulting tone. I was so surprised and shocked I just kept going and didn't respond. It really bothered me."

"Frank darling, I'm so sorry," Nancy said, as she took his hand. "That was uncalled for, but he was probably upset at losing and just venting."

"Nancy, his team won; that wasn't the reason. I know I've been under pressure from the whole Paul situation. Maybe I've been distracted on the field and my performance has slipped," he said. *I can't tell her the real reason and that the coach was right, or what he really said.*

"But you haven't had any bad reviews from the league, have you?"

"No, that's true, I haven't."

"And I haven't noticed you being distracted any more than usual, which is amazing with what we both have been going through with Paul. Just chalk it up to a bad day. Try to put this behind you."

"I know. I just don't like being called out like that. It's normal coming from a player, but I've never experienced it from a coach. I work so hard to be the best, fairest official I can." His false words tore into his soul.

"Frank Ohlendorf, you are one of the best in the league, and I know your passion for the game of football. Don't let anybody bring you down with their comments because I know better!" she said with emphasis. She got up and wrapped her arms around him. "Please try to put this in perspective and put it behind you. Why don't you relax in the living room with your beer and the paper while I finish getting dinner ready."

"I'll do just that, Nancy. Thanks for the pep talk."

She beamed, and he headed into the living room, knowing he had the best wife in the world, who always held him up on a pedestal, so strong was her admiration for him.

He hated the deception. The paper remained open on his lap, but his mind wandered as that last thought lingered.

What have I become? Am I like my mother?

———————

Frank was thirteen when his father left the family for a younger woman. His mother kept telling Frank and his siblings that their father would return, and she invented one excuse after another until they no longer believed her. Her deceptions about their father had the negative effect of keeping their hopes alive that he really would return to them, making it even more crushing when they realized the truth. Frank was furious with his mother for a long time about that, until he was older and realized that maybe his mother *was* holding out hope that her husband would return, not wishing to face her own reality. His anger at her deception was the only negative thing Frank felt about his mother; otherwise, she was his role model in love and devotion to one's family.

Frank's spirit sank to an unimagined low as he accepted that he had done the one thing he had vowed never to do.

———————

Frank arrived at Riverfront Park on Thursday promptly at six o'clock, his normal meeting time with his contact from the diner, Steve. Sweat formed on Frank's forehead, and he thought he would vomit as he saw his contact eyeing him from a secluded booth.

"Not good weekend, Mr. O. Nyet! A fuckup. But we don't think it your fault. Not let it happen again! Try harder. Remember, don't fuck up!" he said as he handed Frank the customary envelope.

"Steve, I've been sick all week, and now I have a fever. I don't know if I'll be able to work the game. The league wants forty-eight hours' notice when you're sick," Frank said, concentrating on holding down his stomach.

Steve replied, "That your problem, not ours," as he walked away, leaving Frank distraught.

CHAPTER TWENTY-FOUR

Frank really was sick, taking decongestants and antibiotics by Saturday and feeling truly lousy. He showed up for the game and did the best he could, but it was a bizarre, very low-scoring game with neither team generating much offense, and very sloppy, inconsistent play. The only scoring came from field goals, with the final score six to three. Frank had not been involved in any plays remotely close to drawing a penalty, apart from one play late in the third quarter. He was just pulling the flag out of his pocket when the whistle blew, calling the play dead. Once again, it was not Frank's fault, and he hoped there would be no repercussions.

He got home late that evening to a very distraught Nancy. She was almost inconsolable, and her speech was difficult to understand as sobs racked her body. Frank was puzzled and trying to understand when she simply took him by the hand and led him to a corner of their backyard. There was Nancy's beloved cat, Rufus, a mangled mess of barely recognizable flesh and bone, only his distinctive collar verifying his identity.

It took Frank just a few seconds to comprehend what had really happened to their pet, and he quickly spun what he hoped would be a plausible explanation for Nancy. "Rufus must have gotten mauled by a coyote that's been reported in the area. I thought that they had caught it. Maybe there was more than one. I'll bury him in his favorite corner of the yard. You go in and rest, Nancy."

After Nancy left, Frank had the unpleasant task of disposing of the remains, but it gave him time to think about what to do next. The message was clear, and the speed with which it was sent alarmed Frank. Fear, anger, and a new realization now forced his hand.

———

Over the next two days, Frank weighed his few options. The previous week, their son had been kicked out of rehab for violating their no-drugs policy. He was so totally remorseless and unappreciative, and Frank and Nancy finally realized they could do no more for him. The slaughter of Rufus was the final blow.

Frank decided on a plan with a certainty he found empowering. When he got home that night, he told Nancy that he needed to visit his brother the next day in Tucson, Arizona, about a matter with the family trust set up by their parents. It was a completely fabricated story, but one that Nancy found credible and did not challenge. Frank fervently hoped that this would be the first step to end his deceptions.

After a very early flight, he arrived late the next morning, called his brother and told him he was in town for business, and they agreed to meet for dinner. Frank told his brother he also wanted to talk about the trust, to give his story some validity with Nancy.

Frank had done his research, so he knew where to go the next day for the main purpose of his trip. He had reached another point of no return but was certain of the direction he must go.

He walked boldly into the building and pushed the elevator button for the sixth floor. The Federal Bureau of Investigation occupied the entire floor, and Frank calmly walked through their front door and told the official-looking lady at the front desk that he had a serious matter that he needed to report. When she asked him if he could be more specific, he declined to give more information, citing the need for the utmost confidentiality. This got her attention, and she excused herself for a moment. She soon returned with the senior agent in charge, Andrew Stone, who introduced himself and ushered Frank into his office.

"Mr. Ohlendorf, what brings you to our office today?" he said.

"Mr. Stone, I am being blackmailed, and my recent noncompliance with their demands has led to a direct threat on my family. I don't know who is behind this, but I believe they will do anything to get what they want, and I've put my family in danger. I realize I may have committed a crime, and if so, I ask for immunity in return for my full cooperation. I also ask for protection for my family."

Eyebrows raised, Stone replied, "Mr. Ohlendorf, I can't make any promises until I know your situation in detail. You have the right to legal counsel before you begin."

"I know that, sir. I am waiving that right at this time. I'm afraid whomever I'm dealing with could find out about my going to a lawyer. My excuse for coming to Tucson is to visit my brother and talk about a family matter, which I didn't think would arouse suspicion."

Mr. Stone produced a yellow legal pad and turned on a tape recorder, saying, "I need to record this conversation. Please start from the beginning."

Frank inhaled deeply, and for the next twenty minutes provided a thorough explanation of his background, Paul's addiction history, and his career as an NAFL official. He asked for a glass of water, which Mr. Stone provided, and continued. In complete detail, he revealed everything up to the recent finding of his cat. Mr. Stone would occasionally stop him to ask a question for clarification and took extensive notes as Frank spoke. When Frank finished, there was an awkward silence as Mr. Stone glanced at his notes and then looked up and asked, "Mr. Ohlendorf, my first thought is why didn't you report this to the league, as I'm sure you're required?"

"Mr. Stone, please call me Frank. Sir, I don't have one hundred percent confidence in the confidentiality of the league, based on my years of experience and the seriousness of the people I'm dealing with. For all I know they may have contacts within the league. I thought going straight to you was my only option."

"Frank, thank you for your confidence. You did the right thing coming to us. Whoever is behind this is obviously part of a larger organization. Russian, Eastern European, and Asian organized crime, as well as home-grown syndicates, are all trying to get a piece of professional sports, and they are ruthless. I will immediately contact our Organized Crime Division. As far as protection for yourself and your family, that's not possible at this point. We would have to build a specific case for the idea of witness protection to even come into play. My best advice right now, believe it or not, is to continue to play along with them as best you can, to stall for time while we investigate this. I don't think there is an imminent danger if you continue to be of value to them. Try to keep giving them just enough to keep them happy. I know this'll be very difficult."

"How long will I have to do this?" Frank asked, his voice barely a whisper.

"I don't know. I will move this along as quickly as I can. I think your reputation and position will get some serious attention. Do you have a cell phone other than your regular one—a burner, as they're called? One that nobody knows about?"

"I don't, but I'll go out and get one."

"Good. Call me when you get it. Here is my personal number," he said as he handed Frank a blank card with only a number on it. "All communications will be through this, and I will text you before I call. Erase all calls and texts afterward. I don't have to emphasize you need to be as cautious as you can. If OCD picks this up, and I'm sure they will, they will probably keep me as your contact," he said, standing and extending his hand. "Good luck, Frank. Again, I want to emphasize that you did the right thing."

All Frank could say was "Thank you" as he shook Stone's hand and left his office. One huge weight had been lifted off his shoulders as another replaced it. He worried that things could become even more dangerous. He had to play his cards carefully, and he prayed the FBI would act quickly.

———

As soon as Frank left his office, Agent Stone rewound his tape recorder to the beginning and reviewed the entire conversation, following along with his handwritten notes and adding additional ones. Next, he wrote a detailed report of their interaction and sent a copy to his supervisor at FBI regional headquarters in Phoenix and a copy to the Organized Crime Division in Washington, DC. He included with the Washington copy a summary sheet of pertinent details to be used as a quick report that could be directly forwarded to all FBI offices. All of this took an hour, so the report arrived in Washington at approximately 2:30 p.m. Eastern time.

———

Nick St. Angelo arrived back in his office having spent the last forty-five minutes at the indoor FBI range, performing his required firearms proficiency. He grabbed a cup of coffee and sat down to review the daily FBI bulletins and his own emails. The daily bulletins were ranked in order of priority established in Washington. The third one caused Nick to bolt upright in his chair, almost spilling his coffee on the computer keyboard.

It was from the Tucson field office, routed through Phoenix and marked *Priority Urgent* by the Organized Crime Division. It detailed a meeting with an individual who came into the Tucson office claiming to be a referee in the NAFL and reported being blackmailed into making questionable calls during games with the intent to influence the outcome. The Tucson office had verified his identity and his position in the NAFL. Nick finished the bulletin and then accessed the full detailed report of the meeting. He was astonished at what he read and immediately realized he now had to tell his boss about the meeting with his uncle. He dialed Thompson's extension.

"He was expecting your call and wants you up here now," Thompson's secretary relayed. Nick raced to his boss's office and was ushered in at once.

"You saw the Priority Urgent bulletin from OCD I presume?" Thompson questioned without a greeting.

"Yes, sir. It blew me away. Pretty serious stuff." He was about to continue, but Thompson cut him off.

"It certainly is, but remember, it's only an early lead until we can find out who's behind it. This guy must be really scared or had a major attack of conscious to come out like this. We might be able to get him immunity, but his career is over." Thompson looked up at Nick, who was just about to speak. "Something to add, Nick?"

"I may have information that could be tied to it." Scott Thompson's eyes drilled into Nick's, but he simply raised his right hand slightly as a sign for Nick to continue.

"Approximately three weeks ago, my uncle, Tony Stravnicki, who is an assistant defensive coach for the NAFL Columbus Colonels, requested a meeting with me. Tony came to ask my advice concerning multiple observations that he and his assistant had noticed involving questionable calls, beginning last season. Tony believed that many of these calls altered the outcome of games and team standings and therefore the playoff picture.

"Mr. Thompson, I have known my uncle for a long time, and he was a major influence in my life," Nick stated. "The urgency and tone of his preliminary call and the subsequent meeting is unlike anything I've ever experienced with him. While he noticed these last season, he didn't think much about it until it continued this season. His assistant, who has experience in sports analytics, performed an in-depth analysis of this season and, using sophisticated statistical software, determined that there was a high probability that these events were not random."

Nick paused briefly, his eyes not deviating from Thompson's, who had not said a word nor moved a muscle. Taking a deep breath, Nick continued. "My uncle is neither an alarmist nor a conspiracy theory nut. He's one of the most practical, levelheaded men I have ever known. Quite frankly, I was astonished by what he told me, and I couldn't help but think that maybe there was something to it, knowing that OC groups are always trying to get involved in sports money. However, I was noncommittal, and I left it with him that I would investigate whether our OC division had any reports of such activity. I asked him to keep me informed as time went by. To date I have not heard back from him."

"So, this meeting with your uncle was on the same day as one of our major meetings, and you decided not to inform me. Is that correct?" Thompson asked.

"Yes, sir. Considering the magnitude and importance of my forensic analysis work, which was the focus of that meeting, and knowing that what my uncle provided was not much to go on, I decided not to tell you at that time. And it *was* my uncle," Nick said. He waited for his boss to lower the boom.

"Well, the Tucson report clearly gives credence to your uncle Tony's observations, which also backs up what the official said. He lives in the Chicago area, so I'm going to push OCD to have the Chicago office put him on surveillance and limited protection. Maybe this will result in a tangible lead we can follow."

Thompson looked hard at Nick but not as severely as before. "I want you to inform me if your uncle contacts you again. If he does, we'll meet and discuss how to handle the next meeting. Understood?"

"Yes, sir," Nick replied.

As he reached the door, Thompson added, "And for what it's worth, Nick, I probably wouldn't have told my supervisor about my uncle under those circumstances, either." There was a sincerity in his voice that Nick had never heard before. He was grateful that he hadn't been read the riot act. Now the pressure was on to deliver.

CHAPTER TWENTY-FIVE

The jarring chime of the cell phone alarm announced the beginning of another Monday. Five forty-five was an unnatural time for Gena Compagna to get up, so used to years of awakening at nine. With a loud sigh, she reached over and turned off the alarm, declaring, "This is too early," knowing that Nick was already awake.

"Good morning, beautiful. It's a perfect time to begin another great day," Nick answered. "Whose turn is it to make breakfast, anyway?" he asked, well aware it was hers. He wrapped his arm around her and pulled her naked body to his. She didn't resist as there was no better way to start the day than to be wrapped in the arms of her best friend, the man she adored.

Snuggling often led to more vigorous activity, and upon completing their under-the-cover aerobics, he headed for the bathroom to get ready while Gena made breakfast. She brought his coffee to him as he finished dressing and stated with a kiss, "I guess getting up this early does have its benefits, come to think about it."

They were a couple destined for each other. Casual acquaintances growing up, they had met again by chance nine months ago, and the chemistry was like a match to gunpowder. Their work schedules often conflicted, so they made their time together special. Working as a model for the Austin Agency, Gena traveled extensively, while Nick rarely did. His job was more private than hers, as he couldn't tell her much about his work at the FBI. Gena, on the other hand, told Nick many details of her work, from the boring, monotonous, time-consuming photo shoots to the exciting travel locations and people she met. Nick was amazed at the scope and diversity of the important, powerful people Gena knew, and their lavish lifestyles.

When Nick got into the office that morning, he was intrigued by an urgent email from his team, directing him to a link involved with the Cayman situation. He was just about to call the team together when the phone rang.

Scott Thompson's voice boomed through the receiver. "Nick, I need you to come to my office *now*. We've got a development regarding the Cayman situation."

"Yes, sir, I'm aware of that. I was just about to call my team together."

"Really? You can't possibly know what I'm talking about." He hung up abruptly.

Nick's head spun as he gathered his laptop and headed to Scott's office. The door was open, and Thompson, who was on the phone, motioned for him to come in.

"Yeah, this could be the break we've been wanting, and apparently St. Angelo also has something else new concerning the Caymans. I'll call you back later." Turning his attention to Nick, he leaned back in his chair and said, "What do you *think* you have that is so important?"

"Sir, the email I received just a few minutes ago from my team indicates that they've tracked sources to five cities in the country, and that's just the beginning. I was just about to assemble them to see what our next step will be."

"That is good news, especially in light of why I called you here so urgently. You remember that I told you about our agent in George Town, whose job is to watch over our informant? He has advised us that he discovered a possible threat to her from an individual known to us from past history. This individual is Pavel Lyubov. He's a Russian who holds an H1B visa, although he has never worked in high tech that we know of. That's likely his cover, as he is actually former Spetsnaz.

"He's been on our radar for being associated with Eastern European syndicates, purportedly acting as intimidator and muscle for them. He has a reputation as being one nasty dude. He's clever, careful, and we've never been able to pin anything on him. Hell, we don't even have a really clear photo, but what we do have shows a prominent facial scar. I want you to take a quick trip down to George Town to meet with our operative there, review the situation, and see if you can come up with anything else. Spend today and tomorrow with your team on their new leads, fly down Wednesday morning, and come back Thursday afternoon. We'll meet here first thing Friday morning." His briefing was nonstop, barely taking a breath.

"Yes, sir. Glad we're getting movement on this," Nick replied, but Thompson's focus had already shifted away from Nick.

―――――――

Since Gena was traveling and would not return until Friday, Nick spent twelve-hour days Monday and Tuesday working with his team. Reviewing the paper trails from the five cities was tedious, but by late Tuesday Nick was able to piece together enough leads to strongly suggest that New York City could be the common origin point. He left his team with detailed instructions on how to proceed and texted Gena that he needed to travel and would see her again Friday night after work.

His flight to the Caymans left early Wednesday morning, and he settled into his hotel with early check-in by two, meeting his FBI counterpart in a secluded restaurant at three. Nick recognized the agent from his file. Jorge Portanas, born and raised in Puerto Rico, was a seasoned FBI veteran whose area of operation was the Caribbean. He had an extensive background in surveillance and counter-surveillance.

"We're secure here, Nick, but we'll still be careful. We've got an interesting situation developing. My associate and I have been following our friend, and we have observed Lyubov trailing her on several occasions, but we've been out of position to get good photos. He contacted her yesterday afternoon after work, tried to intimidate her by telling her to mind her own business and stop asking questions or she might have an accident. He's a scary-looking guy with a prominent facial scar, but our friend doesn't scare easily. She told him that she had no idea what he was talking about and quickly disengaged from him. She contacted me last night on a secure phone we had provided her. I advised her to act as if she'd gotten his message and keep a very low profile until after you and I met today."

"That's good advice, Jorge. She's done a great job, and it's helped us immensely. We'll certainly follow up on Lyubov and see where that takes us. I would like to meet our friend tonight after work. I understand she likes to take walks on the beach."

"Yes, she would enjoy that. I'll have her meet at five thirty, adjacent to the marina. I will be nearby." The men shook hands, and Nick headed back to his hotel.

Nick was on the beach by the marina at five fifteen, and noticed a confident-looking, attractive woman in her mid-thirties sitting on a nearby bench. Nick approached her, and when he got close, he introduced himself.

As they walked the beach, she provided a detailed history of her work in the bank, her connections with other workers, and reviewed what she had forwarded to the bureau. "An interesting point is that there have been several references by my coworkers of these accounts being linked to a pro sport in the States. But I haven't been able to verify that on paper."

Nick pressed, "A pro sport? Nothing more specific than that?"

"Sorry, just what I've told you."

"That's fine, Paula. No problem. That could be big if there is anything to it. Focus on that aspect, if you can without being obvious."

She nodded in agreement, and they discussed her interaction with Lyubov. Nick thanked Paula for her resourcefulness and courage, and he emphasized caution above all.

He had an early-morning flight, but because of weather delays, it was late afternoon before he got to his office. Once there, he called his team together in a nearby conference room for an update.

Knowing he could accomplish nothing further after that, he headed back to his empty apartment. It was a beautiful day, so he decided to take a jog through Central Park to get some badly needed exercise and to organize his thoughts for his meeting tomorrow with his boss. The possible connection of the Cayman file with a pro sport was foremost on his mind.

———————

He was at Scott Thompson's office at eight sharp, and his boss rolled in ten minutes later.

"Well, Nick, what's the update from the Caymans? Anything additional to report from either there or your team?"

"It was a good trip, boss. I met with Jorge and Paula. Both impressed me, and I think they're doing the very best they can. I clarified more of the details on the stuff she has been sending us. With her information and my team, it is very likely the central connection is in New York. She emphasized that a sports connection was mentioned by several people on several occasions. She's been careful and felt that Lyubov had people of his own who were spying for him. She's given us enough to go on for now, but we need to keep her out of danger. Jorge indicated, and I tend to agree, that Paula doesn't scare easily and would be more than willing to look for further information, should we need her to do so."

"Well, right now, our most solid lead is Lyubov. Where there's smoke, there's fire. Nick, I'm giving you point on finding him, trailing him, and determining who he is reporting to, in addition to your work with your forensic accounting team. Can you handle both?"

"Yes, sir, no problem. I have strong confidence in my team. Who will be my liaison in surveillance and counter-surveillance?"

"I'm going to have you work with Harvey Tankersley. He will control his team but will be under your guidance in terms of the overall mission. Do you know him?"

"Not personally, but I know of his reputation. I'm fortunate to be able work with him."

"Get going on this right away. I want you and Harvey to find this guy Lyubov fast and get a tail on him. He's the only concrete lead we have right now with the Cayman business. Report to me Wednesday morning with your detailed plan for the op after discussing it with Harvey. Use all resources necessary, and don't worry about overtime. Make it happen, Nick. I feel something big here." Thompson picked up the phone, meeting over.

Nick returned to his office and called Harvey. He was an old hand and used to working with up-and-coming junior agents who had operational control of a mission. He knew surveillance and counter-surveillance like the back of his hand, and no one was better at it in the New York City office. Nick asked to meet in Harvey's office as a sign of respect.

When Nick arrived, he provided Harvey with a complete recap of the Cayman operation and Pavel Lyubov, with Tankersley listening and taking notes. When Nick finished his report, Harvey looked up and said, "Usually the hardest part is locating the individual initially, then the teams can take over surveillance. It shouldn't be too difficult for Jorge to find out if and when Lyubov left and his destination. If he does return to New York City, we'll cast a wide net using any information the bureau already has on him and hope we get lucky. Agent Thompson has prioritized this op, so I'll get moving. I suggest we meet Monday afternoon at the latest. Let's swap cell numbers so we can stay in touch over the weekend, should something develop."

Nick thanked Harvey. He was pleased how the meeting had gone and once again felt fortunate to have a much more experienced agent as a sort of mentor. He had hoped to get an opportunity for fieldwork, and this assignment held great potential to provide just that.

Back at his office, Nick concentrated on reviewing the progress his team had made, and after several hours of effort he hit a wall and headed home. It had been a busy, productive week, and he was looking forward to getting home and seeing Gena, who would be arriving later that evening.

To his surprise, Gena was home. She ran to the door, and they embraced as passionate young lovers do.

"Gena, this is great. I didn't expect you until at least eight o'clock," Nick said, concentrating on her soft, hazel eyes framed by flawless, tanned complexion.

"I had an opportunity to catch an earlier flight, and I hoped you would be home early. Seems like more than five days, doesn't it? How was your trip? Can you tell me where you went?"

"It's been a hectic five days, hon. It does seem like more than that. I had a quick down-and-back trip to the Cayman Islands."

"Cayman Islands! Sounds more like fun in the sun than work to me!"

"No such luck. Pretty basic forensic accounting. I'm sure you'd find it boring. Had to interview a couple people and head right back. Very tiring. May have developed a lead which points to the city here, and I've been tasked to follow up with a field team to work on this lead. You know I've wanted a crack at fieldwork, and this is it," he said, wide eyed.

"That's great, Nick, but it won't be dangerous, will it?"

"No. A more senior agent oversees the technical aspects. I'm just a liaison. So, tell me about your trip. It's got to have been more exciting than mine."

"Not really. Pretty standard photo shoot in Denver for a major beer company. Long hours. Lots of retakes. Most of the time shuttling between the hotel and locations. But one interesting piece of gossip that one of the girls told me is that our agency has landed a major contract with the NAFL. I guess they want to improve the image of some of the teams' cheerleaders, and they want us to consult about how to do that. Several locations, lots of travel, but something different than usual."

"Well, that sounds exciting. Do you get to go to any games or meet any players?"

"Since it's not yet official, I don't know any details. I should find out more next week. Hey, I'm starving. Let's head out to eat and make it an early night."

"Great idea," Nick said, not realizing the potential implications of Gena's upcoming assignments.

CHAPTER TWENTY-SIX

The next day, he called Harvey Tankersley, who was out but expected back soon. While he waited for a return call, Nick retrieved all his summary reports on the forensic accounting investigation. What had started in the Caymans had now led back to multiple companies across the country, all connected to the entertainment industry. The companies themselves appeared to be ghost companies with no fixed addresses, just postal boxes or mail drops. Nick's team was now concentrating on these with hopes that they would lead to something more substantial. As Nick was reviewing these reports, Harvey called.

"Hi, Harvey. Scott wants us to pull all the stops to find this guy Lyubov. Have you been able to spot him in New York yet?"

"No, not yet, Nick. I've reviewed what the bureau has on him, but it's slim. What few photos we have are three to five years old and not high quality. Jorge's team didn't get a photo of him, and they didn't track him when he left. An updated photograph is crucial. We have information on his past contacts with known Russian and Eastern European mob associates, and I have two surveillance teams working that angle now. I contacted Jorge, and if Lyubov reappears there, he knows getting a high-quality photo is top priority. He was apologetic for not getting one of him before, but the opportunity just didn't present itself. Providing security for their asset, Paula, was their top focus at the time."

"As it should be. Harvey, Scott has authorized any necessary overtime to find this guy, so use as many people as you need. I've been mulling an idea to get Lyubov back to the Caymans to get a photo and pick up his trail. What would you think of Paula getting active again, asking questions, with the hope that he would reappear to warn her? I met Paula, and I think she would be up to doing this. Lyubov is a nasty dude capable of anything, so Jorge and his team would have to be certain of their ability to protect her."

"Nick, that's very risky and way above my pay grade and yours. Scott would have to approve something like that."

"Agreed, Harvey. I think if I put together a solid plan with safeguards, he'll go for it. I'll work on it and contact him today. In the meantime, get eyes on anyone or anyplace that we know Lyubov's been around."

"Will do, Nick. Keep me informed!"

"Certainly, Harvey. Good hunting."

Nick got a fresh cup of coffee and a new legal pad. He needed to come up with an idea that would work and which Scott would agree to authorize. After much thought, he had a plan. While it looked pretty good to Nick, he first needed Jorge to approve, which he did. Nick edited the proposal until he was certain he was ready. Again feeling fortunate, this time that Thompson was in his office, he requested and was granted an immediate meeting.

Thompson was talking to his secretary when Nick arrived, and waved him into his office. "Didn't think I'd hear from you so soon. What's up?"

"Sir, I've spoken with both Harvey and Jorge. It's apparent we have very little to go on right now concerning Pavel Lyubov, and I don't feel we can afford to wait around until something happens.

For now, Harvey is going to extensively ramp up surveillance on his known places and associates, but that's a crapshoot. I've come up with a plan to try to get Lyubov back to the Caymans where we can get the pictures we need and begin to tail him."

His eyebrows raised, Thompson asked, "And how do you propose going about doing that?"

"We use our informant, Paula, to draw him back again. He's personally threatened her once, and it seems likely he'd be the one to follow up if she makes waves."

"St. Angelo, I wanted you to get aggressive, but have you lost your mind? We can't put a low-level informant in harm's way with a guy like Lyubov. How could you possibly guarantee her safety or be sure that he'd even show up?"

"Sir, I had a long phone call with Jorge. I'm familiar with the place, and I've met the key people. Paula does not scare easily, has shown that she can keep cool under stress, and has the established record of drawing his attention. Jorge is confident he can assure her safety. And I'll be right there with her."

"You'll be there with her? And what exactly will you be doing?"

"My cover will be as a forensic accounting expert sent from a New York bank to look into some of the Cayman accounts under suspicion. I'll ask a lot of questions and create as big a nuisance as I can, and Paula will help me do this. If we make enough noise, Lyubov's people will contact him and he'll get down there, pronto. At some point, he's likely to contact one or both of us, and that's when we'll get our pictures and begin our tail. We'll act like we're scared. Paula will promise to quit so she can't snoop anymore. Jorge's team will maintain tight watch over us, and I will be armed in case things turn nasty."

Thompson said nothing as Nick spoke, listening intently with no change in facial expression. "You've thought this out carefully, and you obviously have a lot of trust in Jorge and his team. It's unconventional, but not unheard of." He stared out the window, lost in deep thought for almost a full minute before continuing.

"I don't need to go higher to get approval for this. But I want backup plans to ensure her safety and yours, too. I know you've always wanted to try undercover work, Nick. I'll give you your chance. I just hope it's not a case of regretting what you ask for. How soon does this begin?"

"I'll contact Jorge and make sure Paula is on board with this. Once we have her go-ahead, I'll get down there as soon as possible. I'll get going on my phony credentials while I'm waiting."

"Good luck, Nick. I want portrait-quality photos of him," he said.

"Will do, Mr. Thompson." Nick smiled and walked confidently out of the office, pleased that Scott actually paid attention to him as he left.

———————

When Nick returned home, he was greeted by the aroma of Gena's lasagna, one of her specialties. "What did I do to deserve this?" He beamed in delight as he picked her up and she wrapped her legs around him.

"I know it's one of your favorites, and I haven't cooked a really good meal in a while. I figured we both deserve it, working as hard as we do, and it seems like we're just getting busier and busier with our jobs. My agency's contract with the NAFL is about to kick into high gear, so I'll be doing a lot of traveling."

"Me too, hon. I've just been assigned co-lead in a major project in addition to my ongoing forensic accounting mission. I have to go back to the Caymans for a day or two later this week."

"Caymans! Tough duty again!"

"Actually, it will be, involving very boring paperwork, and endless poring over thick stacks of documents." He didn't dare tell her about going undercover, preferring to hide behind a half-truth. "Tell me more about this football contract your agency has. How involved will you be?"

"We're working with an NAFL vendor called FAE Productions. My agency has divided us into groups, each of which will work with three or four squads of team cheerleaders. I'm in charge of them. We will review makeup, uniforms, and, most especially, their dance routines and how they present themselves to the public. We have been told the NAFL wants to maximize the entertainment value for the fans, and making sure their cheerleaders put on a top-notch show is a big priority. Secondarily, we will appear at league functions put on for their sponsors and luxury box owners."

"And you're complaining about my tough duty!" Nick said in mock indignation. "Cocktail parties can be so challenging and stressful," he said with a laugh, tousling her hair. Turning serious, Nick said, "I know how much you dislike these things." Gena had often remarked how much she dreaded the cattle-call, eye-candy atmosphere.

"I've done enough of them now so that they don't bother me as much as before. I can take care of myself, and I really enjoy meeting other people and seeing how the rich and famous party. And the food is to die for. Speaking of food, let's eat while it's hot, Lasagna Boy."

They enjoyed their meal and time together, each realizing such moments were islands of peace and contentment in their demanding lives.

When Nick got to the office the next morning, he found an urgent email from Jorge about their plan, confirming that Paula was on board. She had arranged to be in the on-call pool of assistants so she would be able to get herself assigned to Nick. He had advised Jorge of his new alias, Richard Valmont, and of his new appearance. His hair would be dyed black, and he would be wearing thick glasses, a conservative suit, and maintain an arrogant, superior manner. He had already checked the airlines and could get down there late that afternoon. He planned to arrive at the Cayman Islands International Banking Center first thing in the morning.

Nick appeared promptly at nine and was pleased to see that the banking center was not yet open, believing in the concept of "island time." He jumped right into character.

"How do you people get anything done down here when you open up ten minutes late!" he bellowed. A young associate apologized and ushered him to the main office area where he would be working. He showed his fake credentials and launched into a series of questions and demands involving the suspicious accounts Paula had uncovered. She and two other associates tried their best to work with and placate Nick. He created an uproar with his overbearing manner and sarcasm. When he complained about the other two women and stated he only wanted Paula to help him, the supervisor was only too happy to oblige.

"Thank you, Ms. Sandoval. It's reassuring to know there's at least one competent professional who can help me," he proclaimed for all to hear. The other women were upset when Paula used them as her "gofers," but the supervisor allowed it, not wanting to upset him. Nick's attitude and his insistence on only working with Paula did not go unnoticed. By midmorning, Lyubov's people had reported to him that not only was Paula again looking at the accounts but now she was helping some bank guy from New York City. The reaction was immediate, and an infuriated Lyubov boarded a private jet out of Teterboro New Jersey and arrived in George Town by four that afternoon. He picked up a car and was in position outside the International Banking Center forty-five minutes later.

They worked throughout the day and only took a short break when lunch was delivered. Nick took great delight in his role, continuing to infuriate the staff, and they were very happy to see him leave at five. They were not happy when he barked over his shoulder on the way out, "I'll be back at nine sharp tomorrow; I'll expect you to be fully ready by then." Unfortunately, Paula had to stay until five thirty, and her coworkers gave her a very hard time until then.

Nick was pleased how the day had gone. They had certainly stirred things up, but did they draw the fly to the honey?

He and Paula had agreed to meet at five forty-five at the same restaurant as his last visit. As he left the hotel, he was reassured to see Jorge's overwatch team.

———————

Pavel Lyubov waited in his car, observing everyone who left the banking center. He was rewarded at five when a man matching the description of the troublemaker exited. The man was alone, so he decided to wait for the woman he had warned before and deal with her tonight. He would leave the man for tomorrow. She exited at five thirty, and Lyubov followed her until she entered a restaurant just before five forty-five. Ten minutes later he took a seat at the bar where he was able to see her in the restaurant, and as luck would have it, her dinner companion was the troublemaker. Lyubov reviewed his plans for them, sipping his favorite vodka. The man appeared weak and would be a pushover. Lyubov was angry that she had not taken his warning. He vowed to make sure she understood him this time.

Nick and Paula ordered drinks and reviewed the day, both getting a kick out of the scene they had created. About fifteen minutes later, Nick received a text from Jorge stating they had observed Lyubov in the restaurant bar, and security cameras had recorded a reasonable photo. Jorge had two agents in the restaurant as well as two positioned outside.

"The bait's been taken, Paula. Lyubov is in the bar," he whispered to her. She didn't even pause to look up, merely continued to eat.

"Jorge has two men inside and two outside, and I'm armed. We'll get a text when Lyubov leaves. My guess is he'll really try to scare the hell out of us, and I want us to play along with that. I'll play like he's gotten to me, and you need to do the same this time, unlike before."

"After our starring roles today, I think I can handle that," she said. "I enjoyed my role."

Nick looked sharply at her. "We can play it up, but we don't want to push too far. Remember that this is all about getting a good photo and establishing a tail. Not about a provoking a violent confrontation."

"Of course, I fully understand. I will follow your lead."

Nick's phone vibrated an hour later. The text indicated Lyubov had left the restaurant and was observed waiting in the southeastern corner of the parking lot. Nick and Paula would have to go through this area to get to the street.

"It's almost showtime, Paula. Jorge has indicated where Lyubov is waiting. We'll head that way, laughing and pretending we don't have a care in the world. You ready?"

She nodded and reapplied her lipstick in a mirror while Nick paid the bill. Strolling outside, they lingered by the restaurant entrance, letting their eyes get accustomed to the dim light before walking toward the street. Nick could just barely see the outline of a man in their path. As they approached, Lyubov stepped from the shadows into a small patch of light, and Nick saw the long, jagged scar on his face. They attempted to go around him, but Lyubov blocked their path.

"You two much trouble today, poking around and asking questions," he sneered in his thick accent. Nick had noticed something in Lyubov's right hand, and it came up quickly, hitting him in the stomach, doubling him over. A click followed as Nick recovered and stood to find a six-inch knife inches from Paula's face.

"I warn you, lady, but you not listen. You think this joke?" Paula started to sob, and Lyubov turned his attention to Nick, grabbing him tightly by the collar, the knife close to his nose.

"And you, Mister Hotshot New York Bank Asshole. You want go home in pieces?" He lowered the knife just a fraction, giving Nick an opening, but he decided to wait.

"Please don't hurt us. We're just following orders, all just routine paperwork," he stammered. Nick trembled as hard as he could, his eyes bulging wide but his right hand a coiled spring, ready to launch if needed. He quickly assessed his options. His opponent thought he was merely a nerdy accountant, but Nick had training, confidence, and the element of surprise. He decided to give his acting another shot.

"I'll go back tomorrow, and I'll report that I didn't find any problems," he whimpered in a high pitch.

Lyubov released his grasp slightly, moving his face inches from Nick's, the smell of vodka strong on his breath. Paula's sobs had turned to a wail.

"Da. You do that, asshole. If I find you cause problems back home, I hunt you down and gut you like a fish."

Lyubov expertly flicked his wrist, and the point of his knife sliced the side of Nick's face. With a cry of pain, Nick's fingers jumped to the wound to staunch the blood. Lyubov followed this with a backhand across Paula's face, sending her reeling.

"Don't go back to work tomorrow or I will kill you."

"Yes, yes. I'm done. Please don't hurt us," she moaned.

Just then, a trio of boisterous, drunken men came out of the shadows, approaching them.

"No more warnings," Lyubov said, and disappeared into the darkness.

Nick turned his attention to Paula, oblivious to his bleeding wound. "Are you alright, Paula? Are you hurt?"

Her sobbing stopped, and she rubbed her jaw tenderly. "Nothing that I haven't experienced before with an ex," she laughed, until she saw the blood on Nick's face, trailing down to his collar. She pulled out some tissues and held it to the cut, doing little to stop the flow.

The drunken men were now mysteriously sober, and Jorge's voice cut through the dark.

"Are you both alright? Nick, you're bleeding. Let us see how bad it is." The other "drunk" produced a flashlight, which Jorge held. "It doesn't appear serious, just superficial." The agent produced a compress bandage, and Nick held it to his face. Jorge shined the flashlight on Paula, revealing a swollen area on the side of her face. "You'll have a nasty bruise, but probably not more than that. I'm sorry about this; it could have gotten out of hand."

Nick and Paula looked at each other and both had a small smile. "The things we actors endure," he said. "Jorge, I just hope you got some primo pictures, and please tell us you've got a tail on him right now."

"Yes, my friend, he is being followed as we speak. The pictures from the bar are quite good, and I'm sure we'll get even better ones as part of the tail. My men will find out how he is leaving the island, any alias he is using, and his destination. Even if it is a false flight plan, he will be tracked by a Navy P-8 Poseidon and the FAA until he lands in the States, and then Harvey Tankersley's teams will take over. He'll be covered tightly wherever he goes. You guys really put it on the line to enable this. Let's get you both to the hospital to get checked out, and then we'll go to my office for the debrief and paperwork." Both Nick and Paula nodded in agreement.

The hospital trip proved to be cautionary, as Nick's wound was indeed superficial. Only cleaning and a large butterfly bandage was necessary. Paula's contusion would look unsightly for a while but not have any lasting effects.

They got to Jorge's office by nine, and he produced after-action report forms and a bottle of rum and some mixers to ease the process. Nick reviewed their interaction with Lyubov in detail, his report being recorded. "For a guy who has never been undercover, you were very impressive, Nick. And, Paula, not being a trained agent, you were remarkable. You both really kept your cool."

"I wanted to take him down in the *worst* way," said Nick. "But I sensed he only wanted to scare us, not hurt us badly. I like to think I was ready."

"I'm sure you were, my friend. My report to your boss will reflect your calm manner under pressure."

Nick nodded his thanks as Jorge poured them another round of drinks. Nick liked this type of debrief, certain that Scott would not approve.

Jorge continued, "Paula, you must not go back to the banking center. Resign tomorrow. You have done everything you can for us there. For your safety, I am recommending that you leave the Caymans until this case is resolved. Do you have any connections in the States?"

"Yes, I have a sister in New York City. I'm sure I could stay with her."

"Excellent. Then I suggest you leave with Nick tomorrow afternoon. We will take care of the paperwork and provide you with some temporary living funds as well as handle getting your personal belongings to you."

"Thank you. I'm grateful for any assistance you might provide."

"My pleasure, Paula. You've certainly earned it."

"Thank you, Jorge, and your team, for all your help," said Nick. "We don't know where all this is going, but it's important to remember that it was uncovered by you, here in the Caymans." They exchanged handshakes after finishing their reports, and Jorge told Paula that his overwatch of her would continue until Pavel left the island. His office would have their plane tickets by noon.

The flight home was uneventful for Nick, with his wound being only a minor inconvenience. He and Paula said goodbye at JFK, exchanging contact information. When he got back to his office late that afternoon, he had received an email from Harvey Tankersley indicating that Lyubov had been tracked back to Teterboro, New Jersey, and surveillance was in effect. Scott Thompson was out for the rest of the day, so their meeting would wait until tomorrow.

Nick was dog tired, the aftereffects of the adrenaline rush of the mission. Gena was gone until the weekend, so he would be able to relax and prepare for his meeting with his boss. Once in his apartment, Nick flopped down on the sofa, rehashing the past forty-eight hours. He was pleased with his performance in his first real undercover op but fixated on whether he would cross paths with Lyubov again. He didn't get much further than that, as he was soon sound asleep.

CHAPTER TWENTY-SEVEN

It was an epic party at one of Manhattan's most exclusive clubs—not that there was anything to celebrate. Travis Dustin's team had lost another close one, and once again he had played a role in the loss. He partied hard to ease the pain, with his companion a willing participant. It wasn't enough to make him forget but was more than enough to make him not care for a while. There was much to forget: the boos from the crowd, his teammates' stares and silent treatment, the attempts by the sports media to interview him, and the stern dressing down and threats from his coaches.

His companion gave him a quick peck on the cheek before leaving his condo, half-heartedly telling him that things would get better. Soon after she left, his cell phone chimed. Answering without checking the number, he was startled by the female voice on the other end.

"Hello, Travis, it's Tina," she said in a low voice. "How are you doing *today*?"

Tina was Tina Bishop, his friend from college who he had last heard from over a year ago. Even though his head throbbed, and his thinking wasn't anywhere near crystal clear, something in her tone and the emphasis on *today* focused his attention.

"I'm doing just fine, Tina," he said too eagerly, trying to sound normal. "Nice to hear from you. It's been a while. How are you?"

"Frankly, I'm worried about you, Travis. I've seen three of your games on TV this year and most of them last year. There's a big difference. And yesterday. What's going on? This isn't you. Are you hurt?"

"Not you, too!" he exploded. "I'm catching shit from everybody, and I don't need this from some bitch I knew in college. You suddenly some pro scout or somethin'? You studying man-to-man and zone defense? You up on the bullshit rules against defenses which make me look bad? What do you know, woman? And why the fuck do you care?"

His head felt like it was in a vise, and he was breathing hard, bouncing around the apartment like a human Pac-Man.

"Don't you call me that word, Travis. Don't you diss me. I won't have it. I know you too well. I don't like what I've been hearing. Word is, you been partying pretty hard in the big city and in Vegas. Mr. Bigshot now, big lifestyle. They got the hook in you big-time out there, I'm told."

"Oh, so now you're my fuckin' grandmother, is that it? Acting all high and mighty. Who gave you that right, Tina?"

"Don't you dare disrespect your grammy, Travis Dustin! Don't you dare!"

Tina now knew something was *really* wrong. She had never heard Travis say anything against his grandmother, always holding her on a pedestal.

"I have the right because you wouldn't have made it without me, and you know it. You wasting such an opportunity. I didn't put my ass on the line so that you could become a loser. And my ass may still be on the line!"

"I wasn't the only one you put your ass on the line for, Tina. You helped others." His tone was calmer now.

"You right, Trav. But you were special. You weren't like the others; you just needed some help with the books. You didn't have an attitude toward me or feel entitled. Your grammy raised you good, Travis. And how is your grammy? Is she feeling any better?"

The awkward silence cut Tina like a knife. "When you last call her, Travis? Please don't tell me you're forgetting your grammy, not taking care of her."

Silence. "Oh, Trav. What's going on?"

A long pause, a low voice. "Nothin' wrong, Tina. Nothin' wrong. Jus' hard times right now. I'll bounce back. Grammy's fine. It's all good." His words were hollow, his voice distant, lacking the exuberance she had known before.

"Travis, there are people who love you and care for you. Your grammy and me are here for you. Don't ever forget that."

"I know, I know. I'm just tired, that's all. Too much partying last night." He laughed. "Got to cut back on that."

"Well, you do sound like you need some sleep. I'll let you go. But I'll call again, soon."

"Okay. Take care. We'll talk again." He disconnected before she could say anything more.

As she put down the phone, Tina was saddened to realize that her instincts had been correct. Something bad was going on with Travis that he wouldn't tell her. Maybe he'd tell his grammy. She hadn't talked to Mrs. Dustin for a long time but had always gotten along well with her. She collected her thoughts for a few moments before dialing, wanting to choose her words carefully. The phone was answered on the first ring by the elderly, soft-spoken, Southern woman.

"Hello, Mrs. Dustin. This is Tina Bishop, Travis's friend from college. How are you?"

"Hello, dear, nice to hear from you. You helped Travis with his schoolwork, as I remember." The words were breathy, not gasping but clearly requiring some effort. "I'm doing okay. My pressure's up and I don't get around too easily. But the good Lord's taking care of me, so I don't complain. How are you, dear?"

"Well, I'm fine, Mrs. Dustin, staying busy. I was just calling to see how you are and how Travis is doing. Have you heard from him lately?"

"No, Tina, I haven't heard from him in a while. I know he a busy man and he call when he can. I be patient."

"Mrs. Dustin, I just talked with Travis, and something isn't right. I don't mean to worry you, but I think he's in trouble and he won't tell me. He's acting like everything's fine. The fact that he hasn't called you worries me. I know he loves you so much."

"What do you mean trouble, Tina? What you think is wrong?" Her voice was now anxious, her breathing more labored.

"Oh, Mrs. Dustin, I don't know. I'm sorry to bother you. I know I'm getting you upset. Would you call him? Maybe he'll talk to you, and you can find out. I hope I'm wrong, but it just didn't sound like the Travis I used to know."

"Yes, dear, of course I'll call him. I got his number right here. He'll talk to his grammy." The voice was now stronger, more intentioned, her motherly instincts roused from their slumber.

"Thank you, Mrs. Dustin. I'm sure he'll talk to you. I'll call you back tomorrow to see how it went."

"Okay, Tina, thank you for calling. I'll call him soon, after I take my pills. We'll talk tomorrow. Bye."

Tina replaced the phone, conflicted in her emotions. *That was terrible, but I had to do it. I know she was upset. I gotta believe that a grammy's love will find the truth.*

After the call with Tina, Travis got another cup of coffee and sat in his favorite chair, dejected that he had been such an ass. Aware that she had been trying to help, his spirits sank even lower as the thought occurred to him that he was beyond anyone's help.

He moped around the apartment, staring out the window at the great view but not really seeing. He tried to get his mind off it by looking at sports magazines and was successful for a while until his cell chimed again. He was truly alarmed when he realized it was from his grandmother. "Hello, Grammy, how are you? Are you alright? I'm sorry I haven't called lately. I've been so busy."

"Travis baby, that's all right. I'm doing fine. The good Lord's watching over me. I got what I need. Travis, I got a phone call from your friend Tina. She's worried about you and thinks something's wrong." Her breathing was better, the inhaler having done its job. Her voice was not strong, but not frail either. "Tell me, baby. How you really doing? You okay? You can talk to your grammy."

Travis knew he couldn't fool his grandmother; his mind wouldn't even let him try.

He paused, and his emotional dam began to crack.

"Oh, Grammy, I've done bad, real bad. I've got myself into a jam, and I don't know what to do. Some people own me. They force me to do things that hurt other people. Oh, Grammy, I'm so ashamed." He let out a small sob, desperate not to fall apart but so close to the edge, barely able to speak.

"Trav, nobody can own you if you don't let them. Whatever's bothering you, whatever you've done, it's never too late to change. I taught you God's love. He will forgive you. His path is the only path— the *right* path. Come back to the path, Travis. Come back to the path."

The dam gave way, and the emotional tumult followed, unrestrained. His body convulsed with waves of tears, his soul so wounded he had to put the cell phone on speaker, as he couldn't hold it any longer.

"I'm so sorry, Grammy, I'm so sorry" was all he could say over and over.

She replied, "It's okay, baby boy, it's okay. Grammy's here," and she whispered, "Shh, shh, shh" into the phone. She didn't ask him what he had done. It wasn't necessary. Forgiveness was all encompassing. When he had finished sobbing and the storm had passed, she said once again, "Whatever it is, Travis, come back to the path. Come back to the path."

"I will, Grammy, I will. I promise. Thank you, Grammy. I love you. I'm so sorry I've been selfish and haven't called like I should. I'll call you every week."

"I'm fine, Travis. Don't worry 'bout me. But it sure would be nice to hear from you more often. Do what is right, Trav. I'll hear from you soon."

"I will, Grammy, I will. Talk to you soon."

He dried his eyes and went into the bathroom to splash cold water on his face. While he still looked awful, his soul took its first step toward redemption. *Thank you, Lord, for my grammy. I will come back to the path. I know what is right and what I need to do. I just have to figure out how to do it.*

CHAPTER TWENTY-EIGHT

Tuesday went well for Travis at the team facility, including practice. He was determined to act normal and maintain an upbeat attitude, putting forth his very best effort, and this led to a good outcome.

He was due to have a meeting with Mr. Thomas at their usual restaurant that evening to get his next assignment. With trepidation, he walked in and saw Mr. Thomas already seated at their regular booth in an isolated corner. Travis pressed a button, activating a small recorder in his pocket. This was the second meeting he had done this, unaware that Mr. Thomas had been checking for recording devices. Travis had gotten lucky: Mr. Thomas stopped doing so two meetings ago, thinking Travis incapable of such action. He rose as Travis approached and greeted Travis warmly.

"What are you drinking tonight, Travis?" he asked.

"Nothing for me tonight, Mr. Thomas. I won't be staying," he said, not taking a seat. Looking Mr. Thomas straight in the eyes he said, "I won't be meeting you again or continuing with our relationship."

Mr. Thomas fumbled his drink, spilling it on his suit, and said through clenched teeth, "We own you, Dustin. You don't have that option if you know what's good for you."

"I know what's good for me, and I'm doing it." He glared at Mr. Thomas for a second before leaving.

Ordering a double Laphroig neat, Mr. Thomas took a large gulp and then called his boss on their emergency number. "We have a serious problem. We have a bolter" was all he said, but that was enough to set up an ominous chain of events.

Travis walked out of the restaurant, head high, pleased that he'd had the guts, not knowing until just then whether he did. He had kept it short and sweet to not lose courage. This was his point of no return. He congratulated himself on having the foresight to think about ways of protection, some *insurance* for his safety. Now he had to complete its setup.

———————

Travis did not have to be at the team facility until eleven the next morning, so at nine sharp he was in the reception area of the VP of Internal Security for the NAFL. He introduced himself to the receptionist and explained that he had an urgent matter to discuss with Mr. Townsend, who was in his office and came out to greet Travis.

"Travis, welcome. I'm Phil Townsend. Please come in and make yourself comfortable." When the door was closed, he continued, "I was told you have an urgent matter. How can I be of service?" He was confident he could stop this potential train wreck.

"Mr. Townsend, I'll come right to the point. I'm being blackmailed. For the past few weeks, I have been altering my play to try to change the outcome of games, to favor my team's opponents. I don't know who's behind this, but I think it's some type of organized crime syndicate. They knew an awful lot about me, the money problems I've gotten into in Vegas, things like that. They threatened me physically, to end my career, if I didn't cooperate. They promised to square me with Vegas, so I cooperated."

"This is quite serious, Travis. Can you go into more details?" Townsend had carefully rehearsed his role.

Travis summarized the most important events. He reviewed the roles he had played in the games and the results of his play. He omitted any reference to the help he had received in college. When he finished, he simply stared at the floor.

"This is quite a story, Travis. You did the right thing coming to us. It took great courage. I've got to ask. What caused you to stop?"

"Mr. Townsend, I'm very embarrassed about this. This is not how I was raised. I've hurt a lot of people, let a lot down who believed in me. I've got to try to make it right."

"Have you told anyone else about this? Any of your coaches?"

"No, sir. You're the first I've come to. I thought it was my duty. But I made an appointment with the FBI for tomorrow morning."

Holy shit!! Townsend's eyes narrowed, and his voice developed an edge. "That's not a good idea, Travis. It's premature. Let my office handle this. That's our job." Townsend's mind raced. This was not going as he had planned.

"But, Mr. Townsend, I've got to protect myself. I've probably broken laws, and maybe they can give me immunity if I help them. I came here because you protect the league, and hopefully the FBI can protect me."

"Your career will be over if you go to them, but we can try to save it if you work with us. You have a lot to lose. Think carefully about this before—"

"I have thought carefully about this!" he said, his voice rising. "It's not my career I'm concerned about losing at this point; it's my life!" He stormed out of the office before Townsend could reply.

———————

Phil Townsend dialed Commissioner O'Brien's private number after Travis's abrupt departure. Very few people in the league knew this number, and O'Brien picked up on the first ring. "Yes?" No need for a greeting on this line.

"Jimmy, we've got a very serious problem. We need to meet in *the room.*"

O'Brien knew the voice and was unsettled at the request, but quickly recovered. "You first. I'll be down in ten." They both knew the code, and the delay would lessen the chance of running into anyone else.

Ten minutes later they were both in the special room in the basement of NAFL headquarters. The look on Townsend's face worried O'Brien, as it was rare for his security chief to be shaken by anything.

"Whatever's going on, Phil, must be pretty serious. Tell me the problem."

"This is really serious, Jimmy. We have a bolter, and this must be dealt with immediately. He's going to the FBI."

O'Brien had been standing, but on hearing that he slumped into a chair, suddenly pale. "Give me all the details."

Townsend recapped the history of Travis Dustin, and his abrupt change of heart last night. He omitted his part in the assistant's death or the failed attempt on the coach, choosing only the worst problem now. "Up to this point, he has been one of our easiest assets to control. There was no sign of this coming, according to my associate who handles him. Just totally out of the blue at their regular meeting yesterday. He came to me this morning, informing me of what he had done, saying he felt it was his 'duty' to the league. He told me he has an appointment with the FBI tomorrow. I told him we would handle it and he shouldn't go, that we could probably save his career if he cooperated with us."

"Will he?"

"Hell no. He stormed out of my office, saying he wasn't concerned about his career but about his life, and he felt the FBI could protect him, maybe give him immunity."

"Do you think he's told anyone else? Could you be sure?"

"He said he hadn't told anyone else, not even coaches, and while I believe him, there's no way to verify that. This is why it's so critical to act fast. We've got to plan this out right now so we can set it up and complete the mission by tonight."

"Agreed. We've talked about the potential of something like this happening, so we know what must be done. What angle will we use to assure nothing comes back on us?"

"I've already been thinking about that, knowing the kid's history. I'm certain my associates and I can pull this off with no problem." Townsend spent three minutes at a rapid pace outlining a detailed plan. At the end he simply said, "All I need is your go-ahead, and I will make the phone calls to get moving. Time is critical."

O'Brien nodded in agreement. "We have no other option. Make the calls. Eliminate this threat. Afterward we will handle the fallout, do any damage control necessary in the press. Protecting the product is the only thing that matters."

"We absolutely don't have any other options, Jimmy. We won't have any problems with damage control. We've got a lot of experience doing that."

They both nodded, saying nothing more. O'Brien left first, followed ten minutes later by Townsend, who used that time to review the recording he had just made.

Back in his office, using a cell phone equipped with military-grade encryption, Phil Townsend sent coded text messages to Pavel Lyubov and Vincent Taranto. Both men knew the coded texts indicated a top-priority meeting at a specific location at a specific time.

All three men appeared at the designated time at the secure location— the boiler room of a long-closed factory. They were the only people with access.

With military precision, Townsend gave detailed instructions to the two men, assigning their roles. No detail was too small, and both men offered input about the plan, which Townsend accepted. Alternative scenarios were drawn up and reviewed. When all plans were complete, they were verbalized by each man to verify full understanding.

It had been a long, intense day, and Travis Dustin was drained, both physically and emotionally. With his meeting in the morning with the FBI, tomorrow would be no better. He desperately wanted a good night's sleep and planned to have a simple dinner and turn in early. As he entered his apartment, it was dark even though he thought he had left the light on.

He flicked the switch.

Nothing happened.

Shit. The bulb's blown. I'll have to use my cell phone.

It was the final activity of his overtaxed brain.

A massive arm came around behind him and put him in a carotid sleeper hold, while two other sets of hands pinned his arms to his sides. He was unconscious within ten seconds, and they lowered him to the floor while the massive arm maintained pressure on the artery. His assailants removed their night vision goggles, and one turned on lights, revealing a prepared scene. His glass dining room table held an opened bottle of Jack Daniels, several loose alprazolams, and two lines of cocaine with evidence there had been a third. An index card was close by, as well as a blackened spoon with traces of heroin and a lighter.

Wearing nitrile gloves, they removed his coat, threw it over a chair, and rolled up his left sleeve. Following their practiced roles, a short, stocky man used a shoelace from Travis's wardrobe to tourniquet his left arm, while a third man, wearing a Con Ed uniform, produced a syringe preloaded with a hotshot mixture of heroin. The heroin had been laced with a particularly potent form of fentanyl for added measure. The mixture was injected intravenously, and their combined effects were profound and almost immediate. The toxic mixture produced deep respiratory distress followed soon by cardiac failure. In three minutes, Travis Dustin was dead, confirmed by stethoscope.

Continuing their rehearsed sequence, his fingerprints were applied to all the items on the glass table. They propped him in his favorite chair, the syringe and tourniquet still in place. The large man left first, keeping his gloved hands in his pockets and a baseball cap with a large bill pulled low on his forehead, an attempt to conceal his unforgettable face. Five minutes later the second assailant, the stocky one, impeccably dressed, departed. He walked down two flights of stairs before taking the elevator to the ground floor and caught a cab two blocks away. The last man, with the Con Ed uniform, completed a thorough sweep of the apartment, using a mental checklist to verify that no trace of their presence would be found.

He took the stairs to the ground floor, complete with flashlight and professional multimeter in hand, and drove away in an unmarked van parked down the street. Their reconnaissance had revealed that the building lacked security cameras, but every effort had been taken to assure that they could not be identified.

CHAPTER TWENTY-NINE

By ten in the morning, a typical Thursday was in progress at the team facility for the New York Pride football team. With one exception, all players were present. Travis Dustin was absent, which was a serious offense considering the coach's strict rules. Multiple calls to his cell phone went unanswered, and questioning his teammates provided no further information. No one had seen him since yesterday's practice.

At ten forty-five, Dustin's companion called on the special line reserved for players families and registered friends. She had not heard from him since early Monday morning, and he was not responding to his cell phone. She was upset when the team assistant told her that Travis had not shown up as required and the team had been unable to contact him. She expressed her concerns that something serious was wrong, and the assistant told her that the team would send someone out to Travis's apartment.

Head defensive coach Junior Baughman contacted the NYPD and requested that an officer meet him and the building superintendent at Travis's apartment. Arriving a few minutes after noon, Coach Baughman explained to the cop, "This is totally out of character for him. He has never missed a practice, and neither the team nor his girlfriend have been able to contact him."

The superintendent, while searching for the right key, commented, "He's been a good tenant, real quiet, no problems at all. I sure hope everything is alright."

The policeman noticed that the door was intact and locked. The officer knocked on the door, identifying himself, waited twenty seconds, and knocked again. Getting no response, he motioned for the super to unlock the door and step aside, and the cop opened the door slightly, calling, "Mr. Dustin, NYPD. Mr. Dustin?" He fully opened the door with Coach Baughman close behind. "Please stay here, Coach. I'll check things first."

The apartment was dark with all the blinds closed tightly, and the officer fumbled to find a light switch to the right of the door. He found it, but no light came on. Reaching for his Maglite, he scanned the room and found Travis slumped in a chair. Turning back to Baughman he said, "This could be a crime scene. Don't move until I call you."

Baughman could not see into the room from his angle, and the superintendent shrank back into the hallway. The policeman crossed the room to the dining area and flipped a switch with his flashlight. The room was bathed in light, revealing a glass table littered with booze, pills, cocaine and drug paraphernalia. He walked over to Travis, finding a tourniquet in place and a syringe still stuck in his arm. The officer felt for a pulse, then grabbed his radio microphone and called the dispatcher, reporting in code his location and findings and requesting detectives, forensics, and a medical examiner. He then motioned Baughman and said, "Coach, please come here. It's unpleasant, but I need you to provide us an identification. Is this your player Travis Dustin?"

Junior Baughman had been coaching for over a dozen years and had been involved in numerous off-field situations involving players, but he had never experienced anything like this. He walked hesitantly over to the officer and was so horrified he was almost physically sick when he saw Travis. He swallowed hard and took a deep breath before replying in a low voice, "Yes, this is Travis Dustin." He turned to look at the apartment and was aghast at what he saw on the glass table. Walking toward it, he was stopped in his tracks as the officer commanded, "Don't touch anything. Please wait in the corridor for the detectives. They'll want to ask you some questions. And no phone calls until they tell you."

Baughman nodded in agreement and shuffled to the hallway, his head spinning. A few minutes later two detectives appeared, identifying themselves, and he did the same. They said they would take his statement after talking with the officer, and shortly thereafter the forensic people arrived. Five minutes later, the detectives pulled him aside.

"Coach, we're sorry about your loss. This must be a quite a shock for you. Any information you could give us would be appreciated."

"Thank you for your sentiments. I've coached over twelve years and have never been involved with anything like this." Baughman reviewed the sequence of events that morning.

"Was he known as a partier or to have drug problems?"

"Like most young players, he enjoyed his fame and this city, if you know what I mean. But I know he never tested positive for any of our league-banned substances, and I never heard any locker room whispers of something like this. This seems so out of character for him, but I guess you never know. Say, I've got to report this to the head coach, who'll tell the league. Can I do that now? Do you need me anymore?"

"We're done for now, Coach. You can tell your coach only about the death right now, not what you've seen. Tell him one of us will call him within the hour with more details, and we will contact league headquarters and talk about press releases and that sort of thing. Thank you for your help."

———

A subdued Baughman called his boss, head coach Josh McIntyre, with the shocking news. His coach was not happy that Baughman couldn't go into details but was relieved to hear he would be contacted by the detective. Two hours later, he received a call from the detective, who informed him that their preliminary investigation indicated that Travis died from a massive drug overdose, but the final determination would have to wait for toxicology. He added that while they had not found a suicide letter, that possibility could not be ruled out. McIntyre thanked the detective and next placed a call to Commissioner O'Brien's office, citing an emergency.

O'Brien picked up. "What's going on, Josh?" He was ready for his part in the charade.

McIntyre informed O'Brien of Dustin's death and what they knew about it so far.

"Josh, I am so sorry to hear this. It must've been very difficult for Baughman to discover him." He offered his condolences and asked, "Who else knows about this at this time, Coach?"

"No one else yet, Commissioner. I just got off the phone with the detective before calling you. We know he has a girlfriend, and we have a number for his grandmother in South Carolina. These are the only numbers he had on file with us. Should we contact them?"

"Yes. Contact them and call an emergency team meeting to notify everyone. We will let all the other teams know, as well as handle a press release. If the detective contacts you again, please refer them to my office."

"Will do, Commissioner."

O'Brien then placed a call to Paul Johnstone, VP of NAFL Media, informing him of the death and making arrangements for an immediate press release. He told Paul to indicate the cause of death as a possible suicide by lethal drug overdose.

———

At approximately one o'clock, Tina Bishop, working from home on her computer, was startled when her doorbell rang. She was not expecting anyone but was relieved when she saw it was a FedEx driver. She signed for a large, flat envelope, which was not unusual, as she routinely received them for work. Opening it, she was surprised to find two letters from Travis Dustin and two keys. One was labeled with the address of his apartment, the other with the name of a bank and a serial number. The first letter she opened was notarized, giving her location, numbers, and legal access to his safe deposit box in New

York City. Her heart pounding, she sat down and opened the second letter with trembling fingers.

Wednesday
Dear Tina,

It is possible by the time you get this letter something really bad may have happened to me. If it has, it won't be an accident or a suicide although they may make it look like either. If the worst happens, there're things you must do to avenge me and hopefully bring justice down on the people who did it.

I was not blameless in this whole thing, but it took your phone call and that of my Grammy to make me realize what I must do. Thank you so much for reaching out to me and I'm so sorry how I treated you. I have hurt many people with my actions, and I have deep regrets. Please tell my Grammy how sorry I am and how much I love her. She will be well taken care of in my will and there is something for you, too.

The very first thing you must do is go to my apartment in New York City. It may be labelled as a crime scene but hopefully they have not changed the lock. In the hall linen closet next to the bedroom there is a false wall in the back of the middle shelf. Remove the towels, push on the edge of the wall above the shelf and the false wall will open, revealing an audio and video recorder. This is connected wirelessly to two hidden cameras with microphones in the living/dining areas and to my internet router. Remove the attached thumb drive and take the two empty thumb drives which are also there.

Next you must go to my bank and get the contents of my safe deposit box, which will have my cell phone and another envelope. Turn on my cell phone and access it with the enclosed password. Under "my messages" there should be a message containing a jpeg file with all the audio/video recordings from my apartment. This was done on the chance you couldn't get in. Copy the recordings onto the spare thumb drives but personally deliver my cell phone and the original video and audio recordings to Freddie Wilmington. You may remember him from college as my mentor. He's a former pro player and can be trusted and he'll know what to do with these items. His contact information is in the envelope in the box. Keep a copy of the recordings yourself in a very secure place.

Tina, you must be very careful and be on guard at all times. These are very dangerous men who will stop at nothing and with our past

I don't want you involved with them or the police. That's why I want you to give this stuff to Freddie.

Grammy told me to "come back to the path" and I hope God knows I tried and forgives me.

I love you, Tina. I'll never forget what you did for me in college, even though I now realize that it was wrong. I don't know why we never became a couple, because I always felt you cared for me and had my back. It was an opportunity missed.

Don't miss other opportunities in your life!

Love,

Travis

She had held it together while she read the letter but now broke down in uncontrollable sobs. *Maybe he was wrong, or just overreacting. I don't have any proof yet.*

That notion was quickly dispelled when she checked her phone for news and found the press release from the NAFL as the lead story. Another wave of grief wracked her body, and it took ten full minutes to subside. She made herself a cup of tea amid short gasps of sobs and sat down to plan the task that lay ahead of her.

———

Tony Stravnicki had just completed a drill with his defensive backs when Coach Hank Naples walked over to him and told him about the death of Travis Dustin. Tony asked the cause of death and was puzzled when told it was by a drug overdose, possibly a suicide. He tried hard to focus on practice but was consumed with the thought of a young man with so much potential whose life had ended so tragically. Instinct told him that something wasn't right.

His ride home was miserable, and not even his favorite classic rock station could ease the funk which overcame him. About a mile from his house, he got a call on his burner phone, and he found a spot to pull over to answer. It was a very subdued Freddie Wilmington.

"Hi, Tony. Travis was just on the news."

"I know," Tony said, just barely audible.

"Just doesn't make sense, man, just doesn't make sense. I know he liked to party, but I've never known him to be involved with drugs. He was pretty straight as a college player."

"We know his play has been erratic, Freddie. Maybe he just got really down on himself."

"Yeah, that's possible, Tony. Hell, anything's possible. I just don't know what to believe. First Denny and now Travis."

"Freddie, you and Brad see what you can find out about Travis's partying habits. Talk to his teammates. That sort of thing. Maybe he just kept it really well hidden."

"Could be, Tony, could be. If it's true, somebody should know something. I'll ask around. I'll touch base if I hear something."

"Thanks, Freddie."

———

Maggie and the kids had returned from the lake that morning, the kids happy to be home and see their father, but Maggie uncertain how she would find Tony. Her attitude softened when she heard the news about Travis and saw the fading bruises on her husband's arm and cheekbone.

"Tony, I heard about Travis, but what happened to you? Are you okay?"

"Yeah, I'm fine, Mags," he replied, the two tenderly embracing. He stroked her red hair as she laid her head on his shoulder. Almost simultaneously, they said, "I'm sorry" and broke down in laughter.

After a moment, Tony began. "I've been lost with all of you gone, and it's forced me to really think about myself and us." He held her tighter and said, "Maggie, I have a mistress, you know."

She jerked away from him, her eyes wide.

"Oh, she's not what you think. She's game film and a whiteboard filled with diagrams of plays. She's seduced me at times and hurt you and the family in the process. I'm sorry about that," he said simply.

Looking into his emerald-green eyes, she saw the love and sincerity that was the true Tony. "I've been in a real funk over us, and the kids liked the lake but really missed you. I know that football is your life, Tony, but we are too. I know there's room in your heart for both. We just have to keep working at it."

"I will, Mags, but a black-and-white guy like me needs you guys to remind me of the colors in life."

"Speaking of colors, are you going to tell me what caused these? Remember you promised no more secrets."

Tony filled her in about his talks with Freddie about Dennis and now Travis, and how lucky he was with the assault. "Maggie, the police think it was a random attack, just like Dennis. I really don't know what to believe."

"Awful lot of 'random' bad things happening to people, Tony. What do you think about this Travis news?"

"My head is spinning. Everyone's concerned, of course, but no one on the team really knew him. So, the response with us is pretty muted. Freddie was shook up. He mentored Travis in college, got to known him fairly well, and feels this whole situation is way out of character. He and Brad are going to talk to his teammates, try to find out about his lifestyle, that sort of thing. See if they can find anything to support this."

"Maybe he just got in over his head. Couldn't find a way out and panicked out of despair," Maggie offered. "There's so much pressure on these young players now."

"Possibly. Denny's analysis of Travis this year compared to last year is factual, as was Travis's impact on the games and the standings. Sadly, his death is another questionable circumstance along with all the others. We need something tangible. We need all these incidences to come together and point in one direction" he said, his voice rising, chewing gum frantically.

"I know, Tony, I know. Spit your gum out and grab a beer before you blow a gasket. Getting yourself worked up right now won't accomplish anything."

He got the beer and headed to the family room. *Goddammit! Could someone have cracked Dennis's files? Was my attack really random? And could Travis's death somehow be related to all this? No answers, just more questions!*

CHAPTER THIRTY

Tina Bishop got an early start, wanting to be in New York when the bank opened at nine. She had arrived at his apartment at eight, her psyche recoiling against going to where his death took place. But she had a solemn duty to perform, and she did it as instructed, without anyone trying to stop her from entering. Next, she went to the bank, getting there by nine fifteen, and after showing the notarized letter, proof of identification, and the key, she was allowed in the safe deposit box area. She came prepared, with earbuds for the cell phone, her laptop, and accessories that could play and copy the audio and video recordings. She was nervous, not having a clue as to what Travis had left.

The box contained his cell phone and an envelope with the telephone number of Freddie Wilmington. Listening to the cell phone recording, it appeared that an individual was giving Travis instructions on what he expected Travis to do in the game the following weekend. The man's voice was distinctive, sounding self-assured and in command of the encounter. When he was finished with these instructions, he reminded Travis of his "Vegas problems" and stated that they were being taken care of for him as long as he cooperated.

Travis was being blackmailed into influencing games! No wonder he had sounded so depressed and desperate.

She recorded the conversation onto the spare thumb drive.

Opening the jpeg file on the cell phone, she recognized the interior of Travis's apartment. Two side-by-side frames came from two cameras. One camera was positioned so it covered the front door and most of the living area, while a second camera scanned the dining area with a glass table. The cameras Travis used were obviously motion or sound activated, and a *6:15* time stamp from the night Travis died showed a man in a uniform entering the room and looking around. He was followed at five-minute intervals, first by a short, stocky, well-dressed man and finally by a massive man wearing a baseball hat. Tina watched as the men, wearing gloves, worked quickly in different locations around the room. The man in the uniform took several items from a bag and began to set them up on the table. Tina was appalled to see that it included a liquor bottle, some pills, and most horrifying, a white powder he placed in lines on the table. The recordings were high quality and captured glimpses of their faces from time to time.

The well-dressed man worked on several lights in the living area, removing the bulbs and closing all the blinds tightly. They worked efficiently and with minimum conversation as a well-practiced team. The most memorable voice came from the large man, who had a very pronounced accent. When they had finished, they put some sort of apparatus on their heads and shut out the lights, and the recording stopped.

The recording was activated at 7:38 p.m., when the front door opened and a figure appeared. She instantly recognized Travis in the backlight of the hall, and her heart leaped into her throat.

No, Travis! Don't go in there! Her mind screamed a frantic warning that could never be heard. The reality of being powerless to stop what would happen sickened her.

She saw Travis try to use the light switch with no effect, the only light coming from the hallway. He began to walk across the room when someone slammed the door shut, again plunging the room into darkness. The sounds of a struggle could be heard. About fifteen seconds later the lights came on to reveal a stunning scene.

An apparently unconscious Travis was on the floor, one man with his arm around his neck and another bending over him. They had removed his coat, and the well-dressed man had rolled up his sleeve and wrapped something around Travis's left arm while the man in the uniform could plainly be seen sticking a syringe in his arm. They held him down for another minute, then let him go as he experienced a series of convulsions, which soon stopped.

Numb with shock at what she was witnessing, she just couldn't turn away.

After about three minutes of no movement from Travis, the uniformed guy checked him with a doctor's stethoscope, nodded to the others, and they propped him in a chair, the deadly syringe still grotesquely sticking from his arm. They had taken off the equipment on their heads, which Tina now realized must have been night vision goggles, and they bustled about the rooms, completing the setup of the deadly scene.

With the lights on, the men's features were more apparent. The very large man had a prominent scar down his face. The shorter, stocky, well-dressed man had a dark complexion. He smiled once, revealing brilliant white teeth. The last man, most likely the leader, the one dressed in a uniform now clearly seen as Con Ed, had a muscular build and a military-style haircut to match.

Shortly, at intervals, they left. The Con Ed man made a careful sweep of the entire apartment before departing. Once again, the recording stopped.

It took a full thirty seconds of disbelief, in an almost catatonic state, before Tina broke down in uncontrollable wailing, clutching the laptop close to her heart. The wave of emotion passed, and through her sobs, her next thought was rational: *Travis was right.* With her background, she couldn't be involved. She needed Freddie Wilmington and his wisdom.

She packed everything up and, heading outside, found a quiet alcove in the bank where she called Wilmington, only to get his voicemail. She stated that she urgently needed to hear from him because she had information about Travis's death. Having no idea when he would return her call and needing to calm down, she found a nearby coffeehouse. After twenty minutes and a second cup of tea, she became stressed. She played with her hair and drummed her fingers, her mind running on overdrive. *Will he call? Where does he live? How long should I wait?*

Just as she was getting up to leave, her phone rang, and it was him. The corner of the coffeehouse was secluded, and she felt she could talk in private. She introduced herself and explained the letters from Travis and the contents of his safe deposit box without going into specifics. Wilmington stated that he must meet her as soon as possible and recommended one of his car dealerships in New Jersey. She agreed to meet him there in two hours.

———————

Shortly after noon, she pulled up to a dealership in Newark, New Jersey, and Freddie Wilmington was there waiting for her. They acknowledged each other, and with a simple "Follow me please" he brought her to a private office. Turning to Tina, he grasped both of her hands in his. "I'm so sorry, Tina, that you had to get involved in this. You must have been very special to Travis for him to trust you as he did."

"Mr. Wilmington, thank you for meeting me on such short notice. I knew somethin' bad was happenin' with him, but I never felt it would come to this! There's horrible stuff on these tapes. He trusted you'd know what to do with them. I just want to give them to you and go home. It's too much for me!" She handed him the cell phone, the envelope, and thumb drives and quickly turned to leave, saying through sobs, "Find out who did this, Mr. Wilmington. Travis didn't deserve this!"

———————

Tina had barely left the building before Wilmington was playing the first thumb drive, the cell phone audio recording. While he had no idea who Travis was talking to, the implications were obvious. Wilmington grimly congratulated himself that his and Tony's instincts about Travis had been right.

Freddie switched to the recordings from inside Travis's apartment and was mesmerized and sickened by what he witnessed. When he had finished, he called Tony on the burner cell phone and left an urgent message for him to call. Tony was most likely out on the practice field. Freddie went directly to the bank where he had a safe deposit box and left a copy while waiting for Tony's reply. Ninety minutes later, Freddie got the call.

"Tony, I've got some incredible information about Travis's death that can't wait. We must meet soon, preferably with Brad. Has he made your house secure so we can meet there?" a very subdued Wilmington asked.

"From the tone of your voice, Freddie, it's gotta be serious. Brad swept the house, found bugs, and has taken countermeasures. I'll get him to sweep again, presuming he can come soon. If he can't, we won't take any chances, and we'll meet by the side of the road somewhere. When can you get here?"

"I can fly out within a couple hours so we can meet tonight."

"Okay. We'll meet here at seven thirty."

"See you then, Tony."

Tony had a hard time concentrating, his mind a whirlwind of possibilities as to what Freddie might have. Brad was available and would sweep the house before the meeting. He called Maggie at work and was put right through to her.

"Hi, Tony," she said in her typical vibrant tone. "How's your day been?"

"Eh, mediocre day here. There's a pall over everyone because of Travis. I can't concentrate anymore, so I'm leaving soon. I've got a couple guys coming over tonight at seven thirty."

The fact that Tony didn't reveal their names told Maggie who they were, so she didn't ask any questions. "We'll have a nice dinner and talk things over, Tony."

"That's good, Mags, but I'm not all that hungry, so don't do anything special for me. See you later."

"Not that hungry, Tony? Wow, something big—" But he had already hung up.

Maggie came home at six thirty to find Brad Vanderbilt busy sweeping their house, while a somber Tony wandered aimlessly throughout the first floor, frantically chewing gum.

"Maggie, we've got to have a quick dinner as Freddie is due at seven thirty. I need the kids fed and upstairs by then."

"And hello to you too, Tony. Yes, thank you, I had a great day," she said. "Why didn't you start fixing something rather than wasting time? At least for the kids. It's all on me, once again. C'mon, Tony, this isn't fair!"

"I'm sorry, Mags," Tony said as he grabbed her bags. "A little on edge right now. Freddie says he's got something big about the Travis situation, and he was the one who urged Brad to do another sweep. I don't know any more about it than that." He and Maggie worked in silence, putting a supper together quickly, both lost in their own worlds.

Brad ate with them, and Freddie showed up at seven fifteen. Tony and Mags got the kids settled upstairs and told them that Daddy had a real important meeting, and they couldn't come downstairs. Tony suggested they go to the basement family room for more privacy.

"That's good, Tony," said Freddie. "What I have is certainly not for kids." Maggie looked at Tony with a *me too?* look, and he nodded in agreement. Freddie set up his laptop on a table and had Tony connect it to his large-screen HDTV.

"I warn everyone that what you will see and hear is graphic and disturbing."

The three exchanged glances, and Freddie reviewed his meeting with Tina, what he knew of her history with Travis, and the contents of the safe deposit box. He played the cell phone recording first and said, "That was the easy one." He started the video recording.

They watched in silence, riveted to the scene unfolding before their eyes. Maggie gasped at one point, and Brad uttered, "Holy shit" near the end. When it was over, Tony turned up the lights and slumped on the sofa next to Maggie, who tried hard to maintain her composure. Brad sat with his hands tented on his temples, an angry fire in his eyes. Freddie fiddled with his laptop. Tony was the first to speak.

"I've never wanted to be more wrong about something in my life," he said, his voice filled with sadness. "Travis paid with his life to prove we're right. Probably Denny, too. Who are these people, and who controls them? The audio and video are pretty good quality. Did you see that guy with the scar? Someone must know him at least."

Brad spoke next, an edge to his voice. "I have no tolerance for things like this. I'm all in. I don't have any other choice but to continue looking into this."

"I absolutely agree, Brad," interjected Freddie. "But this is also way above our capabilities. Some very powerful group is behind this. We've got to send this to the proper authorities."

"I know just the right person," Tony said and reviewed his relationship with Nick and their previous meeting. "But I want to send it to him anonymously."

They all nodded in agreement, and Freddie continued. "The FBI is the logical choice. I don't feel comfortable just giving it to NYPD. It's too big for that, and being their hometown player, it could end up getting political. This is most likely some type of organized crime we're talking here. We can't take them on."

Brad was next. "No, but we can still be doing our thing quietly, and if we find something, we can pass it along via Tony. We know this is blackmail, so there's a trail somewhere. The cell phone recording alluded to Vegas, so I'll see what I can find there."

"And I'll contact Tina again in person," added Freddie. "Maybe she'll open up to me about college. Something more was going on than I knew when I mentored him. Something's missing there."

Brad continued, "Now we know how really ruthless these guys are. We've got to be incredibly careful. You guys have a family to protect. Tony, Maggie, if you don't have a firearm and proper training already, I would strongly urge you to get one and learn to use it. I can help you with that."

Maggie reacted with a pained expression, but Tony replied before she could.

"I'm not ready for that, yet. You've swept the house. We're clean. Let's remember that nobody knows about these recordings except us and Tina. Travis was a genius to set this whole thing up, and I'm guessing the bad guys would never have thought him capable of something like this. Brad, Freddie, you guys do what you've said, and I'll get this stuff to my nephew. We'll stay in contact at least weekly and more frequently as needed."

The two men looked at each other and nodded in agreement.

Both had a look of steely-eyed resolve, and they all stood and embraced, saying nothing more. Once they had left, Tony pulled out the Jameson, pouring himself and Maggie a small amount.

"To Travis and Denny. And a fervent hope that Nick and company can bring these bastards down," Tony said with vehemence.

"And to Nick, too," said Maggie, clinking glasses with Tony. She rarely drank the hard stuff but couldn't think of a more appropriate time.

CHAPTER THIRTY-ONE

After a fabulous weekend, Nick St. Angelo was in high spirits. On Saturday night, following elaborate preparations at their favorite restaurant, he had proposed to Gena, and she had ecstatically accepted. They would set a wedding date for sometime next year.

Reality began anew when he entered his office Monday morning, with a slew of emails awaiting him. Progress on both the forensic accounting project and the surveillance of Pavel Lyubov had slowed considerably, and Scott Thompson was increasing the pressure. Nick was pleased to see his team had identified six companies, all of which were tied in some way to the numerous shell companies discovered as the result of the leads obtained in the Caymans. Curiously, these six companies were all named by three or four letters, so they were being referred to as the "letter companies."

As he reviewed these, he had a strange feeling that he had heard about them before. But where? It really bugged him, so he forced a change of focus. He put the forensic accounting work aside and reviewed the surveillance reports on Lyubov. An update indicated that they had followed Lyubov to an abandoned factory, and twenty minutes later two men came out at ten-minute intervals, and Lyubov exited five minutes later. An unusual meeting with people Nick didn't know, and purpose unknown. Nick was not happy that the tail on Lyubov was lost about forty minutes later when a traffic accident happened between him and the surveillance team.

At a quarter to ten, the mail courier dropped a small jiffy bag on Nick's desk. Per protocol, it had already been scanned and opened to verify that its contents were not dangerous. There was no return address on the bag, and in it Nick found two thumb drives and a single sheet of paper. The paper, a computer printout, stated that these recordings came from the cell phone of Travis Dustin and included audio and video recordings from his apartment. Nick recognized the name as the Pride player who was found dead last week from an overdose. He inserted one of the drives into his computer; it was audio only. There were two recordings, and it was apparent after listening to both that one person had been giving orders to the second person. That person told the first person in the second recording that he wouldn't be cooperating anymore.

The second drive, containing both audio and video, showed two different camera angles. Nick was stunned by its contents and, not even bothering to call ahead, went to Scott Thompson's office, where he found him in his outer office.

"Boss, I've just received a bombshell in today's mail, sent anonymously, about the death of Travis Dustin. You're not going to believe this or who was involved."

"No idea who sent it?"

Nick shook his head.

Scott sat down, scanned the letter, and reviewed both flash drives, with Nick looking on over his shoulder. Thompson said nothing until the part where the lights came back on, revealing the three men and a prostrate Dustin.

"Damn," he muttered. "That was planned and pulled off with military precision. And shit, there's Lyubov, right in the middle of it. Can't hide that face." He played it again and shook his head. "A hit made to look like an overdose or suicide. Very clever. Does NYPD know about this?"

"I don't know. I can contact the lead detective and ask if they have any new leads. We've had a good relationship with them this past year, so maybe they'd tell us if they did."

"Do that, Nick, but don't tell them about this. Why didn't Tankersley's people tail Lyubov to Dustin's apartment?"

"They trailed him to a meeting with the two other men a few hours before this but lost the tail due to a bad traffic accident between him and our people. They didn't pick him up again until Thursday morning. They've added a third team to make sure that doesn't happen again."

"This guy's too dangerous to let him out of sight, and yet we don't want to pick him up now," said Scott. "I'll see what's going on in Chicago with that NAFL referee who came in. What we've seen today warrants his getting out of there and into someplace safe. WITSEC is justified now."

"What do you think about the other audio recording?"

"It seems he was being blackmailed and finally had enough. Just like the ref. We don't know who the other voice belongs to, but this might come in handy in the future. Between Dustin's murder and the information provided by the ref, we have some organization influencing things in the league. Note that this is not typical blackmail; they're not wanting money from these guys, they want their expertise used in specific key situations. Also, it might be linked to your uncle. Any more from him?"

"No, nothing from Tony." He shook his head. "We've got to link these guys to somebody. They're not doing this themselves."

"Exactly the reason to follow Lyubov twenty-four seven. Look into the jet he used to get from the Caymans back to the States and see where that leads. And push that sports connection we kept hearing about in the Caymans. Dustin's murder and the referee blackmail are all related. Lyubov is the connection. He's our only solid lead. I'll send a good picture of Lyubov to the Chicago office and see if the ref can positively ID him."

"Harvey should have some info on the jet, and I'll get back to the accounting trail. I'll let you know if NYPD has anything."

"You have full access to me, Nick. If I'm not here, my secretary always knows how to get me. Push this hard, Nick."

"Will do, sir."

The rest of the day passed quickly for Nick, with a long meeting with his team and phone calls to Harvey about the jet and NYPD about Dustin's death. NYPD could provide no new information and was still treating it as an accidental overdose as no suicide letter had been found.

Tankersley called him back ninety minutes later with the information that the aircraft Lyubov had used was a long-term lease from a well-known company at Teterboro airport, specializing in short-notice trips. Nick decided to call on them and then head back to his apartment.

He found them helpful, and they gave him complete flight records for the past year, a significant amount of paperwork. The tedious task of reviewing all the files seemed fruitless until Nick focused on invoices to the Caymans for the same time frame as both of Lyubov's known trips. No other trips to the Caymans had been made by the company that year, so these were Lyubov's, who had used the alias Steve Prokogorny, which was good intel in itself.

Further review showed multiple trips to the Chicago area over the past four months under the same name used for the Cayman trips. He would have to contact the Chicago field office and see if these correlated to meetings with the compromised official. What caught his attention most was that all the invoices for these trips were paid for by a company called SPQR Holdings. *A letter company. Now that's a solid link!*

Gena came home around five thirty and found Nick relaxing after his eye-straining research.

"Hey, fiancée, how was your day?"

"Good day, fiancé," she said. "I like the title. Low-key day, mostly preparation for the trip. How about you?" She wrapped her arms around him, and they shared a long, passionate kiss.

"Things are beginning to get interesting but more complex with my assignments. We're finding things out but can't link them to something bigger yet. But I have every confidence we will. Do you have more details about your trip?"

"Yes. This week we work with the cheerleaders of the Philadelphia Razors Thursday and Friday, and then observe them during the Sunday game. We then go to a function the NAFL is putting on for some of its corporate sponsors Monday night in Philadelphia. Today there was a rep from FAE Productions who is the intermediary between us and the teams. We will be working closely with her."

Nick stared at the floor to hide his startled expression. *Holy shit! That was one of the letter companies that I ran across this morning. I knew I had heard it somewhere before!*

He quickly composed himself and turned back, replying, "Sounds like you're going to be in a position to meet a lot of NAFL movers and shakers."

"Yeah. This Monday-night gig will have the commissioner and several VPs as well as their significant others. I've already met one woman, Teri Johnstone, whose husband, Paul, is VP of NAFL Properties, which is responsible for their marketing efforts. She seems nice and acts as an informal liaison between the teams' cheerleaders and the league headquarters."

As Gena related this, the wheels in Nick's head were spinning. It was apparent to him that she would be in places where she might hear things relevant to his investigation. A long shot for sure. Could she help? Would she even do it? Would Scott approve such an idea? He might be interested when he heard that one of the letter companies was associated with the NAFL—and that Gena was a part of it.

Gena had continued talking during this time, and when she glanced at him and saw him staring at the floor, she was annoyed. "Hello? Earth to Nick? Where did you go? I thought you were interested in my work."

"I'm sorry, hon. I am interested in your work. When you mentioned the commissioner, I thought about what a charismatic guy he seems to be and how cool it would be to meet him," Nick said, thinking fast.

"Well, play your cards right and maybe you can someday," she said. "I've been told the league likes to do a lot of PR stuff like that, and they like their executives to be involved. So, who knows where all this is headed?

Nick got into the office early the next morning and couldn't wait to speak with Scott Thompson, but he had to force himself to be patient, as his boss was in a high-level meeting. Nick waited outside his office, and when Scott marched in at his usual frenetic pace, he sighed, "St. Angelo, sometimes you see more of me than my wife does. It must be important. Come on in."

"A few interesting developments since yesterday, sir. First, NYPD has no further information, and they still consider it an accidental overdose."

Thompson just shook his head.

"Second, as I've been reviewing our forensic accounting trail from the Caymans, we've been able to trace back to a series of companies, six as of right now, which all have only letter designations for the name. AKJ Enterprises, FAE Productions, REE Security, OWZ Advertising, DN/CS Hospitality, and SPQR Holdings, which has to do with transportation. As I reviewed this yesterday, something was bugging me about them. I was sure I had heard about one of them, outside of the investigation, but I couldn't put my finger on it. SPQR Holdings is the company Lyubov used when he takes trips, but there was something else."

"Nick, you might have heard about one of them randomly, just by coincidence."

"Well, sir, not exactly."

He let that sink in, prompting a questioning look from Thompson. Nick proceeded to provide Scott with a brief synopsis of Gena's work with the agency and their recent NAFL contract to consult with team cheerleaders.

"Boss, Gena had mentioned FAE Productions a couple of weeks ago, and I didn't think anything of it. Last night she told me FAE is a preferred NAFL vendor, and she will be working directly with them. I had to turn away from her, I was so shocked."

Thompson sat bolt upright in his chair.

"Did you tell her anything about our investigations and the connection?"

"No, sir. Anything I tell her about my work is always very generic, and she understands and doesn't ask questions." Nick summarized what Gena had told him about her assignment. He paused, inhaled sharply, and continued.

"Sir, what would you think of the possibility of using Gena as an asset for the bureau? She is going to be in many situations where she might hear something that could be of value. We've heard about a sports connection from the very beginning in the Caymans, there's the Lyubov connections, a blackmailed official, a murdered player, and now this letter-company connection and my uncle. We can't overlook the possibility that what we're looking for is from *inside* the league and not outside."

It was Thompson's turn to pause, staring out the window. He turned back to Nick, his face grave and intense.

"I'll admit I've had a fleeting moment or two where I've wondered just the same thing. As a former player like yourself, it's a game that means a lot to me. It's hard for me to wrap my head around the possibility that someone from inside the league is trying to influence things. But considering our mounting evidence, we can't rule anything out. So, do you think she would be up for something like what you suggest?"

"Yes, I do. She's always saying how routine and boring her job is most of the time, even if it seems glamorous and exciting to outsiders."

Scott laughed a deep laugh, rarely heard in the course of his day. "Sounds like she's working for the bureau already. I wish I had a dime for every time I've told someone the very same thing. It's unorthodox, but I can authorize this, under the radar. Her involvement would be eyes and ears only, unpaid, of course. No offense, Nick, but I must personally interview her to confirm she can do this safely and discreetly. The NAFL is a powerful organization with a lot of very influential friends, and we must proceed carefully. In light of the Travis Dustin situation, we know whoever is behind this doesn't hesitate to get rough. You're willing to put your new fiancée into harm's way?"

"I have thought about that, sir, and based on the many assignments Gena has told me about in detail, it seems unlikely she would ever be in danger. Her agency takes the safety and security of their models seriously, and Gena is experienced. She's been in a lot of situations before and can handle herself. I think she would jump at the chance to do something like this. Of course, I realize you would have to meet her and make the decision. She leaves in two days for this assignment, so it would have to happen tomorrow."

Thompson glanced at his calendar and looked up. "Ten tomorrow. Talk with her tonight. Tell her just enough to see if she is interested. If she isn't, text me right away so I can use that spot in the morning. If it's a go, I'll tell her as much as I think is necessary, and then you and I must get on the same page about what we share with her. Understand?"

"Completely, Mr. Thompson."

"Okay, Nick. Till tomorrow."

Nick was amazed that Scott didn't hesitate to consider his idea. Now he would have to sell Gena. He spent the rest of the morning trying to find more of the relationship between the letter companies and the blind shell companies that led to the Caymans. While the letter companies seemed legitimate, their organizational structure was convoluted and layered and would require time and effort to sort out. He assigned one of his team members to concentrate on them.

Just before noon, he found that he had missed a call from his uncle Tony, who had left a voicemail requesting another meeting later in the week. Nick decided not to reply to Tony until after he spoke with Thompson tomorrow. That way he could also speak with him about Gena's interview, presuming she agreed. Nick prepared for his talk with Gena, rehearsing exactly what he would tell her.

———————

Nick and Gena arrived at the apartment within minutes of each other and together worked on preparing dinner. After a series of dropped items by the normally sure-handed Nick, Gena looked at him with a curious and concerned look.

"What's up with the fumble fingers, lover? Are you okay?"

I kept my cool in the Caymans but can't hack it with Gena. He looked at her sheepishly, replying, "Boy, you sure know me! Yeah, I'm okay, just a reminder not to play poker with you. You'd clean me out."

"Nick, what on earth are you talking about?"

He poured them both a glass of wine and sat next to her at the island. "Gena, you've always been great about not asking much about my work, and I respect you for that." Her gorgeous green eyes sparkled with curiosity. "There is the possibility that your upcoming work with the NAFL may be of help to a current investigation we are conducting. I can't go into all the details, but I can tell you that there are possible links between what you have already told me about your new assignment and the forensic accounting stuff I've been doing."

Gena's look of wide-eyed, rapt attention now turned to one of bewilderment.

"But, Nick, I won't be involved in anything to do with finances or accounting. How can I be of any help?"

"Hon, you can function as a set of eyes and ears for us. You've said you're going to be involved in a lot of interactions with teams, cheerleaders, maybe coaches and players, and most importantly, high-level league officials. In my time in the bureau, one thing that is common is that people like to talk, especially when they've been drinking, and you can never predict what you might see or hear. I admit this is a very long shot and most likely won't amount to anything. It may be a question of being at the right place at the right time. But the question is, are you up for this?"

Gena slapped her hand on the counter, startling Nick. "Up for it? Hell yes, I'm up for it. Are you kidding? I've told you how routine and boring my work can get. This is awesome!" She hopped off the stool and gave Nick an enthusiastic hug and kiss.

"Whoa, girl! You're not Jennifer Garner in *Alias* just yet. You've got to be interviewed by my boss, Scott Thompson, at ten tomorrow. You would have to have a quick background check initially, and he has final say."

"Gee, do I get a gun tomorrow? Secret recording devices and a pen with invisible ink? Cyanide tablets if I get caught? Seriously, Nick, I'm honored. For all the excitement and glamour of modeling, it can be very demeaning. We are often thought of as airheads."

There was an edge to her statement that Nick had heard before. "I can only guess how upsetting and frustrating that must be."

"It sure is, but I'm mostly used to it. A lot of times they don't look much beyond the physical aspects of things or think that I can string together a complete sentence or a coherent thought. Maybe they'll let their guard down because of that misconception." She paused. "You've spoken with your boss already and he didn't say no, so he must have some confidence in your choice of woman to be your fiancée," she said, the edge gone.

"Well, I'm a pretty good salesman, and I pitched a hard sell," he replied with mock seriousness.

"Thanks a lot, Nick," she said, punching him in the shoulder.

"Scott has shown increasing trust in me, and he's familiar with the excellent reputation of the Austin Agency. I've told him a few things about your background and experience, and he's interested. But you still have to ace the interview tomorrow."

"No sweat, lover. Won't be my first rodeo. I bet I nail it. Speaking of sweat and lover . . . " She took his hand and led him to their bedroom.

―――――

As they both expected, Gena aced the interview. Scott spent over an hour with her, finding her poised, articulate, and engaging. He emphasized that she was to observe, listen, and gather information, reporting anything that might seem unusual or even remotely helpful to the investigation. Like Nick, he said nothing about Lyubov or the details of Travis Dustin. This was not just for security purposes but so as not to bias Gena's thinking. He briefed her on aspects of the letter companies and that she should pay close attention to anything involving them. He also provided her with limited information about the attempts to influence games and teams' standings and asked that she report any talk she heard about these topics. He informed Gena she would not be an employee of the bureau, and therefore, there was no remuneration. Finally, she would be debriefed by him after her assignment.

Gena left Thompson's office and swung by Nick's, only to find him on the phone. He raised one finger to tell her to wait, but she simply gave him the thumbs-up sign with a big smile, a wink, and a see-you-later wave. Nick returned the smile and the thumbs-up. *She got it! That's my Gena! Wonder what Scott will say?*

He didn't have to wait long, as his boss called him soon after he finished his first call.

"C'mon up, Nick. Right away," Thompson said.

Thompson greeted Nick at his door with a wide smile. "She did great. Couldn't ask for a better undercover asset for this phase of our investigation. Now we all have to get lucky and hope she hears something. I will start to lay the groundwork with Legal about the possibility of future electronic surveillance by her; that will take some time and preparation, so no harm to begin now. I want us to review everything so we are seamless in just how much we tell her."

Thompson and Nick spent the next fifteen minutes agreeing on how much to tell Gena, with each of them keeping notes for reference. At the end of this, Scott looked up and spoke.

"Anything else we need to cover, Nick?"

"As a matter of fact, there is, boss. My uncle Tony called me yesterday, leaving a voicemail that he wanted another meeting with me. I wanted to speak with you first."

"Certainly, meet with him and see what else he may have. He was onto something before, based on what we now know, and my guess is he has something more. But you can't tip our hand. I'm afraid you must be noncommittal, almost disinterested again."

"Yes, sir. I understand. It won't be easy deceiving him. I hate to do it, but it's necessary. I just hope he doesn't push too hard. I'll contact you after the meeting."

"Yes, do that, Nick. Good luck with him. It was a pleasure meeting Gena."

"Thank you. Maybe both can help us move this forward."

He returned to his office pleased about Gena but concerned about his uncle Tony. He called him but got his voicemail, so Nick told him that he had an opening the following week and to text him if that would work. The investigation was going in different directions with the involvement of Gena and Tony. Nick had been on enough of them to know that they often followed this pattern in their middle phases, so he wasn't too concerned. But he also had never had family members involved before, which added a whole different dimension. Keeping professionally detached became a lot more challenging. He would have to navigate the slippery slopes of not alienating his uncle and of keeping Gena safe.

CHAPTER THIRTY-TWO

After a single day in Vegas, Brad had what he needed. The next morning, he called Tony. "It's just as we thought. Travis was well known as a big player, apparently in deep with the wrong people, and someone became his 'angel investor'—for a price. Too risky for me to try to find out who that might be, and besides, there are too many of them."

"No, Brad, don't pursue anything further. You've provided what I need to tell Nick. No sense in attracting attention."

"Okay, Tony. I'll head home today. I've got the Richmond-Philadelphia game this weekend, then it's time to get back to my other clients I've put on hold. I'll let you know Sunday night about the game."

"Good, Brad, we'll talk Sunday night. Thank you." Brad had been the first to report back since they had all reviewed Travis's tapes. He expected to hear from Freddie in the next few days. He wanted as much information as possible to present to Nick, hoping for a better outcome than the last time.

━━━━━

Freddie Wilmington had also been very busy since the last meeting with Tony. He failed to learn anything from Dustin's coaches, but his teammates related his fondness for Vegas and a certain New York nightclub, the Top of the Town.

Arriving there, Freddie introduced himself to the manager, a football fanatic who knew Wilmington's history and was more than happy to chat for a while. He was saddened by the loss of Dustin and verified what the players had said: Dustin liked to party. The manager also mentioned that Dustin used the facility for what appeared to be business meetings, often with a short, stocky, well-dressed man. He described the man as meticulously groomed and with a set of impossible-to-forget, brilliant-white teeth. He did not know his name but stated he came across as someone who could be trouble if you crossed him. The manager noticed that Dustin often was very upset after meetings with him and tended to drink heavily at those times. Freddie asked if the club had any images of the guy from surveillance cameras, and the manager shot him a questioning look. Freddie remained silent, his eyes staring intently at the manager, who withered under their glare.

"Only for you, Mr. Wilmington," he said and took him to his office, where he pulled up footage from the last two weeks. "We should have an image. They met here just a little over a week ago. Ah, there he is."

The frames stopped a day before Travis's death. The images taken at the entrance were quite clear, and the manager pointed out the man in question, coming in fifteen minutes before Travis. Freddie Wilmington was not surprised to see that the man at the club was very likely the short stocky man in Dustin's apartment surveillance videos. He asked the manager for a copy of the tape, which he provided, thanked him, and signed an autograph with a personal note, which made the manager's week. He finished by asking the manager not to tell anyone that he had been there. The man, being used to celebrities, assured him that would not be a problem, and Freddie cemented the deal with a C-note.

Tina Bishop was the obvious next stop for Freddie, and he decided to go to where she worked. Knowing her hours, he waited for her shift to end.

"Hello, Tina," he said.

"Mr. Wilmington, you startled me," she replied, trying to hide her annoyance. "I didn't expect I'd be seeing you again. Why are you here?"

"Tina, let's go find a quiet place where we can have some coffee. I have just a few questions for you."

She frowned but agreed to follow him, and he drove to a local Panera, where they settled into an isolated booth near the back. Wringing her hands, she stated, "Mr. Wilmington, I told you everything I know. There's nothing more."

"Oh, I think there is, or should I say, was." That got a reaction from her. "Tina, the person responsible for Travis's death was blackmailing him because of his gambling debts in Vegas and something that happened when you guys were in college. What can you tell me?"

"I don't know, Mr. Wilmington; that was a long time ago." The rapidity of her breathing, her eyes darting around the restaurant, and her fidgeting hands told him she was a poor liar.

"Tina, I can't avenge Travis if I don't know everything there is to know. Did Travis get into some type of trouble with drugs or alcohol in college? As his mentor, I never saw anything like that, but I know there's something that they held over him about that time. What was it, Tina? Help me," he said, leaning forward and touching her hand.

Tears began to run down her cheeks as she replied in a barely audible voice, "He was a good guy, Mr. Wilmington, but not a good student. He needed help and I gave it to him, but I could never have known it would lead to his death." With deep sadness, she related her role in detail in helping Travis academically. "My system worked so well for Travis, I never believed we would be caught. How did someone find out?"

"I don't know. Did you help anyone else? Were you romantically involved with Travis and someone knew?"

"I helped just one other guy. Michael Taranto. He was not an athlete, just someone who helped me out of a situation I got myself in, and I returned the favor. He transferred to another school midway through junior year, and I never heard from him again. I didn't help him to the degree I did Travis. I'm sure he didn't know about my helping Travis. We were never a romantic thing, Travis and me. We were close but not like that. It just never went there. Am I going to get in trouble about this?"

Freddie paused before replying. "Not from me you won't. We can't undo what's been done. I don't think you are in any danger because you can't connect anyone to how you helped Travis. Just be cautious and aware of things, and call me if you get contacted by anyone else."

"I will, Mr. Wilmington. I hope you can help solve this."

Freddie could only nod in agreement as he walked her to her car, not willing to tell her that Travis was just a part of something much larger.

———————

Tony had just finished cutting the grass when the secure cell phone rang. It was Freddie. "Hey. What have *you* found?"

"A couple of things. Talking to Travis's teammates, I verified he was a partier both in Vegas and New York. Following a lead, I went to his favorite New York club and got the manager to let me see images from their security cameras. No surprise that one of Travis's attackers was a guy he often met there, probably blackmailing him. But the big surprise was with Tina Bishop. She admitted she had helped Travis academically get through college. Someone must have found out about this in addition to his Vegas fun."

"Along with what Brad found in Vegas, this nails the blackmail theory. But we still don't know who. For now, it's just more information. I'm going to contact Nick again. Well, thanks, Freddie, and keep me informed."

"Certainly, Tony. Good luck with your nephew."

Luck won't cut it with Nick, but the facts I have certainly will.

CHAPTER THIRTY-THREE

Tony Stravnicki was deep into the refrain from "Don't Stop Believing" on his way home from work the next day when the burner cell chimed. It was Brad.

"Hey, Brad, figured I'd hear from you tonight. How was the game. Anything to report?'

"Sorry I didn't call last night, Tony. I was dog tired when I got home. The game itself had no incidents that I noticed, and nothing seemed unusual, but I did run into a guy I played football with in high school, Tom Overholt. We were close back then but just drifted apart. He recognized me, and it turns out he is the head game-day frequency coordinator for the league. He wondered why I was there, so I told him that I was writing a novel about football, but my main gig was security and investigations. The game was about to begin, and we didn't have much time, but he got real serious, looked me in the eye, and says, 'Something weird's going on in the league, Brad, and I don't know where to turn. I need some advice. Can I contact you tomorrow to talk?' So, I gave him my secure number."

"Don't know him, Brad, but that's not unusual. Maybe I'd recognize him. I take it you have some trust in him if you gave out your number?"

"Yes, but I also ran an in-depth search about him, finding nothing, so I was willing to listen to what he had to say."

"And?"

Brad filled in Tony on the extensive conversation he'd had with Overholt about the comms issues, Phil Townsend, and an unknown EMT who mysteriously was seen around the communications area at a time they were having problems. "Townsend explodes at him, telling him to leave security to his department, and throws Overholt out of his office."

Tony's pulse quickened. "Phil Townsend is a nasty prick with a reputation as someone you don't mess with. He was the one who got me in trouble with my coaches, and I was warned I could get fired. This Overholt guy needs to be careful. Go on."

"Too late for that, Tony. Wait till you hear the rest. That night after their meeting, on the way home from grocery shopping, he mysteriously gets a flat tire, and when he pulls over to fix it, he gets mugged by two guys, one with a foreign accent. The guy claimed to read his name tag, which lists him working for league comms. He warns Overholt to 'get his shit together' and then hits him a couple of times. Nothing serious, but it got his attention. Later that night, as he's replaying the whole scene in his head, he realizes there is no way they could have read his name tag in the low light. He believes he was targeted by Townsend as a warning not to ask any more questions."

"That's incredible. A guy with a foreign accent? Same guy in the Travis video? Did he see a scar or any other description?"

"No, he didn't see much. The light was too poor, it happened fast, and he was doubled over after getting hit. He has no idea what to do, and the best I could tell him was to lay low and just do his job as best as he can. I don't think he wanted me to investigate, but he did ask me to check his house to try to improve security, which I said I would do."

"Good. That will keep you in contact with him, bolster his

confidence a little, and I bet he'll tell you if things develop. It's another piece in this puzzle, Brad. Maybe a big one, as this seems to point *inside* the league, not *outside*. After my warning, I began to wonder if something funny was going on with Townsend and this supports it. I'll certainly mention this to my nephew when I see him next Tuesday. Thanks Brad. Keep up the good work."

"This one just fell into my lap, but maybe it'll lead to something. I'll be in touch."

The call ended, and Tony was left in silence, alone with his dark thoughts. The accelerating pace and the possibility that someone whose job it was to protect the sport might be the one doing this sickened him. His mind shut down at this thought, refusing to accept it. He decided not to talk about any of this with Maggie tonight but to have a quiet night of focusing on the family.

Phil Townsend was just leaving his gym after an intense, ninety-minute workout when his secure phone buzzed just as he reached his office. It was one of the many contacts he had scattered across the country in venues where people with trained observation skills had proved valuable to him. This one was in Las Vegas and reported that someone had been asking questions around the casinos this past weekend about Travis Dustin. The contact didn't know much more about it than that but did have a reasonable photo of the guy that he would email. Townsend thanked the man and waited impatiently for the photo.

When it came, he flew into a rage, slamming the mouse on his desk with a loud "Shit!" The image was that of Brad Vanderbilt, the friend of that coach, Stravnicki. Apparently, the threat of being fired had not bothered him, and he was still poking around where he shouldn't be.

Townsend thought about it for a minute before making his decision. Normally he knew what he would do, but considering his recent dealings with the player, he knew the response, at least for now, must be more aggressive and more personal. A quick call to his associate, a brief discussion of options, and the response was set in motion. The associate already had intelligence on his target, so it was simply a question of execution, but he had to get there first. Once again, a short trip on a leased jet. Not a bad way to commute to work.

———————

It had been a busy, stressful day for Maggie Stravnicki, and she was beat as she headed for her car. Dusk came earlier now, and she didn't notice a light was out near her parked car, leaving only one several rows away to provide some illumination. She also didn't notice that no one else was in her part of the lot after she said goodbye to her coworkers closer to the hospital, or that the hospital security car was on the other side of the lot. So she was blindsided when a hand clamped around her mouth, her legs were kicked out from under her, and she found herself down on the ground with a large man on top of her, unable to move or scream.

Bringing his face close to her, his foul breath almost made her gag as he hissed in a thick accent, "Your husband dumb. Not get message last time. Maybe he get it this time."

His massive right hand grabbed the front of her lab coat, ripping it down the front, exposing her scrubs. Thwarted by the toughness of the material, he released his grip on her face just enough to allow Maggie to turn her head and clamp down on his hand with her teeth. He yowled like a wounded animal, and she peeled back his left index finger as hard as she could, dislocating the joint and accentuating his pain. The damaged hand released er, but the other hand followed up with a hard fast jab to her face, breaking her nose. A sea of blood clouded her vision.

"You bitch, I teach you!" he screamed as he tried to lift her off the ground for another blow but couldn't use his injured hand. Maggie wiped blood from her eyes with her sleeve as best she could, trying to get a good look at her assailant.

He paused his attack and tried to rearticulate his finger, and in that moment his face was caught in the dim light. An unforgettable prominent jagged scar ran down the side of his face. The sight triggered immediate panic in Maggie, recognizing him from the murder of the player.

"You think you fuck with me, lady?" he roared, hitting her again with another quick jab, this time on her left cheekbone. His hand now moved down to her scrub top as he put his full weight on her legs with his knees. Intent on his revenge, he hadn't heard or seen the security vehicle pull up behind them.

Marty, the well-liked guard, yelled, "Hey you, get off her," as he reached for his can of Mace, his only defensive weapon, as the guards were not authorized to carry sidearms. As Marty advanced, the attacker, realizing his tactical advantage was lost, released his prey and pivoted toward the guard. He used his injured left hand to block the can of Mace before it could be activated while simultaneously using his right hand to deliver a knife-hand blow to the guard's wrist and then to the right side of his neck. The can of Mace fell harmlessly to the ground. Marty stumbled backward just as a front kick followed by a spinning back kick finished the job, knocking him to the ground. The assailant disappeared.

Maggie recovered somewhat, not sure who had saved her but grateful that they had. She got to all fours, some blood still in her eyes, and was able to make out the prostrate form of the security guard. Even injured, her training and experience kicked in, and she went to help her savior. Marty was dazed, and his right wrist lay at a weird angle. She propped him up against a car and yelled for help. Hearing the commotion, other hospital workers came upon the scene, with more security guards. Two gurneys arrived, taking them into the ER.

It could have been so much worse. Maggie had a broken nose and a nasty, swollen bruise on her left cheekbone, but no damage to her upper jaw, teeth, or vision. Marty had a broken right arm, and a severe bruise on his sternum from the kicks and was held overnight for observation.

Maggie was effusive in her thanks and praise of Marty's heroic actions, but in typical fashion, he minimized his role, just saying he had done his job. He did add that he would make a strong push with the hospital administration for the right to carry a sidearm, and Maggie pledged her full support. She called Tony, telling him she had been involved in an "incident at work" and that he needed to come pick her up. She refused to tell him any more over the phone, and while waiting for him, she and Marty were interviewed by the police. Maggie gave a good description of her attacker, including the scar, but none of his comments, and the authorities felt it was just a random assault.

Tony arrived and was shaken by the condition of his wife. "Mags, honey, oh my God, you look like hell," Tony said, his voice cracking, his eyes moist. "An *incident* at work?"

"It's not as bad as it looks, Tony. It could have been a lost worse if hadn't been for Marty. I don't have a clue who the guy was," she lied because others could hear.

Tony picked up on his wife's tone and eye contact, aware she was not telling him everything right now.

They completed the discharge paperwork, and the head of the ER told her he would personally evaluate her prior to her return. Unsteady on her feet, they used a wheelchair to get to Tony's car, as the adrenaline high of the attack began to wear off and reality started to settle in. Maggie was silent on the ride home. Tony said nothing, his mind racing, while he gave his wife time to rest.

He had sent the kids over to a neighbor's house for the night, and as soon as they got in the door, Maggie headed for the sofa and burst into tears. Tony held her close, her body shaking.

"Tony, I'm so sorry. I thought I was handling this, but it just hit me. Can you make me some tea? It will help calm me."

"Of course. Are you sure you don't want anything stronger?"

"No, tea is all I can handle right now. I need to tell you everything while it's still fresh in my mind."

Tony microwaved some water and got her favorite tea, quickly returning. He wrapped a quilt around her, stroked her long red hair and kissed her on the forehead. "Take your time and tell me what happened."

She took a long sip of tea and took a deep breath, color beginning to return, back in control again. She recounted in detail the tiring day at work, and not being aware in the parking lot, followed by the sudden vicious attack.

"It happened so quickly, and he knew what he was doing. He pinned me down, one hand on my mouth and the other on the top of my lab coat. He had awful breath and a thick accent."

Tony blanched but said nothing and she continued.

"I think he intended to rape me, and he said, 'Your husband is dumb, didn't get the message, maybe he will this time' or something like that. When he tried to rip my lab coat, his hand shifted, and I bit him and pulled back his index finger of the other hand, dislocating it. I was determined to fight back and get a look at his face. That enraged him, and he hit me, breaking my nose, yelling he would 'teach me.' He tried to rearticulate his finger because he couldn't grab me to lift me up, and when he rose up slightly, his face was visible in what little light there was. Tony, he had an awful, jagged *scar* on his face. I'm sure it was the same guy in the Travis Dustin video!"

"Jesus Christ, Maggie! Are you sure?" Tony's mouth dropped open, his eyes wide.

"As much as I can be. I couldn't forget that scar! He hit me again, but I was able to turn slightly so it hit my cheekbone. I was dazed and in pain, and he was about to rip off my scrub top, when, thank God, Marty showed up. Tony, I think this guy was not only going to rape me but maybe kill me, too! Marty was so brave, and all he had was Mace. They're not allowed to carry a gun. So, his attention turned to Marty, who he attacked, and then he just left."

"That's the sign of a professional. He knew when to leave. Thank God for Marty! Maggie, you were so brave. I'm so proud of you! To think I could have lost you tonight." He paused before adding in a low voice, "I'm so sorry about this. I never intended for my family to become a target. They must have found out about Brad in Vegas or someone Freddie talked to, and you were the warning. Someone is very intent on keeping me quiet. I think we need to change our attitude and take Brad up on his offer for gun training. Perhaps he can advise us even more."

"Tony, don't blame yourself. I admit I'm scared. We're in deep with this. We definitely need to reconsider our protection and the kids' safety. But as I told you before, I'm all in with you. I won't get caught again," she said with force.

"Brad and Freddie have all given me significant updates. I'll fill you in on them tomorrow. With all the new information and everything that's happened, Nick must take me seriously now. C'mon, we need to call it a night. I'm going to put you to bed, and I'll sleep in the other room. You sleep in tomorrow. I've got a couple things to do, and then I'll be up."

"No. I need you next to me tonight of all nights. Do what you need, but don't take long. I'm going to take a hot shower."

Tony did not have anything to do, but he desperately needed to be alone for a few minutes. He poured himself a good amount of Jameson and sat in his favorite chair in the dark, his head in his hands. Trying to be quiet, sobs racked his body for a full minute, pangs of fear and sadness overcoming him. *My God, I almost lost her tonight! It was really close. What have I done?*

He took a long sip and sat back, a fierce rage building. He would back off, not make any waves, and he'd insist on the same for Brad and Freddie. He wasn't giving up, just didn't know what more he could do. He was resigned to leaving it up to Nick, the professional, for now.

Tony drained the glass and headed upstairs, thankful to be able to wrap his arms around his sleeping wife.

CHAPTER THIRTY-FOUR

Tony sat impatiently in the spartan common waiting area on Nick's floor, replaying all that had happened since their last meeting a few weeks ago. What had seemed questionable to him then was definite now. The deaths of Dennis and Travis Dustin followed by the vicious attack on himself and Maggie had hit home with a vengeance. There was no doubt in Tony's mind that his cherished sport was being compromised, but who was responsible and why still remained a mystery. He decided to leave out his own assault. Armed with facts rather than conjecture this time, Tony was confident Nick would take him seriously and imagined how Nick had handled the Dustin recordings. Would he mention them?

His thoughts were interrupted as Nick welcomed him with a hearty "Tony, great to see you again. Come into my office."

"Hi, Nick," Tony replied as they warily eyed each other.

"You're looking well. How is Aunt Maggie?"

Tony paused before answering, popping a stick of gum into his mouth, holding Nick with a steady gaze. "She's better now, and went back to work yesterday, after a few days off last week. Nick, she was attacked after work in the hospital parking lot."

Nick stopped mid-stride, a grimace on his face. "Tony, that's terrible. Did she get hurt? Tell me all about it." They settled into chairs, Nick leaning forward at his desk and Tony appearing unusually calm considering what he had just said.

"She was very lucky. She came away from a vicious attack with a broken nose and a severely bruised cheekbone. It looks like it was an attempted rape. She fought like hell—you know Maggie—but if a security guard hadn't shown up and taken on the guy, the outcome could have been much worse. And he only had a can of Mace. The attacker took him out, and he spent overnight in the hospital, but he'll be all right."

"Oh my God. Did he get caught or anybody see him? What did the police say about it?"

"He did get away, but she did get a brief look at him. A big guy. Had a large, nasty scar on his face and spoke with a thick accent, Russian, she thought."

Nick rearranged some papers on his desk, avoiding Tony's eyes, and coughed, covering his mouth.

That shook him! He doesn't know how to respond. Tony let that sink in, and when Nick looked up, his eyes betrayed him. *He knows it's probably the same guy on the Dustin tapes. Bet he doesn't mention them to me.* Tony continued, "Not much to go on, and the police think it was random, but Maggie and I know it wasn't. She didn't tell the cops everything, Nick."

Nick sat bolt upright, eyes piercing into Tony. "What are you saying, Tony? Why didn't she tell the police everything?"

"Because the attack was a warning meant for me. The attacker told her that I was dumb and didn't get the first message but maybe I would this time."

Nick sat back in his chair, hands folded on the desk. "I don't understand. What do you mean about not getting a first message?"

"You may remember that I told you I had contacted three assistant coaches and sounded them out about questionable calls?

Well, one of them complained to the league, and the VP of Internal Security, Phil Townsend, called the owner of my team and accused me of trying to get coaches to bad-mouth officials, which I wasn't. The owner came down on my head coach and me like a ton of bricks, totally overreacting, and I was threatened with firing. My talks with these guys were brief and low-key, but somebody took exception. And Operations handles things like this, not Internal Security. Very strange. So that was the first message." He paused. "You remember my assistant, Dennis, who did the statistical analysis?"

His nephew nodded.

"Nick, Dennis was killed a couple of weeks ago after leaving my house, in what the cops think was a robbery gone bad. He had just reviewed with me his findings of all last season and this one. He looked at an incredible number of variables, looking for correlations, and, boy, did he find them. You can't ignore what Denny's work shows: someone is screwing around with the outcomes of games." Tony handed Nick the thumb drive containing the data, as well as a second thumb drive with the encryption key, explaining to Nick how to use it. "Nick, the only thing they took was his laptop. He gave his life for what's on those drives."

"Tony, I'm very sorry about Dennis. We will certainly look at what your assistant had done, but while it might show some correlations, it still doesn't indicate more than that. We need—"

Tony cut him off, holding up a hand. "I'm just getting *started*, Nick. There's more. After the warning, I knew I had to keep a low profile, so I contacted two guys I played college ball with who I trust." Tony went into detail about Brad and Freddie, their backgrounds, and what they had been doing. He reviewed the communications problems that were plaguing the league, and the odd presence of the guy near the GDFC just when comms problems occurred.

"I was able to get Brad sideline credentials for a few games to observe around the comms area, and he had his credentials challenged. Somehow, he must have been linked back to me because the warning happened right after that, not back when I had talked to those coaches. Nothing was ever said to me about Brad."

Tony then went into detail about Brad's meeting and conversation with Tom Overholt, specifically detailing Townsend's outburst at Overholt and his attack that evening. Tony noticed that Nick's interest had picked up on that and he was even taking notes.

Tony paused to push another stick of gum into his mouth.

Nick tapped his pen on his desk and was the first to continue. "Uncle Tony, this is certainly curious, at the least, I can't deny that, but it's all circumstantial. After our last talk, our guys in OC investigated this, and so far have found nothing."

"Nick, you must be familiar with the death of Travis Dustin. That whole thing doesn't make sense, and his play against my team was unusual! Freddie had mentored him in college, stated he never did drugs; his teammates said the same thing. It doesn't add up. What do *you* know about it?"

"Nothing more than the report we saw from NYPD. The overdose, whether intentional or accidental, is a fact. Seems straightforward. People often change for the worse in life. It happens all the time." He said this with no emotion in his voice, but the sweat on his brow and his pursed lips undermined his attempts at maintaining control. Deceit burned his gut like bad spicy food, stoking the cauldron inside.

The gum took a beating, Tony's jaws pounding away, his heart racing, palms sweaty. *He doesn't know that I know he's lying! What else does he know but can't tell me?* The cat-and-mouse game continued.

"Nick, you can't tell me this is all just coincidental. The warning for me to 'stick to coaching,' Tom Overholt's issues with Townsend, Travis Dustin's unusual play and death, Dennis, and now the attack on Maggie with a reference to me," Tony's voice rose in volume and emotion as he spoke. "What am I supposed to do, just ignore all this?" he yelled at Nick.

"You get emotional, Tony, and you lose your objectivity and perspective," Nick countered, words clipped, his volume matching his uncle.

"Well, how about Dennis's work? That isn't emotional, and it certainly couldn't be any more objective. And I went with Brad and Freddie to get different perspectives." His face red, Tony was almost out of control.

"Tony, I'm not your enemy here. I don't appreciate you yelling at me. I told you we're looking into this, and we will look closely at what

Dennis has given us. But we need something *concrete* and someone we can legally tie it all to."

Tony shook his head, snorting dismissively. "So, I do *nothing*, is that it, Nick? I sit on my ass and be a good boy while someone plays us like puppets and attacks my family!" he said, his voice thick with sarcasm, bile rising in his throat.

That pushed Nick to his own edge. Pointing his finger at Tony he fired back. "What you do, Tony, is to leave it to the professionals. You're in way over your head. Stick to coaching like you were told, and protect your family!"

Tony just looked at Nick with fire in his eyes and, saying nothing further, rose and quickly left the room, slamming the door behind him. Nick did not follow him but slumped in his chair, his head in his hands, dejected and ashamed. It could not have gone worse, and he regretted the necessity of treating Tony so poorly.

His tormented mind raced in overdrive as he replayed the encounter. *He didn't deserve that. I can't remember the last time I've felt so shitty. Have I damaged our relationship for good? I couldn't tell him about the referee Ohlendorf, or the Dustin recordings, or the forensic accounting investigation, or the Caymans, or Gena. And certainly not about Lyubov! That had to have been who attacked Aunt Maggie, but what happened to our surveillance? Tony has definitely found something. He's stumbled into a hornet's nest, and it does appear it's linked to inside the league, maybe this guy Townsend. How can I help him protect his family without compromising our investigation?* Depressed, Nick thought about it for a few more moments, fiddling with his pen, until he decided who to contact, and who he could trust to guide him.

CHAPTER THIRTY-FIVE

Nick appeared unannounced at Scott Thompson's office. He was in a meeting that was just about to finish. Nick sat down, so deep in his thoughts that he failed to see two people leave or his boss approach him.

Nick looked up when Thompson said, "Nick, c'mon in. What's going on? You look like you just lost your best friend."

Nick slumped in a seat, replying, "Maybe I have, boss. I just had a really difficult meeting with my uncle." In a dispirited voice, Nick recounted in detail the meeting with Tony, Thompson silent, not interrupting.

Pausing to make sure Nick was done, Thompson replied, "That was a tough one, Nick. You handled it as well as you could, and you really had no other choice. With what you have told me about your past relationship with your uncle, I doubt very much that any irreparable damage occurred."

"I sure hope so, sir. I just hated to lie to him."

"For sure he's pissed, but when he thinks about it, he will realize you had no other options. Your uncle's feelings aside, that meeting was very productive, and we haven't even looked at the data his assistant compiled. Certainly points to someone inside the league now, not outside. We'll take a hard look at this guy Townsend. And the strong probability that Lyubov was again involved is another link to several parts of this whole mess. I want to know why we missed him again. I authorized Tankersley a third team to prevent something like this. We've got to find who's controlling him."

"The fact that he was involved really concerns me," Nick replied. "My aunt was very lucky. Boss, how can we help keep them safe?"

"While I was able to get Ohlendorf and his family approved for WITSEC, it's not possible for your uncle and his family. Their circumstances are different. But we can quietly advise their local PD to ramp up patrols around their house, have hospital security walk your aunt to her car, that sort of thing. They'll have to figure out most of it on their own. The best approach is simply for your uncle to keep a low profile, like he is scared and got the message.

"I hope Tony will do that, but he's mule stubborn. I don't know how he will react."

"Do you think you can call him and talk options over the phone?"

"Not yet. We didn't end on a good note. I'm due to see him in a couple weeks when my mom has us all together for dinner in honor of our engagement. Maybe by then the dust will have settled."

"I'm sure it will, Nick. In the meantime, we've got to keep pushing. Do you have anything to report from Gena or your team?"

"I'm due to talk to Gena tonight. She was reserved and vague on the phone Sunday night, so I don't know what to make of that. My team keeps plugging away, with these letter companies coming up with increasing frequency. We've made a lot of progress but no breakthrough yet."

Thompson sighed. "Just hope we can crack this before someone else gets hurt or killed. That was good work today, Nick, no matter how painful it was."

"Thanks, boss. Yeah, it was tough. Don't want to do that again. Thanks for your help."

Thompson just nodded.

―――――――

While Nick was dejected after their meeting, Tony was downright depressed. Initially seething at Nick's comments, his anger had morphed into a grudging realization that Nick was right. On the flight home he replayed their interaction multiple times and always came up with the same conclusion: he *was* in over his head, and he *should* leave it to the professionals. This thought sank his spirits even lower to the point of powerless despair.

Tony had always worked to be in control of his destiny, accepting the ups and downs of life as his responsibility and not ever willingly play the part of the victim. His black-and-white world was now revealed as a crumbling façade. He had never really given it much thought before, but now it hit him like a lightning bolt: he had been in total denial, partly out of his fear of repeating the past and partly because he had been so *naive.* He allowed himself a few more minutes of wallowing in self-pity before his spirit came back to its true foundation, Maggie.

Sure, they were having issues, but this simple yet profound fact halted his downward spiral of negativism and replaced it with a temporary peace.

―――――――

When Tony arrived home, the haggard look on his face was pronounced. Maggie said, "Why don't you say good night to the kids and pour us a couple glasses of wine while I put them to bed. You look beat and I bet there are things on your mind after seeing Nick." He was on his second glass when Maggie returned.

"That your second glass already? I'm guessing it didn't go as you had hoped with Nick."

"Not even close. I presented what I thought was even more convincing information than the last time, and he blew me off even more. Told me I was 'in over my head' and I should 'stick to coaching and leave it to the professionals.'"

"Ouch. That was harsh. But don't you agree, hon, that it does have an element of truth to it? You were always honest with Nick when you were mentoring him. Now the shoe's on the other foot."

Tony took another sip of wine, shaking his head.

"But that's just it, Mags. I know he wasn't telling me the truth. I asked him what he thought about Travis's death, and he just gave me a stock answer about believing the NYPD. When I told him about your attacker having the scar, that got his attention. He tried to hide his surprise, but it didn't work. I felt like we were playing chess."

"You're being unrealistic. Nick can't divulge information on an investigation. Surely you understand that. Did it ever dawn on you that sending the Travis recordings anonymously to him was being deceptive to some degree?"

"Hey, whose side are you on anyways?" he said. "We all agreed—you, me, Brad, and Freddie—to send it anonymously, because of the circumstances. And I know he can't tell me *everything* he knows. But shit, at least throw me a bone. Don't just tell me 'We need something concrete.'"

"Tony, you *know* I'm on your side—*our* side—in this," she replied. "But I won't just tell you what you want to hear and not what you need to hear. He does need concrete evidence because his job is to put the bad guys away the right way. I'm sure my attack scared him because it *was* one of the guys who killed Travis and he knew that. He's also holding back because he's afraid for us, knows you're tenacious, and he wants to protect us by getting you to let them do their job. How did you leave it with him?"

Tony rolled his eyes. "That's the worst part. I was pretty sarcastic to him, and we both ended up yelling at each other. I stormed out of his office."

Maggie frowned and shook her head. "Oh boy, Tony. Not the way to end it."

"I know, I know. I was so upset, I just had to get out of there. I can't take it back now. I'm afraid I hurt our relationship. It's very depressing to think that," he said in a low voice.

She looked at her husband and saw the hurt and embarrassment in his eyes. Tony thought the world of Nick, and his emotions simply got the best of him, which was rare. Two men in a pissing contest. It happened all the time in life but rarely with Tony.

"I'm sure he was upset, Tony, but I doubt there's any long-term damage. You guys have too much great history together. Nick won't think poorly of you. He loves you and is smart enough to realize that emotions got the better of you both. You have to trust both your relationship with him and his ability to do his job."

"I sure hope you're right, Maggie."

"We'll find out soon enough. Remember, we have dinner at my sister's in a couple of weeks to celebrate Nick and Gena's engagement."

Tony groaned. "I forgot about that. Maybe I won't go."

"You'll do nothing of the sort. That would be the absolute *worst* thing you could do. Two weeks is a perfect cooling-off period for both of you," she said. "Let's talk about what you should do now. How you should move forward."

Tony looked at her and replied, "One thing Nick did say was 'to protect my family,' and I agree with that completely. I'll call Brad to see how soon he can get us going on firearms training, and I want him to advise on what guns would be right for each of us."

"Reluctantly, I agree. I'm not wild about having guns in the house, but Brad can show us how to have them here safely and yet be available. He can advise us on what to do to help protect the kids. Hospital security has agreed to escort me to my car. Overall parking lot security has been ramped up, I'm told."

"Good. Brad can help us get all the permits we need. I'll contact the police to ask for more frequent patrols, which shouldn't be an issue since they know about the assault."

"So, our focus will be on protecting ourselves and the kids. Tony, you need to listen to Nick and lay low for now."

"I thought I had, Maggie. Brad, Denny, and Freddie were doing the investigating, and the warnings have most likely been because of what Brad has been doing most recently. Do you want me to have them stop?"

"No. But the focus has to change. Let's have them over for a meeting sometime this week and see what ideas they have. While they work quietly in the background, you've got to be a model coach, Tony. Focus on the team and the players in ways that will draw attention to you in a positive way, so they have nothing to hassle you about."

Tony reflected for a minute before responding. "I usually don't feel comfortable drawing attention to myself, but with the warning I received, it makes sense to appear to toe the line, try to be as valuable as I can. Having a meeting with Freddie and Brad is a good idea." He gave her a hug and peck on the cheek. Although she had a worried expression on her face, Maggie said nothing further.

As he headed to the living room to make his calls, Tony was deeply discouraged, his world out of control, his thoughts discordant. Visions of job and career over, and his marriage and family in jeopardy, took him down to a place where he now questioned who he really was.

CHAPTER THIRTY-SIX

Kate Forsythe knocked twice, waited ten seconds, then opened the door to Commissioner O'Brien's office without waiting for permission, the double knock her private signal that she was about to enter.

"Hi, Kate, is the meeting at one with Phil Townsend still on? He indicated yesterday he might have to postpone it."

"Yes, he confirmed for one about an hour ago. I was just about to tell you. Also, you have a sticky on the pile I just left to call Justine between eleven thirty and noon."

"That narrow a window, huh. What now? Did she say why then?"

"Said she would only be available at that time. No further information."

"Okay. Thank you, Kate. I've got an errand to run at noon, so I will be leaving at about eleven forty. Maybe I can catch her before then.

I may be a few minutes late for Townsend. Keep him entertained until I return."

Kate tilted her head and looked at her boss over her glasses with an exasperated *thanks a lot* look. Keeping Townsend occupied if O'Brien ran late was never fun. The man insisted on military precision with everything and could be very difficult. However, as the commissioner's personal assistant, Kate enjoyed a degree of protection from his wrath not enjoyed by anyone else in the league.

After leaving the commissioner, Kate made herself a cup of tea and walked to a window with an incredible panorama of the New York skyline, musing on her interaction with O'Brien. She found it odd that he almost never referred to football as anything but "the product," as if they were making widgets rather than managing a sport. And as a woman, she was uncomfortable with his constant irritation with Justine, who had always treated her with respect. She wished he would give her a break. It couldn't be easy being the wife of such a high-powered man who was constantly in the spotlight. Sure, she'd fallen into the wealth and prestige trap that engulfed so many people, but few could successfully avoid that. He didn't realize what a good ambassador she was for him, especially with the Special Olympics, O'Brien's favorite charity. Their efforts were near and dear to Kate, having a special-needs son of her own.

Her thoughts turned to "entertaining" Townsend and her hope that O'Brien would return on time.

———————

Jimmy O'Brien worked diligently on his paperwork until eleven thirty-five, when he called Justine.

She answered with a "Hi, Jimbo. Thanks for calling me now, hon. I'm in between appointments."

"Not a problem, Justine," he said through gritted teeth. He hated being called *Jimbo.* "What's going on?"

"Honey, I just wanted to remind you again to get the stage passes for this weekend's halftime performance. My sister keeps calling about it. Her kids are so excited. I'm sorry to bring this up again."

This was the third time in ten days, and O'Brien didn't believe his sister-in-law was really pushing like that. "Passes will be here tomorrow, Justine. I told you that. Nothing to worry about. Have some faith in me," he scolded.

"Oh, don't be angry with me, Jimbo. I just know you have a lot on your mind, and I'll look bad with my sister and her kids if I don't get this for them," she whined. "And we need to think about moving forward with the Hamptons beach house. At least start looking."

Jimbo again. He took a deep breath.

"The passes are all set, and we will discuss the Hamptons sometime this week, I promise. Look, I've got to run. I'll see you tonight. Enjoy your afternoon." He hung up, shaking his head. *When did she get this way, always bugging me for stuff? It never ends!* He stormed out his private entrance but was calm by the time he reached the street, looking forward to his "errand."

———

After a seven-minute walk from league headquarters and using a private elevator in the rear of the building, he entered a plush, twenty-second-floor condo, titled to Alpha/Omega Holdings, an offshore company he had set up. He was greeted by a dazzling brunette wearing nothing but one of his blue button-down, long-sleeved shirts, the sleeves loose and the top five buttons undone. She handed him a vodka tonic, which he eagerly accepted as the five-foot-seven former model stood on tiptoes to deliver a passionate kiss.

He took a large gulp, and with neither saying a word, she took off his suit coat, undid his tie, and removed his shirt, revealing his muscular chest and flat stomach, impressive for a man his age. He had kicked off his shoes, and when she bent down to pull off his socks, her shirt opened, revealing her own enticing chest. He took another quick gulp. She arose and another passionate kiss ensued, which he followed up by undoing her remaining two buttons and peeling the shirt off her shoulders and down her arms.

Slowly working his way from her mouth, he delivered soft, wet kisses down her neck until he reached his goal. Moving first to the left, his tongue flirted with his target until the desired result was achieved, and then he repeated his action on the right again with a similar outcome. Breathing heavily, she allowed the shirt to fall to the floor as she led him by the hand down the corridor. Following her voluptuous, naked figure, he arrived to candlelight and a turned-down bed. She pivoted to face him, and he gently pushed her on the bed. Quickly removing the rest of his clothes, they consumed the next twenty minutes in passionate sex with each reaching total fulfillment. No words had been needed or uttered, their communications totally physical.

With Teri wrapped in his left arm, the commissioner reached for his drink, draining it. Turning back to his lover, he pulled her closer and kissed her on the forehead.

"That was wonderful, Jimmy."

"Yes, darling, you certainly know how to light my fire. Funny what an unbuttoned blouse and a drink can do to a man," he said, his blue eyes sparkling.

She chuckled and said, "Hey, what about what's in the blouse? Isn't the present better than the wrapping?"

He laughed loudly. "It certainly is. But you wrap the present so well!" Fond memories of her greetings as a sexy schoolteacher, a ravishing serving wench, and the obligatory cheerleader came flooding back. The time she answered the door glistening in a wet cut-off T-shirt and thong was particularly memorable. "We do have our fun, don't we? Just have to catch it when we can."

"We're careful. Not stupid or greedy. I'm thankful for whatever we have, Jimmy."

"Me too, Teri. I'm so glad you're in my life, however you can be."

They held each other for a few minutes before heading off to the shower. Time did not allow for anything more than a few minutes of soapy sexy play, but it was enough to satisfy their desires until their next appointed time. A brief kiss, a long hug, and the lovers parted to go their separate ways.

The seven-minute return to the office allowed O'Brien to reflect on this almost weekly event. *Teri's right. We can't be greedy. Must take what is given and be grateful. Certainly can't have Justine or Paul find out. That would be devastating! Teri is always a counterpoise to Justine. Great timing after that phone call earlier. Justine is getting harder and harder to handle, constant demands and whining. Won't she ever be satisfied?*

He knew the answer to that would take a lot longer than the seven-minute walk to figure out, and he was relieved when he returned to his office—his fortress—where he could concentrate on other things. At least until the next phone call.

Deep in thought, he hadn't noticed the man in the shadows who had seen him come and go. The same individual observed Teri leave forty minutes later. He had taken photos of both of them.

CHAPTER THIRTY-SEVEN

Returning to his office precisely at one, Phil Townsend was just arriving. When O'Brien said hello to Kate, she mouthed, "Thank you" to him. He turned and motioned to Townsend with a "C'mon in, Phil," as he closed the door.

From time to time, the commissioner and Townsend met for an off-the-record report on the business of the NAFL Internal Security Division. This involved information for discussion between the two men before being divulged to anyone else.

O'Brien asked Townsend, "What do you have to report, Phil? Any issues I don't know about that I should?"

"I have several items to review. There have been some suspicious issues recently that I've dealt with," he said. He continued without pause, not letting O'Brien make a comment, ignoring the pointed look from his boss.

"There's been some interest in our offshore companies, apparently connected to a bank investigation into money laundering and drug traffickers. Nothing to be concerned about. I've taken care of it, and the potential threat is over.

"That assistant coach for the Columbus Colonels, Tony Stravnicki, is a concern again. Remember, his assistant pulled all the film, and I had to take care of that. Stravnicki has been upset about some calls against his team and the communications problems. He's been asking questions and even had a former college teammate, who now runs a security firm, poke around in Vegas about Travis Dustin. I came down on Stravnicki hard. He's been threatened with firing by his team owner and head coach, and an even more pointed message was sent to him recently, and that appears to have worked."

"What was the pointed message, Phil?"

"I prefer not to divulge that at this time. I believe in the compartmentalizing of information for security reasons. I've mentioned this *before*."

O'Brien thought about it for a moment, an uneasy silence between them. "Continue," he finally said.

"Our head game-day frequency coordinator, Tom Overholt, tried to push me hard on the comms issues and asked too many questions, but I deflected this back to him and his boss, and that appears to have been the end of that. His boss, Felix Lipton, won't challenge me, and Overholt has been sufficiently warned."

O'Brien nodded, a wry smile on his face. Lipton was a weasel but an efficient manager. He certainly wouldn't confront Townsend. O'Brien said, "Speaking of Lipton, he just informed me this morning that they have been unable to contact one of our officials, Frank Ohlendorf. He called in sick for his game this weekend, and no one has been in contact with him since."

Townsend could not conceal a look of shock at this announcement, and O'Brien noticed. "What do you know about this, Phil?"

Townsend regained control and replied, "Ohlendorf is one of our most useful assets. I didn't know about this, but I'll get right on it."

"He's that important and you didn't know about it? I'm not happy with that, Phil. How did this happen? How long has he been out of contact?" O'Brien's voice rose, his face red and his neck veins prominent as he stared at Townsend.

"Lipton didn't contact me about this, so I don't know how long."

"You're supposed to know about him even before Lipton does! You're supposed to maintain close contact with our *most useful* assets!"

"I don't need a lecture. I told you I would get right on it. I will deal with it," he spat out, refusing to be browbeat.

"An investigation involving our offshore business, an assistant coach and GDFC asking questions, and now a missing ref who worked for us. On top of a player asset who bolted. Do I need more oversight, Phil?"

"No, you don't. This ref business probably has a simple answer. I don't like being micromanaged, Jim. I've got a long track record of delivering on what I've promised. You put me in this job because you trusted me. Our bigger concerns should be the loss of two important assets. It will take time to develop replacements and certainly won't happen this season."

"I want to continue with that trust. I must have assurances that you and your people are one hundred percent confident that nothing can come back on the league or us. We have time to find new assets for next year."

"I need to emphasize again that I have built in redundant safeguards. Commissioner, let me do my job." He said this with emphasis, having had enough of the schoolboy lecture.

"Get to the bottom of this, Phil. I want an update, and soon!"

O'Brien rose, signaling the end of their meeting, and Townsend left without another word. O'Brien settled back in his chair. He accepted the blame for giving Townsend too much latitude and that it would be difficult to get the genie back in the bottle. Townsend had been central to accomplishing his vision, but O'Brien's inability to control him was a very high price to pay. He could only hope that the security chief's self-preservation instincts would protect him at the same time.

―――――――――

Phil Townsend rushed to his office, furious from his meeting with O'Brien and embarrassed about the Ohlendorf situation. His assistant handed him a note that he had received an urgent call from someone named Steve. Using the secure cell, he called Lyubov, resisting the urge to reprimand him until he had heard the full story.

"Sorry, boss, I don't know where he go. We have normal meeting last week; I turn on TV for game and he not there. I try several times but he not pick up cell. Even call his work this morning, not there." He sounded confused through the thick accent.

"Listen, Pavel, get on a plane and go to his home and work. See what you can find. Report back to me tonight."

"Yes, boss. I will find him and he will pay!" Lyubov boasted.

"No, Pavel, don't do anything except find him!" Townsend commanded and disconnected.

Townsend buzzed his assistant and asked for coffee, which she quickly brought. Deep in thought as he savored his favorite, French vanilla, he reviewed all the incidents of the last two months, culminating with this one. Townsend believed that all these things were merely coincidental and, except for those involving Stravnicki, were not related. He doubted the coach was capable of anything serious. But he knew they must be taken as threats to the vision nonetheless, so caution was required. Ohlendorf could be a problem, but even if he had gone to the FBI, nothing could be traced back to them. Townsend wouldn't hesitate to burn Lyubov, having set him up to be expendable with a cover of Russian mob involvement.

CHAPTER THIRTY-EIGHT

G ena arrived at the training facility of the Dallas Riders shortly before one o'clock following a three-hour flight by private jet. The flight was provided by the NAFL, and with her were three other members of the Austin Agency. Accompanying them was Teri Johnstone, who served as liaison between the league and FAE Productions, the company that had retained the Austin Agency to work with some of the cheerleaders. On the flight down, Gena had introduced herself to Teri, and the two women soon discovered they had similar backgrounds in modeling. Being personable and outgoing, they found conversation easy, and a friendship developed. Gena remembered her secondary mission for this trip and, feeling at ease with Teri, began to query her about the details of this project.

"Teri, we are quite pleased that the league chose my agency

to help out with your cheerleaders, but from what I've seen, they already do a pretty good job."

"Thanks, Gena," Teri said, "but the commissioner wants far more than just a *pretty good job*. His vision has been to upgrade the entertainment value of the football experience to provide a superior product for the fans. The team cheerleaders all must be top notch to deliver the image he wants. Some of them are just not up to that level yet, and we are counting on you guys helping to get them there."

"I'm certain we can. We'll start with the basics: hair, makeup, projecting a strong positive image, then review their routines to see what they do."

"That's great, Gena, just what we want. We're looking to really add sizzle and showmanship to their presence." Teri turned to Gena and outlined the schedule for the next few days. They would be long and busy and would culminate in Miami with a private party where the commissioner and several high-level league executives would be present. Teri raved about what great parties the league threw and promised it would be the highlight of the trip.

"These boys know how to party, Gena. Hard work, hard play is an unofficial motto!" she laughed.

Gena's imagination ran away with the possibilities of how her undercover work could help Nick.

The days flew by in a blur, a whirlwind of events beginning in Dallas, moving to Houston, and finishing in Miami. The overwhelming focus of the league was all about producing a Hollywood extravaganza, and the few players she met seemed more than a little annoyed by it all, questioning what it had to do with their sport.

Teri was involved in all aspects of the process, working closely with Gena, and by the time they reached Miami, their relationship had blossomed. Gena was privy to conversations not directly related to her agency work, and she was learning much about the functions of some of the letter companies that Nick mentioned in his briefing.

The league party, to be held at the luxurious mansion of the owner of the Miami Waves, would expose Gena to even more potential intelligence sources, and she looked forward to the evening. Her team members had another assignment and would return to New York, so Gena would be by herself. Despite the many functions she had gone to in her career, she was well aware of how special this one could be; she was not just acting as an "agency girl" this time.

———————

Teri had not exaggerated about the opulence of the party. It was one of the most amazing events Gena had ever been to, and all the league elite were there. Teri first introduced Gena to her husband, Paul, whose pasty complexion, short stature, and out-of-shape physique was in sharp contrast not only to Teri's toned, svelte build but to most of the males in the room. He was pleasant but reserved and seemed uncomfortable in the current setting. After a few awkward moments, he left them to engage in conversation with a colleague, and two tall, athletic, handsome men soon came over to Teri and Gena. The larger of the men introduced himself to Gena as Commissioner Jim O'Brien before giving Teri a quick peck on the cheek. He introduced his companion, Bill Macafee, who smiled and simply shook their hands. Excusing themselves, Bill took Teri aside, leaving Gena with the commissioner.

"Gena, Teri tells me you and your agency have made a strong impact for us. That's wonderful. I'm looking forward to seeing the results this weekend," O'Brien said.

"Thank you for the confidence in us, Commissioner. The squads already had strong foundations, and we were able to bring out their best. It was fun working with them."

"Always good to have fun while you work. Sometimes we can take our jobs too seriously," he said with a light laugh and sparkling eyes. "We're constantly striving to upgrade our product to give our customers, the fans, the best experience possible. There is a special relationship between the sport and America, you know, and we must nurture it."

Gena was just about to reply when Bill and Teri returned, accompanied by a stocky, serious-looking man with piercing blue eyes. O'Brien turned and acknowledged him with a nod and said, "Gena, I'd like to introduce you to Phil Townsend, our head of Internal Security."

Townsend offered his hand. Their eyes locked for a few moments. She got a totally different vibe from him, as if he was assessing her as a threat. *Guess that's what you do when you're head of security,* she thought. She looked forward to seeing how others interacted with him.

Her thoughts about him ended when two women joined them, and Townsend excused himself. The significantly younger woman went up to Macafee, wrapped her arm around his waist, and they kissed lightly. The other woman, not stunning like the first but still attractive nonetheless and more stylishly dressed, made eye contact with O'Brien, and he reached out and took her hand.

"Darling, I would like you to meet Gena Compagna of the Austin Agency. They've been doing great work for us with the girls. Gena, this is my wife, Justine."

"Hello, Justine, nice to meet you. The commissioner has been flattering with his praise for us. We appreciate it."

"Yes, he *is* very good at flattery," she replied, her voice lilting upwards. "Have you found it interesting work, Gena?" she asked, a hint of haughty disdain evident as the imperious woman passed judgment on Gena.

"Oh yes. A different side of the game than what I see on Sundays."

Looking at Gena knowingly, she replied, "There are many sides of this game that aren't apparent to the public, aren't there, Jimmy?"

He laughed and turned his attention to Macafee and the younger woman. Macafee looked at his companion first and then Gena, stating, "And this is my wife, Rachel," who simply nodded. An awkward silence was soon broken by a waiter carrying a tray of champagne, and O'Brien and Macafee handed glasses to the ladies. The commissioner raised his glass, offering a toast. "To a long, rewarding relationship and continuous improvement of our product."

"Here, here," Macafee seconded, and all raised their glasses in agreement. "Ladies, we must leave you for now but will rejoin you at our table for dinner," he said as he followed the commissioner, leaving Gena with the contrasting women. They engaged in meaningless talk for a few difficult minutes before the ladies went their separate ways, leaving Gena relieved.

Gena was honored with a seat at the circular head table and was pleased to be next to Teri and the commissioner. O'Brien held court, expounding on "getting outcomes that we want" and "control of the product" with any talk about football itself revolving only around team standings and television ratings. Banter went back and forth between most at the table, but Gena observed that whenever Phil Townsend spoke, no one except the commissioner made a comment. It came across not as deference to him but more like no one wanted to say anything to challenge him, and the neutral expressions of his tablemates bore this out.

Gena's vibrant and engaging personality assured that she interacted easily with them all. When Bill Macafee spoke about his new yacht *Nirvana* and she asked several pertinent questions, he followed up by giving her an open invitation to join them sometime.

Gena excused herself to attend the ladies' room, and as she pushed her chair back, she dropped her purse under the table. Bending to retrieve it, she noticed *DN/CS Hospitality* stenciled on the underside of the table. *Wait, isn't that another of those letter companies Nick told me about?*

On her way back, she ran into a smiling Teri, radiating excitement.

"Hey, girl, were you ever the talk of the table when you left! I've never seen that crowd take to someone so quickly. For Bill to invite you on *Nirvana* is huge."

"I enjoyed meeting them, Teri. They seemed so welcoming and warm to me, except for that guy Phil. What's his deal?"

Teri waited a few seconds before answering, her expression thoughtful. "You probably noticed everyone other than the commissioner didn't respond much to his comments. He is very intimidating to a lot of people. You *never* want to cross swords with him, and I will leave it at that."

Teri's husband, Paul, came up to them and said something to her. Teri turned to Gena. "I'll catch up with you later." Gena was left with her thoughts when Phil Townsend came up behind her, seemingly out of nowhere, giving her a start.

"Oh, sorry to have startled you, Gena." There was a total lack of sincerity in his voice. "You seem to be enjoying yourself."

"Yes, I really am, Phil. Everyone has been so kind to me and my colleagues."

He nodded but didn't reply to the comment, continuing, "As head of Internal Security, it is my job to remind you and your girls that total discretion is required of you. Nothing you see or hear is to be disclosed to anyone else. Failure to adhere to this could have some severe consequences. *Do I make myself clear?*" he delivered in a hushed yet pointed monotone, blue eyes staring with chilling effect.

"But of course, Phil," Gena shot back, refusing to be intimidated. "That is always standard procedure with all of our clients, and we've worked with many high-profile groups like yours."

A dark expression came over his face, the muscles around his eyes contracting, accentuating his look. "Then you have nothing to worry about. Have a good night," he said and departed.

Gena took a deep breath. *He is one scary dude who doesn't like to be challenged. No wonder no one except O'Brien interacted with him at the table. What a strange coincidence that I just asked Teri about him and then he showed up. Or was it?*

The flight home, on the same private jet, allowed Gena and Teri ample time to discuss the events of the past several days. Gena was cautious in her questions for Teri but still learned enough to give Nick a fair amount of information. Teri was pleased with how the week had gone and hinted that the Austin Agency would be offered an extended contract based on their performance. The two new friends departed with Teri promising to contact Gena soon.

Gena couldn't wait to see Nick to recount all that she had learned, but he had left a note that he would be working late. Although it was only four, she lay down for a catnap, tired from the intensity of the trip. She was awakened by a soft kiss from Nick at seven thirty.

"Hi, beautiful. Is my poor undercover agent worn out from her first assignment? I brought takeout so we can eat and talk."

"Oh, Nick, you're brilliant! I was pretty tired, but I've been asleep for about three hours, so I'm fine now. So much to tell you, hon. Nothing earth shattering, just hope it's helpful. But how about you, any big breakthroughs?"

"Not yet. We keep grinding away at leads. What did you find?"

"It was an awesome experience, Nick. I met and spent time with a bunch of NAFL executives, including the commissioner. Teri Johnstone, wife of Paul Johnstone, VP of NAFL Properties, was my liaison and we became friends. She interacts with FAE Productions and my agency, and I also found out about business with two other companies, AKJ Enterprises and DN/CS Hospitality."

"That's a clear connection. What do they do for the league?"

"AKJ interacts with artists and performers for the league, and DN/CS apparently provides food and beverages." She related to Nick how she found their stencil on the table.

"How about conversations with these executives?"

Gena described in detail the conversations involving O'Brien, Macafee, and Townsend. "The commissioner is very charming and witty, Paul Johnstone is very reserved, almost meek, Macafee comes across as a yes-man, and Townsend is scary."

"Scary? That's a harsh description. How so?"

Gena explained how people were uncomfortable with Townsend and she related almost verbatim his warning to her. "Teri told me he intimidates people and even warned me about him. She told me not to cross him."

"Sounds like you stood up to him, hon."

"Yes, and he clearly isn't used to it."

"How about general conversation?" All this time, Nick had been taking copious notes, which impressed Gena.

"What struck me is that just about all the conversations had to do with the entertainment value of football or the business aspects. They talked about 'going Hollywood' and how to 'monetize the product.' Anything spoken about the game itself revolved around team standings and 'getting the outcomes we want.' *The product* and television ratings were mentioned constantly."

Nick jerked up from his notes. "Someone actually said 'getting the outcomes we want' and 'team standings?' Are you sure about that? Do you remember who said it?"

"Yes, I do. It was an exchange between O'Brien and Macafee, and it was Macafee's comment. I remember the Miami team owner looked perplexed about the statement but didn't say anything. I noticed O'Brien gave Macafee a very brief frown. Could this be important?"

"It's an odd comment." He was not sure just how much his boss had briefed Gena on the attempts to influence games. "Anything else?"

"Well, it was interesting seeing all these people interacting, the dynamics of it. Teri and her husband seem an odd combination, as does the commissioner and his wife, Justine. She wasn't warm to me and came across as haughty. I seemed to pick up on a chemistry between Teri and O'Brien, but I'm not sure about that. Just a gut feeling. But I did hit it off with Bill Macafee to the extent he invited me on his yacht, *Nirvana*. Even Teri was surprised about that, and she hinted that the agency's contract may be extended."

"Invited on his yacht? Now I'm jealous!"

"Don't worry, it will probably never happen. But who knows?" She paused. "Nick, did I do okay for my first attempt?"

"Gena, I think you did great. Exactly what we wanted. Let's see what Scott says Monday. But now I need to make sure *you* reach nirvana." And he took her by the hand.

———

Monday morning, Nick was looking forward to briefing Scott on Gena's trip but was forced to wait until two that afternoon. He used his time to do a full review of all aspects of their investigation and now had a high degree of certainty that influence was coming from sources within the league. But still, they had no direct links or hard evidence. While he waited, he tried to brainstorm ideas but mostly came up empty. It was a tenet that sometimes good investigative work could only take you so far, and you needed a lucky break or the bad guys to make a mistake to crack the case open. But the trick was how to put yourself in a position to get either.

At two, Nick arrived at Thompson's office to find him buried in a desktop of paperwork.

"C'mon in, Nick. I've been looking forward to this all day. What did your future bride discover?"

Nick provided a detailed report from his notes of Gena's debrief, and Scott's attention never wavered, jotting notes and asking an occasional question.

"She did really well, Nick. Certainly supports influence from within, and she's likely to be involved on a continuing basis. Linking more of the letter companies was important. Based on this, I should have no problem getting a judge to approve her use of recording devices. She'll need to be formally debriefed, processed, and trained to make sure she understands protocols and procedures."

"Boss, I can't tell you how happy she was to be involved, and she'll be thrilled to take the next step. We have to move quickly, as she has another group of cheerleaders to train next week."

"Okay, I'll get right on the approval when you leave. We've got to find that inside person. Lyubov has got to be the main outside guy. Harvey's surveillance has failed to turn up anything significant yet. We need a break there too. By the way, the referee Ohlendorf is in WITSEC in New England. His disappearance from the league may lead to some talk that Gena might run across."

"Boss, I'll run a detailed background on all the league officials Gena met. Perhaps something will pop up."

"Great idea. Get right on that today. Top priority. Touch base with me tomorrow, and we'll figure out when to get Gena back in. Give her a high-five for me."

"Will do, sir. See you tomorrow."

Walking back to his office, Nick believed for the first time things might be starting to come together.

CHAPTER THIRTY-NINE

Nick returned to his office with renewed confidence that they were finally making tangible progress and that Gena's observations had been helpful. His priority now was to investigate the backgrounds of the three top league officials Gena had met, and he wanted to meet with Harvey and review the surveillance of Lyubov.

A comprehensive review of Commissioner O'Brien failed to find anything, but the review of William Macafee got Nick's attention. Prior to the league, Macafee had extensive training and experience in international banking, and had even been a consultant for the industry in combatting money laundering by drug dealers. He had often traveled to the Caymans as part of this.

Philip Townsend's history provided such a shock to Nick that he called Thompson, stating, "I found something big." His curious boss delayed a scheduled meeting and told him to come right away. Nick was almost breathless when he arrived, and Scott said nothing, just waving him in.

"Boss, Phil Townsend, the NAFL security guy, has a deep background in covert ops, dating from his time in the Marines, and he spent ten years in the NSA. Much of his government history is unavailable to me, but perhaps you can find out more." Nick reviewed Macafee's background while Thompson took notes.

"Crap. An international banker and a covert ops guy. That's a combination that could do some damage. Finding much about special ops such as his time in Force Recon will be difficult, and his NSA file is sure to be protected, but with my higher clearance, I might find something. I'll get right on this and contact legal to get wiretap authorization for Gena. I want as broad approval as I can get, and I believe the judge will see our justification now."

"Harvey and I have a meeting in thirty minutes to review Lyubov's surveillance tapes and see if we can find any connections."

"Good. Let me know," Thompson said without looking up.

CHAPTER FORTY

Nick arrived at Harvey's office to find a large monitor connected to sophisticated video equipment. "Hi, Nick. Ready for the tedious part of surveillance? We've got many hours to review, and this is a fraction of what we've filmed. My team has already previewed a lot of film and eliminated known individuals of no significance. I hope we get lucky and find something of value."

"Well, Harvey, at least we have some specific people to look for now." Nick gave a quick explanation about a possible connection with the NAFL executives.

"We have very good facial and body-type recognition software and amazing enhancement techniques, so let's get started."

After much fruitless effort, Nick was reviewing a sequence where Lyubov had met someone along the Atlantic City boardwalk. He exclaimed, "Harvey, this may be something. Can you enhance it?"

Tankersley tapped on his computer, refining the image until he turned to Nick and said, "From that distance and angle, that's the best I can do. Who do you think it is?"

The image was not perfect, but to Nick it was crystal clear. "Hank, that's Phil Townsend, I'm sure of it. Can you compare this image to known photos of him we've acquired recently?"

"Absolutely. Just take minute or two." Rapidly pounding the keyboard, Tankersley opened three windows on the monitor. In addition to the surveillance image, a file photo of Townsend from his last year at the NSA appeared. "This third box is our sophisticated facial recognition software. I just click and drag the images from the other two boxes into it and begin the program. We'll know in about a minute." Actually, it was forty-five seconds before the words *confirmed match* blinked on the screen. "There you go," Tankersley said.

Nick's head spun. He needed to get back to his boss. *A solid connection! Influence from within the NAFL! But is Townsend acting alone?*

He congratulated Harvey and thanked him, heading back upstairs. This time Thompson's secretary told Nick that there was an important meeting going on and Thompson had given explicit orders not to be disturbed. Nick gathered his thoughts about how to proceed, aware of the need for concrete ideas. Sustaining momentum was critical now.

―――――――――

Twenty minutes later, Thompson was free, and he went right in. "Boss, working with Harvey, we have visual confirmation that Townsend met with Lyubov. I want Harvey to run the same comparison on the Travis Dustin tapes, but you have to okay that."

"Harvey has a confirmed match? And you think one of the three men in Dustin's apartment is Townsend? We already know one guy is probably Lyubov because of the scar. How about the third one? Any ideas?"

"Not yet. Harvey is going to expand surveillance on Townsend. The Dustin videos may be a crucial link now that we've associated Townsend and Lyubov. It's unlikely Townsend is doing this all on his own."

"Probably not. Being a military guy, he's used to being part of a team. No problem releasing those recordings to Harvey. What other thoughts do you have?"

"Ohlendorf, the ref in WITSEC. I think it's critical he looks at images of the two. If we can link either of them to the Ohlendorf blackmail, that will be another big step."

"WITSEC doesn't like doing something like that, but under the circumstances it shouldn't be a problem. They will want to handle the whole thing by themselves for his protection. I'll set that up," said Thompson.

"That's fine. It needs to be done soon. We've got momentum that I want to sustain."

"I'll get right on it. By the way, broad wiretap approval was granted for Gena. We need to get her in here soon. Does she have any other meetings set up with the people she met?"

"She's not traveling this week, so we can get her in. I'll find out tonight when her next meetings are scheduled."

"Good work, Nick. Contact me tomorrow."

"Yes, sir. Will do. Thank you."

———

Nick returned home to find Gena all dressed up. The look of confusion on his face prompted her to tease him. "Forgotten where we're going tonight, haven't you, Nick?"

He thought for a few seconds and then groaned. "Tonight's the dinner at my mother's for our engagement. I just put it right out of my mind."

"Sorry, Nick, I meant to remind you this morning. At least you haven't been worrying about it all day. Go get ready, luv, and I'll make you a light drink to take the edge off. It's going to be fine. Tony isn't the type to hold a grudge. Just keep the conversation light and neutral."

Nick's mouth twisted like he had sucked on a lemon. "I'll do my best, but be prepared to bail me out if things go south."

"Sure, but I doubt that will be necessary. We'll make it work."

———

It wasn't easy. Both men greeted each other with a palpable

coldness. Maggie and her sister moved the focus to Gena and Nick's engagement, a toast was made, and the ice was somewhat broken. The conversation flowed easily among the women, while the men didn't interact with each other but were otherwise pleasant. Maggie engaged Nick while Gena tried to get Tony to open up a bit. Gena spoke about her recent experiences with her agency and the league cheerleaders, and that got Tony interested. As she described the glitz of NAFL showmanship, Tony increased his attention, asking Gena a series of questions about the process.

"I've never really paid much attention to these things, Gena. I've been too busy as a player or a coach, but from what I've noticed recently, it all seems so over the top. I'm not trying to insult you, Gena; it just appears to have taken on a life of its own."

"Tony, believe me, it's as orchestrated as any reality TV show out there," she said with a laugh. From the quizzical look on his face, she realized she had said too much. "But I've only been working with them for a short time," she tried to backtrack. Fortunately, Maggie came over at that time and asked to look at Gena's ring, leaving Tony to himself, deep in thought.

Dinner was awkward, with the conversation almost exclusively between the women and the men rarely even making eye contact. Nick and Tony remained aloof for the remainder of the evening, the ladies wise enough to let it be. Twenty minutes later, Tony gave Maggie the *time to leave* sign, reluctantly shaking Nick's hand, who reciprocated in silence.

In the car to the airport, Tony let out a sharp sigh and said, "Well, that went well . . . *not!* I told you there might be an issue with Nick. I feel terrible. I didn't know how to handle it, and I was afraid of making things even worse."

"Tony, Nick was clearly uncomfortable too. He's never acted that way. I'm sure he was just as uncertain of what to say and how to act as you. You hurt each other pretty good, and there hasn't been enough distance for any healing to take place. Give it time. I know this is big, but I firmly believe your relationship with Nick is far stronger than you think right now."

Tony was very quiet for several minutes, and Maggie didn't break the silence. In a barely audible voice he eventually replied, "The price of my foolishness is getting pretty expensive. The potential loss of my job is bad enough, but the attack on you and the falling-out with Nick is more than I imagined."

This tripped her Irish temper. "Once again, it's all about you, Tony Stravnicki! Don't you forget that we are *all* in this shit together. You've got a big support network and people who believe in you. You're not being foolish, but your attitude needs some adjustment. Stop the pity party already!"

On the flight home, a chastised Tony barely spoke, too depressed and lost in his thoughts. Maggie was silent. *Great, I've pissed Mags off. Again. What more bad things can happen?*

———————————

"Well, Nick, that was difficult. I wasn't expecting it to be that tense."

"It was very hard, Gena. I feel awful. I just hope that at some point this is resolved, and I can explain things to him, but I don't know if that will happen."

"You had no choice, Nick. Truly between a rock and a hard place. Not much you can do at this point. At least you guys didn't add to the problem."

"How could we? We didn't say anything to each other. I feel badly for Mom and Aunt Maggie, but they handled it as well as they could. Maggie knows about my meeting with Tony, but Mom was totally in the dark. I'm sorry it cast a pall on what should have been a fun time."

"All you can do is go forward the best you can and hope that somehow you can prove that Tony has been right all along. That will go a long way to a reconciliation."

"Well, progress *is* being made. If we can keep up the momentum, something is likely to break things wide open. That's the hope we have. Just gotta keep pushing hard. Speaking of that, Scott was able to obtain authorization for extensive electronic surveillance and recording, and that means we must get you in soon. You've got to be completely competent and comfortable with all the equipment."

"That's good news. Just in time too. I found out today from Teri I'm invited on Macafee's yacht in a week. So, he wasn't just blowing smoke. She told me, in confidence, there's a meeting on the yacht that weekend, some bigwigs from the league. They want me there to give them a presentation on how to market their cheerleaders even more."

"Great! That could be a huge opportunity. Knowing up front you'll be on a ship will enable the tech guys to customize your equipment. I'll let Thompson know first thing tomorrow. You're going to have to learn a lot in a short time. Not just about the equipment but fieldcraft techniques for your safety, backup plans, things like that. You'll need to tactfully learn as much as you can about the meeting and schedule of the weekend as you can."

"Fieldcraft techniques, huh? Does sound like James Bond. Still no invisible ink or a gun?"

"I know you're kidding, Gena, but this is serious stuff. You've met Townsend. He got your attention. Anything's possible with him. Your safety is priority, and we have to think about that in detail."

"I know this is serious, Nick, and there are risks involved. I won't take any chances I don't have to, and I think I've really earned some degree of their trust. There's no reason for them to suspect anything other than the image I show them. That's a big advantage."

"Yes, it is. But we still have to have backup plans to minimize risk." He remembered the backup plans in the Caymans. Without them, the outcome might have been disastrous. "What's your schedule like this week? How available are you?"

"I've got a lot of comp time due, so I'm pretty much free all week."

"Great. Plan on most of the week being with the bureau then."

Gena nodded and changed the subject to this evening, but Nick had already checked out. His mind was racing with the possibilities of what Gena might be able to discover, the threats she could face, and how to deal with them.

CHAPTER FORTY-ONE

Trying hard to forget about last night's dinner and his deepening gloom, Tony got to his office early. He had just popped two pieces of gum in his mouth when his phone intercom buzzed. It was the head coach's secretary.

"Coach T. You're wanted up here right away." Her voice was distant and somber, and she didn't wait for a reply. *Now what?*

When he reached Rocky's office, he was ushered right in by the grim-faced secretary. Team owner John Cane was present with Jones, who motioned Tony to a chair.

"Tony, we've just received word that Hank Naples has been killed in a car crash on the way in this morning."

"That's terrible, Rocky. Is his family aware?" a shaken Tony replied.

"Yes, the family has been told, but we have not yet released anything to the team."

"We wanted to talk with you first, Tony," said Cane. "You and Bob Stratton are the front-runners to take over his defensive coordinator job. Opportunities like this don't come along often. Based on your experience and seniority, you were probably expecting to take over for Hank, but with the problems you've had with the league this year and the position you seem to take about player injuries, we have concerns. We need to hear about your commitment to the team and the league."

Tony tried his best to look unmoved but could feel the fire in his cheeks and the bile rising in his mouth. His head began to spin, but he forced himself to focus and keep in control.

"My commitments to this team and the league have been proven both as a player and a coach and are unchanged. I am who I am, John," Tony said without hesitation.

"You're a very good coach, Tony," chimed in Jones. "We need your continued expertise and support as we make a run for the playoffs. Can we still count on you?"

"Of course I'm still on board, Rocky. Bob is a great candidate and would have my full support. We've always had a great relationship." Stratton was the linebackers coach, and he and Tony had worked closely together. The fire in his face subsided, and his tone was composed and matter-of-fact. He even stopped chewing his gum and parked it in his cheek.

"We will announce Hank's death at a team meeting in a few minutes. Don't say anything to anyone until then, and we'll make a decision about DC by the end of the day."

Tony rose. "No problem. That's your job." He proudly walked out without saying another word.

After he left Cane said, "We know who our man is. That was easier than I thought it would be." Rocky nodded in agreement.

The team meeting was held a half hour later, and Naples's passing was announced, quickly followed by a terse statement indicating Stratton would be the new DC. At the end of the meeting, Tony congratulated Stratton and told him he was looking forward to working with him. Several players tapped Tony on the back but said nothing. He went back to his office, locking his door and shutting off the lights.

Tony was not a big drinker, but he kept a small flask of his favorite scotch hidden deep in his desk just for situations like this; Milky Ways wouldn't cut it this time. He took a good swig of the amber liquid and tipped his chair back, putting his feet up on the desk. He reflected on the speed of their decision and his brief hope that he actually had a shot. The knowledge that this could be a career killer was not lost on him. The thoughts came at a furious pace, churning in his mind as Tony's spirits sank even deeper, the cold reality of it beginning to burrow into his psyche. Another good pop from the flask, and he put it away while pulling out two breath mints to mask the smell. His years in the league, the only way of life he had known, were possibly coming to an end. What would be next?

He'd had just enough alcohol to diminish his mind's inhibitions. Jumbled thoughts and emotions swirled, incoherent initially but slowly coalescing to a somewhat clearer path. There were still responsibilities to see through, to the players and to himself. His character would not let him shirk these. He saw the faint outline of a path through the forest of reflections. A tiny glimmer of hope began to emerge from the darkness of his despair, and, as he had always done, he seized it.

CHAPTER FORTY-TWO

Tony did his best to diminish the pall that hung over the team and his own personal disappointment, and the result was a decent practice, all things considered. They were, after all, professionals, and the game would still be played. The small victory of a successful afternoon buoyed his spirits to the extent that he refused to reflect upon the day as he drove home, instead losing himself in his music.

He had reminded Maggie that morning about the meeting with Freddie and Brad, so she had dinner ready and the kids' homework completed. After supper he retired to the living room and was sitting in his chair, waiting for them to arrive, when Maggie came in, sitting next to Tony on the sofa.

"Penny for your thoughts, Tony. You've been pretty mellow since you arrived."

Tony smiled and kissed her while squeezing her hand.

"It's been a trying day, Mags. Big things happened." He proceeded to tell her of the sudden death of Hank Naples and his getting passed over for the DC job.

"Oh, Tony, I'm so sorry. About both. How is Frannie?"

"Taking it hard, as you would expect. They didn't have any kids, but he told me they were trying."

"This must be really hard for you."

"I'm trying to come to terms with it all. Dennis's death, now Hank's, not getting the job. It's not unexpected considering how they've warned me, but it's a shock how it happened and the reality of it. But I'll be all right. *We'll* be all right. I just want to get the bastards screwing the game but protect my family in the process."

The doorbell chimed just as Maggie was about to reply, so she smiled, nodded, and got up to greet their guests.

Tony rose as Brad and Freddie entered together, shaking their hands with a simple "Hi, guys." When they were seated and Maggie had brought them coffee, he began.

"Sorry we had to postpone this meeting. A lot has happened since we last met."

With help from Maggie, he reviewed her attack in detail. While they expressed shock and dismay, they praised Maggie's fortitude and that of the security guard. Brad and Freddie were not surprised about the probable identity of her attacker.

"He's dangerous and capable of anything, but he's being controlled by someone else. Thugs like him rarely have the ambition or smarts to work on their own," stated Brad. "I can have a plan ready in a day or two to upgrade security and protection, working with the police. I've got weapons permit applications with me, and we will set up training before I leave."

Tony and Maggie looked at each other and nodded in agreement, thanking Brad.

Freddie spoke next. "We need to look for links outside the league that point to someone on the inside or this scar guy. When I spoke with Tina again, she mentioned she had helped another student named Michael Taranto who she didn't think knew Dustin back then. That's a lead for you, Brad. See if you can find out anything about him."

"Will do, Freddie," Brad said, taking notes. "I'll put my best investigator on that right away. Tony, I don't see any reason for me to go to more games. I think we've gotten all we can out of that. But how about Tom Overholt, the comms guy?"

"Yah, no more games. Contact him and review everything in detail. Maybe that will lead somewhere." Tony then reviewed his second meeting with Nick and the subsequent dinner. His description was reserved, matter-of-fact, the lack of emotion belying his true feelings.

"I'm not surprised about Nick's responses, Tony. The FBI is cautious and conservative, and I believe your nephew said the only things he could," said Brad.

Tony did not respond to his comment but continued, telling them about the death of Naples and his getting passed over for the DC position. Dismay registered on both men's faces, the significance understood, and Freddie was the first to speak.

"That's a shame, Tony. You really have something positive to contribute to the game and the players. Others in the league know who you are and how much you care about the sport. This isn't necessarily the end of the line," he said.

"Thanks, Freddie. 'Preciate it, man." He paused. "Maybe you're right, maybe not, but I might as well go down fighting. I can't continue feeling powerless and out of control. I want to blow things up and see who responds."

"It sounds like you have something in mind already, Tony," said Freddie.

"Up to now, the official line about Travis Dustin has been an OD, possibly a suicide. We know otherwise. What if I leaked out information that suggests it was a hit because of extortion and game tampering, with just enough information to give a hint that it came from me, via another source. That's sure to get those involved upset at me. We watch what happens, see who responds."

Brad and Freddie looked at each other, and a stunned Maggie was the first to respond.

"Lead them right to you, Tony, to us? Are you crazy? I'm behind you, but this is too risky."

Before he could answer, Brad jumped in.

"Well, it may be less risky now than earlier. Your attack was foiled, and they must realize your security is going to be ramped up, they just won't know by how much. They probably understand their tactical advantage—the element of surprise—is diminished. With a greater local police presence and the same for the hospital, the bad guys will have a tougher time. And you're going to be armed, trained, and confident when I'm done with you."

"The trick will be how to pull this off. You're getting passed over may be helpful here, as a *disgruntled low-level NAFL coach with ties to Dustin* source might be the route to go," added Freddie.

"Yeah, something like that is what I had in mind. Can you handle that, Freddie? Do you have a media connection you can use?"

"Several. Let me write something up, and I'll call you on the burner tomorrow and we'll decide the timing to release. I want Brad's plans and your training completed first."

"Okay, Brad, let's plan out this week in detail. We both know our schedules."

Freddie let himself out, and Maggie and Tony filled out firearms paperwork. With Brad, they drew up a comprehensive training schedule for the week, and he left about thirty minutes later.

———

After he left, Maggie poured them a glass of wine.

"Whew," she said, as they touched glasses. "A lot happening."

"Yes, there is. Maggie, I think it's a good idea you and the kids stay at Shannon's lake place after Brad's training. Don't tell anyone but her." Maggie's eyes bulged wide, so Tony continued before she could reply. "Brad knows his stuff, and he has my confidence. This is just more insurance."

She waited before replying. "You know, I've seen too much damage from weapons in my career to think about carrying one. But the attack changed all that. I'll do anything now to protect my family and myself. I need to be ready. The lake house is a great idea."

They finished their wine. Snuggling together in silence, both contemplated where their lives were headed next.

———

Over a three-day period, Brad Vanderbilt delivered on his promises by developing and implementing a comprehensive security program for the Stravnicki family. Working with local police, hospital security, and a team of two of his employees, coverage was as extensive and seamless as possible. While around-the-clock protection was not practical for many reasons, not the least of which was cost, the multifaceted approach significantly improved their safety. He had evaluated Tony and Maggie for the most practical and easiest weapon for each of them to use, obtained all necessary permits, and provided them extensive training in all aspects of firearm use, not only on a firing range but in practical, close-quarters situations. Both pupils were intensely focused, athletic, and quick learners, which simplified the process. He emphasized situational awareness at all times. When he was done, he felt that they were as ready as they could be.

"We can't thank you enough for putting together such a great plan. Maggie and I feel confident in what you've taught us, Brad," said Tony.

"It's what I do, and you and Maggie were great students. I'm confident you can protect your family and yourselves if necessary. On a different note, my team has been investigating the Tom Overholt situation. We obtained CCTV video from the grocery store he was at just before the attack and were able to get the plate number of the car that followed him. It matched to a Stephan Pokogorny."

Tony frowned. "Who's that?"

"Undoubtedly an alias, but the picture on the driver's license is the guy with the scar, although he did a poor job trying to mask it. The address is bogus, but maybe we'll get lucky and link him to someone in the time we have."

"We gotta get a break sometime."

"Yeah, we're overdue for that, for sure. I've got another team looking into Dustin's college days, and I'll be in touch when I hear more."

"Thanks again, Brad."

Tony was left with his thoughts, fully understanding how the stakes had been raised.

———————

With Tony's help, Maggie had the van packed and ready to go before the kids got up. They were thrilled about another adventure, and Tony would handle the details about school and Maggie's job.

Their destination was Portage Lakes, about two hours from their Columbus home, an idyllic, isolated setting they had all been to before. Shannon readily agreed, asking no questions, aware of her sister's attack.

As they drove along, singing songs and chatting, Maggie was oblivious to the pickup truck following her the entire way.

CHAPTER FORTY-THREE

It had been a busy week for Gena at FBI headquarters, where she spent significant time training on the use of the bureau's cutting-edge, state-of-the-art eavesdropping equipment. Much of this was classified, to the extent that not even Nick was privy to this technology. Through Teri, Gena had learned that the *Nirvana* would sail out of Miami Friday and remain at sea overnight. Knowing the characteristics of the design and layout of the vessel had allowed the bureau to customize the devices used.

Scott Thompson decided he owed it to Nick to brief him in general terms on Gena's training and the measures in place to safeguard her, so he summoned Nick to his office.

After a brief but warmer than normal greeting, Thompson got right to it. "Nick, Gena's been amazing this week. She quickly mastered everything we've thrown at her—the equipment, tradecraft techniques, some self-defense skills, and emergency procedures. Some of these you've had experience with, and others are classified. She understands she is not to discuss these outside this building. This may end up being a bust, but you never know what might be said. It must be an important meeting for the big guys to be gathered, and being at sea seems to indicate they want real privacy. Now we need to get lucky."

Nick nodded, but a slight frown crossed his face.

"I know what you're thinking, Nick, and we have a strong backup plan in place. I emphasized her safety is first priority. She's smart and comes across as resourceful. She's not the type to do anything foolish."

"I know, sir. I have confidence in her."

"You'll be pleased to learn Ohlendorf positively ID'd Lyubov. It took some arm twisting to get WITSEC to go to his location, but we were vindicated with the result. We've now got enough to pick Lyubov up. I have a meeting scheduled this afternoon with Tankersley to plan the operation, and I want you there. I'm sure you'd like to be out in the field as a part of taking him down."

Nick's eyes widened, and he burst out, "Seriously? I can do that?"

"You've earned this, Nick. Harvey agrees. Three this afternoon. See you then."

When Nick had gone, Scott leaned back in his chair and allowed himself a smile, remembering his earlier days in the bureau when he had the same fire in the belly as Nick. A little taste of action in the field was a just reward for all the tedious work Nick had done without complaint.

Freddie Wilmington had spent the morning deciding how he would leak the information about Travis Dustin. When he was ready, he called Tony, who approved. Using the same burner cell, he contacted the sports editor of *The Daily News*, and was pleased when he was put into voicemail, whispering just enough to be heard.

"You don't know me personally. I'm an assistant coach in the league. Officially, Travis Dustin's death was listed as a suicide. That's not what happened. He was murdered to keep him quiet. I've seen visible proof that NYPD hasn't been given. Dustin was being blackmailed into altering his play to change the outcomes of selected games, to influence the standings. Look at his play this year compared to last at critical points in some games. Not the same guy. Notice what happened to the standings after those games. He had a change of heart, told them he would no longer do it, and he paid the price. Find out who 'them' are."

Wilmington was pleased with his statement, and knowing the sports editor's reputation, this would be a bombshell revelation he couldn't ignore.

===

The sports editor nearly fell off his chair when he reviewed his voicemail. He often received quirky phone tips, but this one had an air of authenticity he couldn't ignore. He had covered Dustin during his career and believed the official report on his death was too quick and neat. He also knew a decision on this was above his pay grade, so he made a recording of it and immediately called the managing editor for advice. After reviewing it and a brief discussion, a strategy was determined on how to handle it; they would publish the information in the next day's edition and begin their own investigation. They could hardly believe what had been dropped in their lap.

Tony was on his way home when he got a call back from Brad.

"Hey, Tony, got some more big news. My team hit pay dirt with Travis's college days."

"What did they come up with?" said an excited Tony as he unwrapped another stick of gum.

"Using official school ID photos and social media, we were able to find out more about that other student, Michael Taranto, who Tina Bishop had also helped. His father's name is Vincent, and he had been associated with the mob in New Jersey in the past. There are several pictures on Facebook of Michael with his family. Tony, Vincent Taranto is clearly the same guy on the CCTV tapes from the Top of the Town."

Tony whistled and said, "Let me guess. He's also on the tapes from Dustin's condo."

"Very likely. Body type's the same. We're stretched pretty thin right now, Tony, but we'll follow him as much as we can and hope something turns up."

"More dots being connected, Brad. Just gotta find the Big Kahuna."

"We keep plugging away, Tony. That's all we can do."

Tony once again thanked Brad and continued his commute home, leaving the radio off, lost in his thoughts.

———

Tankersley was standing at a whiteboard in Thompson's office when Nick arrived. He stopped writing on the board and said to Nick, "I told Scott that we picked up a conversation between Lyubov and Townsend about Ohlendorf. They are very confused and concerned about his disappearance."

Nick beamed and turned to his boss. Thompson said, "Don't look so happy, Nick. We don't want them to go underground because of this. We've got a warrant to pick up Lyubov on blackmail and extortion charges, and we've got a strong enough preliminary case that he will be considered a major flight risk and held without bail for a while. Harvey has come up with a good plan, which I approve. Lyubov is unlikely to go quietly, so our SWAT team will be there with you. I've got to finish the paperwork for this operation, so I'll have you guys go down to Harvey's office to finalize the details. Good luck, gentlemen. Be careful with this guy. Remember his background."

Nick and Harvey spent the next two hours reviewing all aspects of the plan, and afterward Nick spent another hour checking all his personal equipment and weapons. He double-checked everything until he was certain he was ready. The same anticipatory high that he experienced before his second Cayman trip began to form. He had waited a long time for this opportunity, and it was finally here.

———

Nick and Gena had a quiet night at home, both subdued during dinner. Afterward Gena put the finishing touches on the program she would present for the league officials that weekend. A distracted Nick had not told Gena anything about his upcoming mission, and they awkwardly avoided speaking about hers. They turned in early and snuggled in bed until a profound passion engulfed them, and their concealed thoughts and emotions were unveiled in rapturous lovemaking. Completely consumed, they fell blissfully into deep, peaceful sleep.

Nick was awakened early by his watch alarm, not disturbing Gena. He silently exited their apartment, but not before kissing his princess and leaving a note on her night table.

CHAPTER FORTY-FOUR

The Daily News published the Travis Dustin leak in their Thursday edition with a headline across the top of the front page leading to the main article in the sports section. It was a small, brief article, complete with Dustin's picture, but its impact was out of proportion to its size. The reaction was widespread and immediate, creating a buzz among New Yorkers usually reserved for higher profile news. In the age of instant information, the effect was not so much like the ripples after a pebble is thrown into water but more like tsunami waves after an underwater earthquake. The New York Pride and the Columbus Colonels, due to play Sunday, soon found out, and then word spread rapidly throughout the league. Nowhere was the news more explosive than at league headquarters where Commissioner O'Brien summoned Phil Townsend.

Arriving at the commissioner's office, Townsend found his boss to be just barely in control. O'Brien's normally steady demeanor was replaced by frenetic pacing alternating with staring out over the city skyline. As soon as Kate closed the door, O'Brien stomped toward Townsend with balled fists, the veins on his forehead prominent, stopping a foot away.

Towering over him, he screamed, "How the hell did this happen, Phil? You told me it was taken care of." The volume through clenched teeth was so loud that Kate in the hallway flinched.

"Settle down, Jimmy. The whole floor probably heard that." Townsend's tone was even, almost soothing, totally in control, but his blue eyes shot O'Brien a warning look that had its desired effect. O'Brien stormed over to his liquor cabinet and poured a quick shot of Laphroig, not bothering to offer one to Townsend. Returning to the expansive window, he downed it, took a deep breath, and turned back to Townsend.

"So, what is your plan to solve this now?" he said, control reestablished, embarrassed he had lost it in front of Townsend.

"It will be taken care of *permanently* this time. Stravnicki's behind this somehow. Sour grapes for not getting the defensive coordinator's job. I was too soft on him last time. That won't happen again. The paper can do all the investigating they want but will find nothing. The report of visible proof is bullshit. When that comes up empty, the *News* investigation will go away. And they'll look like fools."

"You fucking better be right, Townsend. We'll talk about it this weekend." O'Brien turned back to the window, nothing more to say, trying to maintain some measure of command. Townsend walked out, a telling smirk on his face.

———

It had been a fun and uneventful time for Maggie and the kids, and she was glad for the break from all the drama. The only downside was poor cell service, and by Thursday night she had been unable to contact Tony. She was anxious because of this and decided that tomorrow she would take the kids into town for dinner, where cell service was normal.

The kids were already sound asleep, worn out from their day, and at nine Maggie decided to have a small glass of wine, then call it an early night. She had just shut off the light and was passing through the kitchen when she saw a brief shadow cast across a partially lit section of the driveway. She thought she had imagined it until she saw one again, now outlined on the van.

She gasped as an electric shock ran up her spine, and momentarily froze before reacting as Brad had trained her. He had emphasized having her weapon always loaded and close by. It would have been difficult to do this and keep the weapon away from the children, but Brad had provided an innocent-looking, hollowed-out book for this purpose. She quickly retrieved it, flipped off the safety, and assumed a shooter's stance in a prepared position facing the door, the only entrance from the outside. *I will not be the victim this time!*

Less than a minute later, the door slowly opened, the lock having been picked. The dim light over the stove was the only illumination, but it was enough. Maggie could see the outline of a long-barreled handgun first, followed by a black-clad figure wearing night vision equipment. He located Maggie, aimed the weapon, and stated, "This is for your hus—"

He didn't complete the thought as Maggie fired twice, and he was hit in the right thigh, dropping the weapon. As taught, Maggie fired twice more, directly into his ballistic vest, propelling him back into the doorframe, knocking him out. She rapidly turned on the kitchen light, picked up his weapon while keeping her automatic trained on him, and tore off his balaclava. His square, tanned face seemed familiar to her. As she was trying to remember, a man ran up onto the porch, shotgun in hand, shouting, "Maggie, Maggie are you alright?" It was George, the next-door neighbor, who had known Maggie for years.

George guarded the assailant while Maggie took the kids to his house, using the landline to call the police. They arrested the man and sent him to a regional trauma center for his wounds. George returned and invited them to spend the night there, which Maggie quickly accepted. He praised Maggie's strength and calm, and they fondly recalled their memories of the gap-toothed, freckle-faced girl she had been long ago. Having had enough excitement for the night, he went to bed, and Maggie, with the aid of a second glass of wine, called Tony.

A phone call after eleven at night was rarely good news, and Tony's mind raced faster than his pounding heart as he answered it. Given the hour, he was perplexed at the conversational tone of Maggie's voice.

"First of all, the kids and I are okay. But I need to tell you about something that happened tonight." She described in detail the evening's events, a shaken Tony not interrupting. "You're probably a target too, so be ready. Brad trained us well, Tony. Just be on the lookout."

"Not again, Maggie. I'm so sorry." His voice was a whisper, despondent.

"I was ready this time, Tony. You and Brad made sure of that for me, and for the kids. I wasn't going to be a victim again."

"What a night . . . I am so proud of you. Thank God for Brad. I'll be watchful, for sure. I think it's best you and the kids stay up there a couple more days."

"Yes, I agree. The police are going to patrol more, and George is close by. Despite what happened tonight, I think it is safer than home, and the kids love it, so we'll stay until Saturday."

They talked about the weekend, then ended the conversation. Tony was alone with his thoughts, once again in awe of his amazing wife.

―――――――

Scott Thompson was more alarmed than mad. The release of the Dustin story by *The Daily News* had the potential to screw up the bureau's operation, putting his people in danger or causing the bad guys to go underground. It was now apparent that they must accelerate their plans and pick up Lyubov now. It had been planned to take him when he exited his building, but Scott contacted Tankersley and approved an immediate breach of Lyubov's apartment, using the SWAT team on standby.

The apartment had been on continuous surveillance, and they saw him enter and were certain he had not left. A six-man SWAT team would gain entry while other agents provided backup. Nick and Harvey were overseeing the operation.

The front door crashed open from the effect of small explosives on the locks and hinges. The team stormed in, highly trained in breaching and close-quarters combat tactics.

"FBI, Pavel Lyubov, you're under arrest." No immediate resistance was encountered, so the team methodically went room to room, calling, "Clear" multiple times until all rooms were searched. Nick and Harvey, close behind with ballistic vests on and weapons drawn, were astonished when the team leader came to them, saying, "We've got a dry hole. I thought you had complete surveillance on him?"

An incredulous Nick just looked at Harvey. "That's impossible. He's got to be hiding somewhere. Check again."

The team leader looked at Nick, cocking his head to the side. "This isn't our first rodeo, Agent. Look for yourself," he sneered. Quickly going through each room verified that Lyubov was not there. There was no fire escape, and all windows were closed and locked from the inside. The apartment was modest, with basic furnishings and no weapons or useful evidence found. Harvey went back to the team leader, who had a disgusted look on his face. "I tell you our look was tight. We didn't miss him."

"Then where the fuck is he? He Houdini or something? We're outta here," the SWAT commander barked.

"Something isn't right here. I'm going to have a team rip this place apart. He had to have a way out," said Harvey. The leader just shook his head wordlessly and departed with his team. A dejected Nick wandered around, not believing what had happened. Smoke from the flash-bang stun grenades still hung heavy in the air. He looked everywhere, unsure what he was hoping to find.

In a rear bedroom closet he found a small three-drawer bureau, about half the width of the closet. It contained a few shirts and pants, nothing remarkable. Nick leaned against it, gathering his thoughts, and was surprised that it seemed strangely solid for its size. He tried to move it, but it wouldn't budge. "Harvey, come here, I've found something weird."

He came running.

"Try to move this bureau, will you?" It wouldn't move for him either.

He gave Nick a startled look and then reached for the microphone of his radio. "Strike Team Leader, this is Tankersley. I have a situation here. I want your team to immediately breach the units directly below this one and the adjacent unit. Strong suspicion of a hidden escape route. My responsibility for this call. Acknowledge."

"Copy that. Your call. Will do." No sarcasm, just professionalism.

Harvey turned back to Nick. "This bureau's probably part of an escape hatch to the unit below it. I've seen something like it before in a drug bust we did. Let's get downstairs."

They arrived just as the assault team gained entry, but once again, no one was there. But this time things were different. They discovered an ingenious system where the bureau upstairs could be retracted into the adjacent unit, exposing an opening with a ladder leading to the lower unit. Here they found a large cache of weapons and money. A console of sophisticated video surveillance equipment linked to cameras in the neighborhood and in the building, with a bank of radio scanners, filled a small room. But most chilling was extensive material for disguises, including makeup and wigs and a closet full of uniforms.

"Shit, he knew we were coming and had plenty of time to change his appearance and bug out. He might have gone out right under our noses," said Harvey.

The SWAT team leader overheard this and came up to him. "Don't blame yourself. This is the most sophisticated setup I've ever seen. You couldn't have known. I apologize."

Harvey just nodded and murmured, "Thanks."

Nick was processing the whole thing, his mind churning with possibilities. Scott had briefed them on the *Daily News* article and how it might trigger a response from Lyubov. Something about the article was bugging Nick. It had mentioned the source as an assistant coach. Tony's team was in town for a game and were having a walk-through today. *Tony?* A chill ran down his spine. Tony was the target! He didn't know how Tony knew about the Dustin videos, but that was not important now. Time was critical, and Lyubov had a lead.

"Harvey, we've got to leave. I'll explain it on the way, just trust me. You drive. I've got phone calls to make."

———

Pavel Lyubov got the call from Townsend soon after he had left the commissioner's office, outlining what must be done and that failure was unacceptable. Lyubov jumped into action, having been monitoring the actions of the FBI with the equipment Townsend had provided.

Townsend had set up the escape route into the lower unit as well as providing everything else—the weapons, cash, and items involved with changing one's appearance. He had trained Lyubov well, and with his Spetsnaz experience, he was prepared for anything.

With confidence developed from practice, Lyubov had taken on a different look. He cut his hair to a flattop, dyed it blond, thinned his eyebrows, and a bulked up his nose. But his crowning achievement was to mask his facial scar. He donned a Con Ed uniform over his ballistic vest, with matching baseball cap pulled low, and loaded a specially made toolbox marked *Con Ed* with his Heckler & Koch MP7 submachine gun and extra magazines. Also armed with a Smith and Wesson nine-millimeter pistol and a Fairbairn-Sykes commando knife, he was determined to have a better outcome than his last mission.

He was able to slip out of the apartment building by a practiced route down to the electrical room in the basement and out a side door. He had used his surveillance equipment to find blind spots in the FBI coverage, so it was easy to get to his Con Ed van three blocks away.

———

As Harvey drove, Nick tried repeatedly to reach his uncle but was unsuccessful. He did reach Scott and quickly apprised him of the situation. Harvey contacted the SWAT team and local police near the Meadowlands, requesting immediate backup there, but he and Nick would arrive before either of them. Pulling up to the parking area closest to the team entrance to the stadium, Nick was surprised by the number of cars there. This could pose a marked security problem, giving Lyubov options for cover and concealment, and would take critical time to sweep and establish a perimeter.

As he quickly scanned the area after exiting the vehicle, nothing seemed unusual or out of place. The only person Nick noticed was a Con Ed employee near an official van, two rows of vehicles ahead of him. Harvey was to Nick's right and said something about a needle in a haystack, but the remark was lost on Nick.

Remembering the cache of disguises and clothes they had discovered at the apartment, Nick drew his weapon, turned to Harvey, and whispered, "Harvey, that Con Ed guy two rows ahead. He's the same height and build as Lyubov, and the uniform was used at Dustin's murder. Let's check him out."

Harvey drew his weapon, nodding that he understood. They slowly worked their way one row forward and had a clear view of the utility man, who was holding a Con Ed toolbox and was heading toward the entrance. Nick stood up, leveled his weapon, and announced, "FBI. Drop the box and turn around."

In one lightning-quick, fluid motion, Lyubov flung himself to his right, finding cover behind a small sedan, and with practiced speed, he opened the box and had the MP7 ready. Nick had moved three steps forward immediately after his command, amazed at how fast his target reacted. Peering around a vehicle, he saw nothing, so he rose slightly in a crouch and continued cautiously. When Nick became visible, Lyubov fired a burst, then ducked and moved two cars to his right.

Only one step into the open, Nick felt a hammer-like blow to his left arm and a searing pain. The simultaneous sound of rounds impacting metal registered in his mind that he had been hit by an automatic weapon. Slumping to the ground, he was confused at the size of the red pool beneath his arm. His weapon still in his right hand, Nick's last conscious thought was the need to protect himself, and he tried to sit up, but his body wouldn't respond to his brain's command.

Fifteen feet away when Nick issued his command, Harvey too was amazed at the reaction speed of their suspect. Unlike Nick, Harvey held his position, so when Lyubov fired off his burst, Harvey returned fire, in two 2-round sequences. He thought he saw the man go down, and when he ducked and looked toward Nick's location, he didn't see his partner. As he closed the distance to Nick's last position, he was aware of no further gunfire and did not see Nick anywhere.

Rounding a vehicle, he saw Nick's slumped body, blood pumping from his arm, terminating in a large puddle. Recognizing an arterial bleed, Harvey quickly scanned for threats, then crouched down and retrieved his combat tourniquet with one hand. He held the tourniquet and weapon with one hand while taking Nick's carotid pulse with the other. Miraculously, it was present but very weak. Harvey placed the device and turned the windlass until he could no longer feel Nick's radial pulse. Scanning the area once again and finding nothing, he called for immediate medical assistance, describing the situation. The SWAT team leader came on frequency, and Harvey gave a terse briefing. They were two minutes out.

The SWAT team, local police, and medical help came within minutes while Tankersley provided security and checked the still unconscious Nick. His pulse was weak but steady, a good sign, as bleeding had decreased significantly. The teams of officers secured the perimeter and worked their way to Nick and Harvey, and soon the ambulance came and began IV replacement fluids before departing for the hospital. They told Harvey it would be close.

The SWAT team located Lyubov's last location and found a blood trail leading toward the stadium. Proceeding cautiously, they hadn't gone far when Lyubov rose up, letting loose a sustained burst of fire, wildly inaccurate compared to earlier. A SWAT overwatch sniper team, positioned high in the stadium, put two rounds in his left leg, taking him down. They had been on orders to use lethal force only as a last resort. The men subdued the wounded suspect, confiscating all weapons and body armor. Harvey's fire had grazed the left side of the Russian's neck and shot off part of his left ear. Harvey arrived as he was being handcuffed and used wet gauze on the left side of Lyubov's face, removing the makeup and revealing his signature scar. He said a silent prayer that Nick would live to learn his hunch had been right.

———————

Inside the stadium, Tony was busy with the walk-through when he heard gunfire close by. Not having his cell phone, he was out of contact and unaware of the events happening. The team quickly sheltered in place in an internal corridor until given an "all clear" by an FBI agent. Tony approached him, identified himself, and stated that he had a nephew in the local office of the bureau. The agent asked his name, and when Tony mentioned Nick, the agent blanched and told Tony he needed to speak with the senior agent in charge.

A jolt of adrenaline shot through Tony, and a lump in his throat almost caused him to vomit. He frantically ran to find the agent in charge, who only stated that Nick had been wounded, stabilized on scene, and transported to the hospital. *Nick's been hurt, maybe even killed! This has got to be linked to me. What have I done?* Distraught with grief, Tony left for the hospital, not even thinking about the team.

CHAPTER FORTY-FIVE

Thirteen hundred miles away, Gena was oblivious to the plight of her fiancé. Deplaning from the sleek private jet in Miami with Teri Johnstone, they were whisked by limousine to a suite in an exclusive beachfront hotel. They were scheduled to meet the next day with the cheerleaders from the Miami Waves and then board Bill Macafee's yacht, *Nirvana*.

The bond between Gena and Teri continued to grow, and conversation touched on many things yet was devoid of work-related topics. Teri spoke very little about her husband and more about Commissioner O'Brien, leading Gena to wonder if there was more to the relationship. She had found Paul Johnstone to be very reserved compared to the charismatic O'Brien, who seemed a better match for Teri's bubbly personality.

Friday passed quickly, with Gena restless and bored with her cheerleading consulting. She was excited to begin her mission on the yacht, hopeful that she could contribute even more than earlier. Her participation was much more involved this time, with a higher degree of risk. Her training, while limited, had stressed her safety, and she felt confident in the backup plans should they become necessary. Scott had insisted she activate these plans at the first sign of trouble, briefing Gena on the possible ruthless nature of these men.

They got to the *Nirvana* just after five, and Gena's eyes reflected her awe. She had seen much in her modeling career but nothing like this! Bill Macafee was waiting on deck to greet them with champagne and a kiss on the cheek for her and Teri.

"Welcome, ladies, to my home away from home. Let me give you a tour."

Nirvana was a fine lady, with long sleek lines, and she projected a powerful image, one to rival its owner. At almost 170 feet long and 32 feet in width, she was a magnificent sight.

"She was built in Holland three years ago. We can cruise at fifteen knots, which is pretty good, and we have a range of forty-two hundred nautical miles." They followed him forward, rounded the bow beneath the bridge, and headed aft on the main deck. They reached a large open area with sliding glass panels, which gave the option of enclosing the space against weather and offered multiple comfortable seats and small tables. "This area can be configured for either business or entertainment and will be where you will make your presentation tomorrow, Gena." Gena took in everything as she made mental notes on possible places to position her bugs. "Make yourselves comfortable, and join me on deck when you please."

"Bill, may I come in here again later, so I will know how to set up for tomorrow?" Gena asked.

"Of course. I'll have an attendant meet you here in a half hour to review how it will be set up."

"That's great. Thank you."

Teri turned to Gena and said, "Mind if I skip that, Gena? I'm pretty tired and feel a headache beginning, so I'd like to lay down for a while."

"Oh, I'm sorry to hear that. Of course. I can check it out with the attendant. Hope you feel better."

"Me too. A little rest will probably do it. I want to be good when everyone else comes on board later," Teri said as they each headed to their separate cabins. Once inside, and after being sure her door was locked, Gena examined all her equipment, making certain that everything worked. She had several devices to use, all disguised as ordinary-looking items: an iPhone charger, a bottle of suntan lotion, a pair of sunglasses, an earring, three pens, and an official-looking Austin Agency binder. Their capabilities were varied, and they were designed for redundancy so that they could be used simultaneously, transmitting their signals to her cabin. Here they were received by a cell phone identical to her real phone except this one retransmitted the signals via encrypted burst transmissions to a satellite and from there to the bureau. All devices were supposed to be undetectable, minimizing her risk.

She left her room with only some of them, intending to try to place some now and others tomorrow. Counting on the fact that the high-level meeting of the NAFL executives was supposed to meet right after her presentation, in the same location, any of her seemingly innocent devices should capture what was said and by whom.

She made her way to the meeting area where the attendant was waiting. He had a mobile podium set up with complete audiovisual capabilities, which he reviewed with her. Once she was alone, Gena practiced her presentation while moving around the room, placing three of her devices. Pleased that she had been undetected, she returned to her cabin to prepare for the evening.

All guests were on board by seven, and the *Nirvana* cast off, leaving the stunning sight of the Miami skyline behind. Drinks were in a luxurious bar area followed by dinner in the formal dining room. Gena was seated between the commissioner and Phil Townsend, with Teri and Paul at the far end of the table.

Macafee sat across from her. "Well, Gena, what do you think of *Nirvana?*"

"Its name is fitting, Bill. Spending time on her is certainly peaceful."

"It usually can be, except for those times we have a meeting." He laughed. "Not always peaceful then!"

O'Brien chuckled, but Townsend said nothing, giving Macafee a disparaging look. Gena remembered her previous encounter with Townsend and vowed to avoid him as much as possible this trip.

Sitting next to him didn't help. She was just trying to figure out how to leave when Teri come to her rescue.

"How about a nightcap up forward, Gena? I want to make it an early night."

"A drink under the stars with this relaxing breeze. This *is* nirvana."

O'Brien and Macafee laughed and rose, bidding the ladies good night. Townsend didn't move a muscle.

The two ladies enjoyed their drinks, engaging in conversation centered on the traveling they had done. After a while, a chilly breeze picked up, so they decided to call it a night. Soon after Gena had retired to her cabin, there was a knock on the door. Thinking it was Teri, she quickly opened the door only to find Phil Townsend standing there with some type of electronic device in his hand.

"I'm going to do a check of your room and electronics. Give me your cell phone." It was not a request, and he brushed past her before she could answer, making a circuit of the room, waving the device around. "And the phone . . . " She opened her handbag and removed her real cell phone, handing it to him.

"Unlock it," he commanded, which she did. He circled his device around the phone, expressionless and silent. The device made a buzzing sound, and she worried what that signified.

"Once again I will remind you of our confidentiality policy. In addition, after your presentation tomorrow, you must leave the aft area and stay in your cabin or forward of the bridge until informed otherwise," he said curtly and slammed the door.

The encounter left Gena annoyed rather than shaken, sick of his bullying tactics.

CHAPTER FORTY-SIX

Gena's presentation was scheduled for ten in the morning, and she had been allotted one hour to present and answer any questions. Five men were there, all members of the Committee, and all except Townsend greeted her warmly. He just gave her an unsettling stare but said nothing. Gena smiled back at him with a "Good morning, Phil," and set up her materials, placing one of the pens and the binder on a shelf in the podium.

Her presentation and recommendations were well received, and they asked several pertinent questions. Preparing to leave, she waited for her opportunity, and when they were all momentarily turned away from her, she dropped an earring in an inconspicuous corner of the floor. She left her sunglasses on a small side table and the bottle of suntan lotion in a built-in shelf. As instructed by Townsend, she departed the meeting area.

Five minutes later Townsend walked the perimeter of the area, making sure their meeting would be private. It bothered him that his equipment had registered something in Gena's room, even though it was far below a normal level of significance. Unfortunately, O'Brien called the meeting to order before he could check the area electronically.

"We have some really important developments to discuss today, in addition to our regular update. Bill, you go first, followed by Paul."

Macafee took about ten minutes to present his reports on the business aspects of the league, emphasizing the enormous success the league was experiencing. He went into detail on the success of the letter companies, the Cayman shell companies, and how all this affected them financially.

Next, Johnstone and St. George together reviewed the increase in media response the tight team standings had generated and confirmed their success with various contracts. O'Brien thanked them and then turned his attention to his security chief.

"Phil, I know I speak for us all when I say we were blindsided by the *Daily News* story," he said, a slight edge to his voice but radically different than the other day. "What's going on?"

"It's a fishing expedition. Nothing can come of it. A brazen attempt to discredit the league from an assistant coach who got passed over for a promotion. The *News* investigation won't find anything because there's nothing to find and the story will die. That assistant coach won't be making any more problems for us," he said.

"How can you be certain?" asked Johnstone.

"Because I was personally involved. I know what happened because I fixed it. My best associate has taken care of him."

"Taken care of him? What does that mean?" shot back Johnstone.

"This isn't the Boy Scouts, Johnstone. What do you think it means!"

Johnstone glowered at him but said nothing further.

Macafee spoke next. "On a different subject, but still under your purview, I understand one of our officials has gone missing. No one can contact him. Just fell off the face of the earth. Is he one of the people you've used, Phil?"

Phil Townsend looked uncomfortable, a rare event. Taking a deep breath he responded, "Yes. He's one we've used. Always did what we told him. But I wouldn't be too concerned about him. He's got a lot of problems, been a heavy drinker and gambler, has family issues. He's probably on a bender somewhere. I'll locate him with resources no one else has." His attempt to make light of this did not go over well.

Anthony St. George, silent up to this point, spoke next. Looking alternately at Townsend and O'Brien he said, "It appears to me things are unraveling. We have a ref who's influenced games for us disappearing and a bombshell report on a dead player who had done the same. We have considerable risk as it is with the Cayman situation. Where are all the safeguards you and Bill talked about?"

Townsend's anger was simmering just below the surface, and O'Brien recognized the potential explosion. Turning to Macafee, he attempted to take the pressure off Townsend. "Have there been issues coming out of the Caymans, Bill?"

"None that I'm aware of. I'm confident in how I set them up. They can't be traced back to us," he said, and he looked over at Townsend.

"No. Quiet there. Everything's been normal," Townsend lied. Looking from man to man with an intimidating glare, he continued, "You all happy with your money? Like the *Nirvana*, Bill? Pleased with that new house in Aspen, Tom? Those fancy trips to the Pacific keeping Teri happy, Paul? You all knew there would be some degrees of risk involved. So don't play high and mighty with me. Let me do my job as only *I* can. I remind you again, we're all in this together!"

"Yes, we're all pleased with the money, Phil," said O'Brien. "But it's also time to dial it back, let things cool down a bit. Suspend your work about influencing games and concentrate on solving these two problems now. Is that clear?"

Townsend nodded his agreement, his face red, teeth clenched. One by one the others voiced their approval of that course of action. O'Brien then declared, "Let's take a break. Good time for a drink."

CHAPTER FORTY-SEVEN

Four men hurried to the bar, but Townsend held back, pacing, seething at the scolding he had just received. As he made his rounds, he noticed the pens and binder on the podium and the bottle of suntan lotion. All seemed conspicuously out of place, as Macafee was an obsessive compulsive who insisted on absolute neatness. He then realized that these items were Gena's, and it caused him a momentary start; he had not swept this aft area just before the meeting.

Reaching into his bag, he retrieved equipment and began to check those items. They all seemed innocuous enough, but when he reached an iPhone charger plugged into an outlet, his device registered something. Not a conclusive reading, but not normal either. He raced to Gena's cabin, pounding on the door, getting no response. Traveling forward to the open bow area, he found Gena and Teri sunbathing, the stunning pair in their Versace and Saint Laurent bikinis.

"Gena, come with me *right now*. There's an issue we need to discuss."

Gena tried to play it cool but was alarmed by his tone.

"What's this all about, Phil? You can't be ordering her around," Teri exclaimed.

"Stay out of this, Teri. I'm well within my authority."

"It's okay, Teri. I've nothing to hide, and besides, I've had enough sun for now." She put on her matching cover-up. Townsend began to head toward the cabins, making sure Gena was following. He turned and had her go first.

"We're going to your cabin."

Saying nothing, she forced herself to saunter, trying to portray an air of confidence she no longer had. Reaching her cabin, she opened it and, turning toward Townsend, said, "Going to check my cabin with your gizmo again?" He gave her a rough shove through the doorway and pushed her onto the bed. "Hey, what—" she began but her words were silenced with a sharp backhand across her face.

"Shut up." He quickly scanned the room, his device again indicating unusual readings, this time higher than on the aft deck. He failed to notice as she took the transmitter cell phone off the nightstand and quickly hit the "home" button three times, the emergency signal, before hiding it behind a pillow. He turned toward her.

"Who do—" Again another backhand, harder than the first, sent her backwards, her head striking the headboard, stunning her.

With practiced skill, he produced a Taser and gave her a jolt, her body jerking into submissiveness. Producing rope, he tied her arms and legs to the bed in a wide V and bound her mouth with duct tape. From his bag he produced a syringe and vial, a flat rubber truncheon, and a surgical scalpel. She moaned slightly, the effects of the Taser wearing off. He went into the bathroom, returning with a large glass of cold water, and threw it on her face, reviving her.

"Now, this is how it's going to work. I'm going to ask questions, and you're going to tell me the truth, or things will go very badly for you. I don't know what you're up to, but I *will* find out. I've *never* failed," he sneered. "It's just a question of how much pain and disfigurement you want to go through first." He waited a few moments to let that sink in.

The horrified look in her eyes brought a smile to his face as he produced the blade and held it in front of her, terrorizing her even more. She struggled against her restraints to no avail. Grabbing the material of her cover-up, he cut it from neck to hem and ripped it off. "I can cut you so you'll never work in modeling again," he whispered. He moved around the room, holding the scalpel, her eyes following his every move.

"Who are you working for, and where is the receiver for your bugs?" He ripped the duct tape to the side.

"I work for the Austin Agency. You know that. Your office vetted me through them," she gasped.

"That's your cover, honey. Who really?"

"No one. I—"

He roughly pushed the tape back. He produced the rubber truncheon and gave her left thigh a hard, sharp whack.

She tried to scream, but the tape was too effective. Three more sharp slaps, alternating left then right thigh. The sickening sound resounded in the small room. More squirming and moaning. Bruising was already starting to show, sweat forming on her forehead, her breathing coming rapidly through flared nostrils.

"We've only just begun, sweetie. Far more to come. I can make it look like anything I want to: a nasty fall, or maybe you just slip over the side." He went over to the closet and came back with a small flat iron, plugging it in.

"Ready yet? Who?" he asked, bending over her, his voice a whisper, his eyes cold, devoid of emotion. He ripped the tape off again.

"Austin Agency, you psychopath," she spat.

Enraged, he shoved the tape back and backhanded her across the face, splitting her nose. Blood poured across the tape, down her chin and throat, and trickled in between her breasts. He gazed at her nearly nude body, picking his next target while the iron heated.

He grabbed the flat iron and held the tip in three places: on her calf, the instep, and then the sole of each foot, the smell of burning flesh filling the air along with an intense but muffled scream. The pain overwhelming, her breathing grew increasingly labored, and she passed out.

Three miles away, just over the horizon, the Coast Guard Legend-class Maritime Security Cutter *Hamilton* headed toward the *Nirvana* at twenty-five knots. Five minutes earlier, a short-range Prosecutor rigid-hull inflatable had been launched from her stern ramp, carrying an eight-member maritime security response team, followed one minute later by an MH-65C Dolphin helicopter, with four additional members of the MSRT.

The MSRT teams and the boat and helo crews had been maintaining "hot alert" status and spun into action when given the go-ahead by the FBI's Special Agent Scott Thompson, after receipt of the emergency distress signal from Gena. The Dolphin would reach the *Nirvana* in approximately two minutes, with the Prosecutor arriving almost simultaneously and the cutter seven minutes later.

On the bow of the *Nirvana*, Teri Johnstone was stunned by what had just happened. She remained numb, paralyzed for a few minutes before summoning her courage and quickly dressing. She headed for Gena's cabin and, arriving there, heard low moaning sounds.

"Gena, Gena, are you alright? It's Teri. Let me in," she yelled, pounding on the door.

"Get the fuck out of here, Teri. Leave me alone if you know what's good for you," screamed Townsend. "You're not beyond my control!"

Teri, now beside herself with fear for her friend, hurried aft to get help from Jimmy. Townsend had gone too far this time. Frantic, focused on stopping Townsend, the whine of the approaching helo failed to register in her distraught mind.

Townsend became enraged at the interruption, throwing a coffee pot against the wall, turning back to his unconscious victim. Retrieving more cold water, he was so engrossed in his evil he failed to hear the now-hovering helo. "You will suffer until you tell me what I want. I'm in control here, not those idiots topside!"

Teri arrived at the aft area just as the helo arrived and was as startled as the four league executives when a commanding voice came from the chopper. "This is the Coast Guard. All of you lie down on the deck with your hands clasped on your heads." Simultaneously, four heavily armed MSRT members fast-roped from both sides of the helo and landed with M4 carbines leveled.

Teri lay down on the deck as commanded and yelled at one of the guardsmen, "Go to cabin number five. Hurry! There's a woman in danger." The team leader nodded to two of his colleagues, who headed below, leaving the stunned Committee prone on the deck. The Prosecutor arrived, and eight more men quickly boarded, fanning out across the ship and securing the crew, separating Teri from the others.

Once again revived by the cold water, Gena moaned behind the duct tape, the searing pain from her burns engulfing her.

"Last chance before I rearrange your face and have my way with you." He pulled the tape off while simultaneously cutting through her bra and making a deep incision. Gena screamed loudly, bleeding heavily from the fresh wound.

"Talk, you bitch."

The door exploded with a loud bang as the two guardsmen crashed through, the first one firing two shots, hitting Townsend in the right arm and shoulder, causing him to crash to the floor, dropping the blade. The guardsman roughly rolled a screaming Townsend over and handcuffed him while the other rushed to Gena's aid, expertly placing a combat gauze containing the hemostatic agent TXA to staunch the bleeding. He cut Gena's bonds and covered her up as best as possible, making certain the bleeding had stopped. Only then did he turn his attention to Townsend and provide medical help. He radioed the approaching cutter that medical services and evacuation would be needed.

On the aft deck, the four members of the Committee had been handcuffed and forced to kneel. The *Hamilton* came alongside, moored to the *Nirvana*, and Thompson and two other FBI agents boarded her. He immediately went looking for Gena, while they stayed aft. One of the MSRT guys showed him to her cabin, where Thompson was appalled at what he saw. The medic gently moved the covering from her legs: Thompson saw the large purple bruises, the ugly red burns, and the blood staining the cover by her breasts.

"She's one tough lady, sir," the medic said to Scott. "I've given her something for the pain."

He knelt beside her and gently took her hand.

"Oh, Gena, I'm so sorry. I never thought something like this would happen."

"Did you get them? Did I do good?" she gasped.

"You did outstanding. We got 'em. They'll be going away for a long time. These guys are going to take good care of you now. We'll talk later."

He took a quick look at the handcuffed guy and was disgusted but not surprised to see it was Townsend, who was badly injured but would survive. He then hurried aft to confront the cabal of football executives.

"You have no right to board us. We haven't done anything and are in international waters," Macafee fumed when Thompson returned.

"Do you know who I am?" O'Brien yelled. "You can't treat Big Jimmy O'Brien like this! I'm going to sue your ass off. You'll be counting paper clips in Alaska when I'm done with you!"

A smiling Scott Thompson slowly walked up to the four kneeling men. "You are all under arrest for extortion, blackmail, money laundering, wire fraud, murder, and conspiracy to commit murder, to start," he said. "We're not in international waters, genius. By the way, it wouldn't matter if we were, *Big Jimmy*. Tommy, read 'em their rights and get 'em out of here. The United States government will provide accommodations for you, but probably not up to par with this," he said, taking in the *Nirvana*. They were stood up, all quiet and sullen now, and transferred to the *Hamilton* for transport back to Miami.

Gena and Townsend were stabilized and then flown by helicopter to a hospital on the mainland. Thompson was lost in thought as he toured the mega yacht, which was being thoroughly searched. The mission was a success, but the cost had been perilously high.

CHAPTER FORTY-EIGHT

A gentle touch, usually calming, registered in Gena's brain, but something wasn't right. The memory of terror, pain, and the unknown invaded her psyche like a swarm of angry bees whose hive has been disturbed. "No, stop!" she thought she heard herself scream, but then she remembered the tape muffling her anguish. Thrashing wildly in the bed, the horror once again replayed. But now her constraints were not harsh rope biting into her flesh. Something softer was on her wrists and ankles, and something was in her nose and arm.

"Shh, shh, my love. I've got you. You're safe. I've got you."

A tender hand grasped hers, a gentle kiss settled on her cheek. Another hand softly stroked her hair. "Gena, Gena, darling. Wake up."

Her eyes slowly opened, struggling to focus, the voice reassuring and loving, not harsh and menacing. Like a vessel coming out of a fog bank into sunshine, her mind finally registered the smiling face of her lover. "Nick, Nick," she cried, tears no longer of pain but of joy, streaming down her face, her arms attempting to touch him.

He released her left arm from its restraint followed by the right, allowing them to embrace. "You were struggling in your sleep, Gena, having terrible nightmares."

She nodded, sitting up slightly, and only then noticed that his left arm was wrapped from shoulder to wrist, with his own IV line connected to a bag on a pole.

"Nick. You were hurt too? What happened? Are you alright?" she said, the tone of her voice distressed, confused.

"I'm fine, hon. Nothing major. I just forgot to duck," he said with a small smile.

"You were shot? Oh my God!"

"I'm okay, Gena, really. We can talk about it later. You've got to get your rest."

She settled back into the bed, and he held her tenderly as best he could until she fell asleep, then returned to his bed next to hers. Once deemed stable, Nick had insisted on being transferred to the same Miami hospital as Gena, and the bureau flew him down on a special medical flight. He had only been told a few details of her injuries, but it was apparent she had been through hell. His prayers for Gena had been answered.

He had been told the seriousness of his wound and that Harvey had saved his life. It had been so close for both, but they would still have their tomorrows.

———————

That afternoon, Scott Thompson came by to see them, bringing flowers for Gena and a bottle of Nick's favorite beverage. Gena was still quiet from being lightly sedated. Nick peppered Scott with questions. He had turned on the television news, which was all abuzz with a breaking story, details not yet available, about a scandal involving top executives of the NAFL, including the commissioner. Nick demanded to be briefed.

"Nick, things are happening quickly, and this is not the time nor place to explain. I understand you are being released in a couple days and hopefully Gena a few days later. You damn near died, and they want you to rest for two weeks, which I know isn't going to happen. I'm ordering you to rest. We'll get you and Gena home and settled, and then you can come in. I'll bring you totally up to speed. I need your help to wrap this whole thing up . . . but only on limited hours. I don't want to hear another word," he said, only somewhat sternly, heading for the door.

"Boss?" said Nick.

Thompson turned, expecting an argument.

"Thank you for rescuing Gena. And thank Harvey for me," he said.

"I will, but you'll see Harvey soon enough. I'm awful sorry Gena went through all she did, Nick," he said through misty eyes, and left.

Two other visitors came later that afternoon, Tony and Maggie. Gena was much more alert by then and was thrilled to see them. They brought more flowers for her and candy for Nick. While Maggie effortlessly occupied Gena with family and local gossip, Tony and Nick initially were reserved, remembering all too well their last encounter.

After a short period of awkward silence, Nick spoke first. "Some big breaking news, eh, Tony?"

"Lots of rumors going 'round. Know anything about it?" he asked, eyebrows raised.

Looking directly at his uncle, Nick replied, "Yeah, I know a lot about it. But I'm missing a few details because, as you can see, I've been somewhat indisposed."

Tony showed a quick smile, but his face tightened into a frown, and his eyes darted around the room before settling on Nick. In a barely audible voice, Tony said, "I should have listened to you. It was because of me and my actions that you and Gena were hurt, almost killed. I'm so sorry, Nick. I can't forgive myself for that." Tony decided not to mention Maggie's latest attack and swallowed hard to control his emotions.

"Tony, don't blame yourself for this. The bad guys are responsible, not you. We have a lot to talk about. There's so much I couldn't tell you before; I hope to be able to soon. I hated to have to lie and deceive you, but I had no choice."

Tony nodded slowly. "You weren't the only one being deceptive, Nick, but I'll save that for our talk."

"We're good though, right, Uncle Tony?"

"We never weren't good, Nick," Tony said, understanding in his eyes, lightly punching his nephew's good right shoulder. "We need to let you guys rest. C'mon, Mags, let's give this couple some privacy."

"You'll hear from me soon, Tony." A wave from Tony and kisses from Maggie and they were gone.

———

Nick was released from the hospital two days later and Gena the next, and they were flown to New York City by FBI jet. Although both were exhausted from their ordeals, Nick was eager to learn the details of Gena's mission and help Thompson build the case against what he now knew as "the Committee."

At the bureau, Nick received a hero's welcome with many congratulations on his work on the case and wishes for a full recovery. Entering Thompson's office, he was elated to see Harvey already present. Their reunion was emotionally intense for both men. Harvey was his humble self, but there was now a bond for life between the two men. Thompson gave them their moment before beginning.

"We've got 'em, Nick. We've got 'em good. We have layers of evidence—so much that at least for now there is no bail for the five of them, as setting them free would constitute an unacceptable flight risk. We're working quickly to secure grand jury indictments. The press knows that they were arrested and are being detained, but that's all they know. The league is in a hot mess as we comb through their headquarters, and the next level of executives is scrambling to just keep things going." He paused and his voice softened. "I'll fill you in on Gena's mission, but Harvey wants to brief you first."

Nick looked at Harvey and said, "All I remember is Lyubov standing up in the parking lot. That's it."

Harvey reviewed the encounter and his use of the combat tourniquet, the FBI snipers taking Lyubov down, and his total refusal to cooperate. "He's a real hard case. We've got a lot on him, and once we present it all, he may change his tune."

"Speaking of tune, one of the Committee is already offering information in exchange for a reduction in charges or sentence," said

Scott. "Paul Johnstone claims he knows a lot. He's pissed because he suspected his wife was having an affair, hired a PI to follow her, and discovered she was seeing O'Brien at a condo not far from league headquarters. We won't cut any deals yet."

"I saw the report from my team, and it's solid. We should have no problem getting indictments for racketeering, fraud, and money laundering," offered Nick.

"Yes, your team did an outstanding job. Very impressive. I've received several compliments on it from the higher-ups."

Scott paused, Nick looking at him expectantly.

"Nick, what Gena got us *makes* this case. The audio is high quality and unprecedented for a rookie. The evidence is irrefutable, and they incriminated themselves about the letter and shell companies in the Caymans and their manipulating the outcome of games by extortion of officials and players. Gena couldn't have done any better, but she paid an awful price, Nick, and I apologize for that." Scott detailed the MSRT raid and how they got to Gena just in time, and he described what Gena had suffered at Townsend's hands and how tough she had been.

Nick paled when he heard this, but quickly recovered after a few moments of awkward silence. "I'm thankful you had such a strong backup plan, boss. You saved her for me," he whispered, almost unable to speak. Thompson could only nod.

"There's more. We have affidavits from the ref and the comms guy Overholt against Lyubov. And it looks like we will have positive IDs from the Dustin tapes. All solid stuff. Just has to be presented correctly." His intercom buzzed and a voice stated, "Coach Stravnicki is here, Mr. Thompson."

Thompson looked at Harvey and Nick. "We ready for him?"

Affirmative nods responded.

"Send him right in."

CHAPTER FORTY-NINE

Tony strode in confidently, a different attitude than his last visit. Greetings were exchanged, and Thompson took the lead. Tony slowly inserted a stick of gum.

"Coach Stravnicki, this pretty much began with you. While we can't go into every detail, we can explain a lot now. You should feel confident that things will be very different in your league now that we've broken up this so-called Committee. I think it's only fitting that your nephew fills you in or some of the details. I may need to step in if I think he says too much," he said.

"Understood, Mr. Thompson." Tony turned to his nephew.

"Tony, when you first came to me, I really wasn't sure you had anything other than a bunch of subjective coincidences, reinforced by your assistant's statistical analysis. But by the second visit we had begun to have our own suspicions, and you only reinforced that." Nick gave a summary of his team's forensic accounting efforts, including some basic information about the Cayman connections.

"We were starting to realize there might be a connection, especially after we anonymously received video and audio recordings of Travis Dustin's murder, linked to a person of interest we were investigating. Tony, I felt awful lying to you, deceiving you, but I had no choice. I was also very concerned about you and your family's safety."

"Well, Nick, that was quite the cat-and-mouse meeting we had. I had told you about Maggie's attacker, and I knew you knew about Dustin, and I wanted to see your response."

"How did *you* know about Dustin, Tony? No one outside the bureau knew about that."

A wry smile crossed Tony's face, and he paused, enjoying the effect. "That's not true, Nick. Several people had seen what was on those thumb drives before you did."

Nick was slack jawed and wide eyed, Thompson leaned forward in his seat, and Harvey remained impassive, arms folded.

"Nick, I was the one who sent all that to you. I felt then that surely you would support me, but Maggie later made me realize I was expecting too much from you."

Nick's mouth was still open while Thompson's eyes bored into Tony. "Coach, you need to explain to us how you came into possession of that material."

Tony reviewed in detail the sequence of events with Tina Bishop and Freddie Wilmington. "I simply didn't feel comfortable giving it directly to you, Nick, in light of our first meeting. Freddie, Brad, and Maggie all agreed with me. We felt we should continue to work things from our side, and I was concerned you'd order us to stop. I was just too emotionally invested in this, Nick; you were right about that."

A few seconds passed, Nick too stunned to respond, Thompson tapping a pencil on his desk, and Harvey shaking his head, looking incredulous. Finally, Thompson broke the ice. "Any other surprises you have for us, Coach?"

"I dunno, Mr. Thompson. How much do you know about a Vincent Taranto?" Tony asked, receiving blank looks from all three FBI men.

"Who is that, Tony?" asked Nick.

"He was Travis Dustin's handler and one of his murderers. Brad and Freddie discovered the link between them. I think he was involved in the death of my assistant, Dennis Jalmond. He tried to kill Maggie Thursday night. He's in jail in Ohio." Tony gave a full review of what his friends had discovered, and Maggie's attack and takedown of Taranto, as Thompson and Harvey furiously scribbled notes and Nick listened in awe.

"I think you know everything else, Mr. Thompson," Tony finished. "But my team and I deserve to know what you've found out."

"Your actions have been highly unusual for a civilian. But the bureau is grateful for your help. We will need to do in-depth interviews of your friends, Brad and Freddie, and you and your wife. It's likely you will all need to testify," said Thompson.

"We're all committed to helping, however you need us, sir."

Thompson sighed and with a hard look at Tony said, "What I have told you is completely confidential. You speak of this to no one, not even your wife. After we have done our interviews, I will personally brief all of you together to provide as clear a picture as is legal." Thompson rose, extending his hand to Tony. "I'm sure you and Nick have a few things to say in private, Coach."

The three men filed out. Harvey shook Tony's hand and simply thanked him. Nephew and uncle were left standing in the corridor.

"He doesn't say much, does he?" asked Tony.

"No, but he saved my life. C'mon, Tony, let's get some coffee and go to my office."

Once there, Nick slumped wearily in his chair, propping his feet up on his desk. *I'll be damned if I'm going to have my uncle be kept in the dark about what's going on.*

"Tony, you don't have to wait for Scott. I'll give you the outline of what we've found, and how Gena and I got hurt." For the next ten minutes, Nick summarized what the bureau knew, but with more detail about his getting shot and the ordeal Gena had endured.

Tony was spellbound, barely moving a muscle, shaking his head now and then. When Nick had finished, Tony could only mutter, "Wow. I never wanted to believe this was coming from people *inside* the league, although I did wonder. Makes sense now why so many people were afraid of Townsend." Thirty seconds passed, both men sipping their coffee in silence.

Nick broke the heavy stillness. "Maggie took down Taranto? Where'd she learn that?"

Tony reviewed Brad's extensive training, after reviewing his own attack and the probable motive. "So much for me to process, Nick. So many emotions right now. I'm so sorry I didn't listen to you. You guys suffered because of me."

"Tony, sending that info on Dustin to *The Daily News* was a ballsy thing to do. It forced our hand and could have ended badly in several ways."

Tony was quiet for a few moments. "Maggie was right, Nick. I'm a black-and-white guy in a gray world. How did it get so out of control?"

"It's what I see all the time in my job, Tony. Greed, power, arrogance, the insatiable quest for money. Same vices, different venues. I'm just more exposed to it than you."

"How do you constantly deal with it without it consuming you?"

"The only way I know how—I believe I'm making a difference. Without that, it's *meaningless*."

Tony sat looking down at his hands, humbled by those words. He stood and walked over to his nephew, his hand extended.

"Thanks, Nick." Nick took his uncle's hand, and they embraced.

"You taught me well, Tony," he replied.

The coach turned quickly and hurried out, not wanting his nephew to see the developing wetness in his eyes.

———————

Unable to drive yet, Nick enjoyed being chauffeured by the bureau and looked forward to spending time with Gena. Her physical wounds were healing rapidly, but he was more concerned about any lingering psychological trauma. They hadn't spoken about her ordeal, and he was uncertain how to approach it. She did have an appointment with a bureau psychologist next week, standard procedure after a mission involving an injury.

Entering their condo, he was pleased to see her in the kitchen cooking, her favorite home activity. She was moving to the beat of a popular song and doing her best to mimic the singer. A lovely singing voice was not one of her talents, but the fact that she was doing this brought happiness to Nick.

"Hey, Gena babe. Smells great! What you cooking?" he said, coming behind her and planting a soft kiss on her neck.

"One of your favorites, my lasagna. I hope you have an appetite," she replied, turning to kiss him on the lips.

"That's awesome, hon, but don't you think that's overdoing it for now?"

"Nonsense! I feel great. Just a little tender to walk with the bandages on my feet. But I'm much better than yesterday, and I've had enough lying around."

He cleaned up the cookware as she finished each step and poured them both a generous glass of wine.

"Hey, you do pretty good for a guy whose arm is in a cast!" she toasted as they touched glasses, settling in at the island.

"I'm not an invalid, but I sure like being driven around," he laughed. They sipped in silence for a while. "It's great you're feeling well and healing, Gena. How are you *really* doing?"

"I'm good. Surprisingly good. I had some bad dreams in the hospital but none since. I've thought about it quite a bit—what could have happened if the Coast Guard hadn't come when they did. I've come to terms with it. He hurt me; the pain was *real*. He's psychotic, would've done anything. But I didn't give in to him during that attack, and I won't give in to him now. If I let him stay in my head, always thinking *what if*, he wins, he dominates me. And I won't let that happen." Her voice was strong, resolute.

"The other part about this experience is how *alive* it made me feel and the enormous sense of pride and accomplishment about what I did. Nick, I haven't felt anything close to this since my very first modeling gig so long ago. This didn't break me down, Nick; this empowered me, and I'm so very grateful you and Scott had the faith in me," she said. "This may sound crazy, but I'd be open to helping out again, if the opportunity ever arose. Perhaps to even work together."

He tenderly held her hand, his fingers massaging her smooth skin, his emotions just barely in control. He had come close to losing her and her incredible spirit. His love. His rock. What other adventures lay before them?

CHAPTER FIFTY

The midwinter owners meeting of the National American Football League was unlike any which had preceded it. The universal topic was the recent indictments of the five members of the self-anointed Committee, chief among them former commissioner Jimmy O'Brien. Such was the severity of their alleged crimes and the strength of the government's case that none of them had been granted bail, despite multiple vigorous attempts by their high-powered lawyers. The government held their cards close to their vest, and speculation ran rampant as to the full extent of their crimes. Words like racketeering, fraud, extortion, money laundering, assault, and even murder had been leaked, fueling conversations in the three months since their arrest.

The league did all it could do to get through the remainder of the season, with new interim executives scrambling to maintain some semblance of normalcy. The principal business task of this meeting was to elect new senior officials and chart a new course for the league.

The keynote speaker of the opening ceremonies had been nominated by two individuals who had, ironically, just a few short months ago, almost certainly ended his future in the league. But considering what was now known, this individual, formerly a pariah but now held as the courageous savior of the sport of football, had been unanimously chosen.

Tony Stravnicki initially scoffed at the idea put forth by team owner Cane and Coach Jones, rejecting the offer out of hand. But they gave him time to think about it, and the persuasive powers of Maggie prevailed.

"You have a message the league needs to hear, Tony. You can say things that no one else dares to say, and you will be believed because you *live* those things. They're not just words, they're *who you are*," she had told him. He had listened to her and taken her advice to heart, and now here he was. But he insisted it be done his way or they'd have to get someone else.

He had given in and worn a tux, a concession to Maggie, and he nervously made his way to the podium, accompanied by polite applause after a benign introduction. At his request—a demand, really—giant high-definition monitors were installed behind him for all to see. No one knew what they were for or what he would say. He had also insisted that his speech and what would be projected on the screens be recorded, so that players, coaches, and other non-owner personnel of the league would be able to view it at some point.

He cleared his throat and, looking out over the assembled gathering of rich, powerful people, flipped a switch on the podium. Behind him images appeared, chronicling the history of the league since its inception, replete with clips of famous players and memorable plays. He began, his voice clear, his New York accent unmistakable.

"Thanks for your kind reception. I won't take much of your time. I'm here tonight because our beloved game of football has been under assault by misguided individuals who have, in my humble opinion, come very close to destroying the essence of it.

"Football is a sport where hard work, dedication, determination, discipline, and team effort should be our core values with fairness of opportunity the guiding principle. Yes, our sport is a business—a wildly successful one—employing tens of thousands not only in the league but across our great country. These provide opportunities for countless individuals to better their lives and provide for their families. But it is a fatal mistake if one places the *business* of football over the *purpose* of football. We have come perilously close to just that, and it is up to you, the owners and governing body, to pull us back from the abyss. You must remember that football is a game, to entertain us as participant and spectator. But at its core it is first and foremost a learning tool for life lessons.

"Let us not forget our players, for they are the lifeblood of our sport, yet too often treated like an endless commodity. They are not to be used as pawns in a massive game of chess," he said, his voice rising in intensity.

"Our sport is far more than another venue in this nation's entertainment industry. Yes, we provide entertainment. But we should also provide an opportunity to showcase the values that made this country great and continue to do so.

"You, the owners, have your work cut out for you in light of the recent troubles. But you also have a unique opportunity to *do it right*," he said, his voice now rising to a crescendo. "Seize this opportunity to remake the game, remember the spirit of those who have gone before us, and right the wrongs of the past! Thank you." His words ended almost simultaneously with his video presentation.

Tony turned and began to leave the stage but was stopped in his tracks by a thunderous sound. Glancing over his shoulder, he was astounded to see they were giving him a standing ovation. He raised his hand and nodded his thanks and hurried off stage into the waiting arms of a beaming Maggie.

Six months later, the Committee was probably not enjoying their post-football lives. The government had presented a complex, successful case with multiple layers of evidence. Paul Johnstone, incensed at discovering his wife's affair with O'Brien, provided state's evidence on the others in return for a reduced sentence, resulting in convictions on multiple counts.

O'Brien's wife, Justine, filed for divorce, with a hefty settlement.

Phil Townsend tried unsuccessfully to minimize his role, blaming all the others for virtually everything. The evidence and the testimony of his codefendants easily negated his attempts. To the very end, he refused to believe that Travis Dustin had tripped him up. His arrogance and disdain for the victim would never have allowed the possibility of him being outsmarted. Even the explosive story in *The Daily News*, detailing Dustin's brilliant, heroic recordings, failed to convince him.

Vincent Taranto was convicted of accessory to commit murder and conspiracy to commit murder and extortion, after trying unsuccessfully to deflect blame on O'Brien, Townsend, and Lyubov. Travis Dustin's audio tape of their meetings provided a key piece of evidence. There was not sufficient evidence to indict him in the death of Dennis Jalmond.

Pavel Lyubov was the toughest nut, never giving an inch, but they had enough solid evidence on several charges, with testimony from the referee Ohlendorf, to keep him in prison forever.

All but Johnstone would spend the rest of their lives behind bars.

———————

After his impassioned speech at the owners' meeting, Tony was flooded with job offers, from head coach to front-office positions, even in league headquarters itself. With Maggie's counsel, he evaluated them all. Finally, his dream of becoming a head coach in professional football could happen. But he had doubts, realizing he had to find a way to balance his passion for his family against his passion for football. As he considered all his options, Tony remembered Nick's words about making a difference. He remembered his past, the good past.

On a crisp fall day, a man with a booming New York accent and a backward baseball cap calmly walked the sidelines of a small suburban stadium. Clutching his prized clipboard, his jaws worked overtime chewing gum. A player came up to him agitated, and the coach put his hand on his shoulder, looked him in the eyes, and quietly counseled him, calming the storm.

Tony Stravnicki had found his place in life when he accepted the joint positions of athletic director and head football coach for Mid-Ohio Catholic Prep, a high school just outside Columbus. Here, he could influence lives and make a real difference, as he once had with a favorite nephew.

ACKNOWLEDGMENTS

M any individuals have helped make what were vague, random thoughts over ten years ago into this, my debut novel.

Thank you to my early readers: my wife, Ferol; my children, Kenneth, Rebecca, and Rob; and Kathy Baronas, Deb Pelletier, and John Cole. Their encouragement gave me the fuel to move forward.

Thank you to my New Hampshire Writer's Project critique partners, especially Karen Goltz. Her many insightful comments proved invaluable to the shaping of the story.

Thank you for the many fine courses developed by Writer's Digest that answered so many of my questions and guided me along the journey.

Thank you to John Koehler and his wonderful team at Koehler Books for believing in my story and providing the pathway to make it happen. A special thanks to KB's editor Becky Hilliker for making the dreaded editorial process easy and informative.

Thank you to all the writers I have met through KB and at conferences and workshops, including the New England Crime Bake, for all your encouragement and sharing of knowledge.

And finally, a reach out to Journey for "Don't Stop Believin'" and Kelly Clarkson for "Breakaway." Their iconic songs jump-started my motivation at the beginning of every writing session.

ABOUT THE AUTHOR

Richard "Dick" Groves retired from a thirty-eight-year career in Navy and private practice dentistry. A lifelong football fan, his debut novel, *The Hidden Game*, combines his love of the sport and his passion for writing crime suspense and mystery.

Dick is a member of the New Hampshire Writer's Project and critique group as well as the New England Crime Bake. He is currently working on a follow-up novel and enjoys writing short stories and flash fiction.

A graduate of Northeastern University and the Virginia Commonwealth University School of Dentistry, he served six years in the Navy Dental Corps with two years in Guam. In retirement he has participated in two humanitarian missions to the Far East and Pacific on board the hospital ship USNS *Mercy* and the USS *Pearl*

Harbor, and two Mission of Mercy endeavors to Appalachia, helping to provide much-needed dental treatment to these areas.

Raised in Arlington, Massachusetts, Dick resides in Merrimack, New Hampshire, with his wife, Ferol, and their two rescue dogs, Lily and Lucy. He finds quiet inspiration for his writing in the tranquility of Waterville Valley in the White Mountains.